THE BRIDE BLUNDER

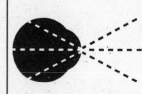

This Large Print Book carries the
Seal of Approval of N.A.V.H.

THE BRIDE BLUNDER

KELLY EILEEN HAKE

THORNDIKE PRESS
A part of Gale, Cengage Learning

GALE
CENGAGE Learning™

Detroit • New York • San Francisco • New Haven, Conn • Waterville, Maine • London

GALE
CENGAGE Learning

LIBRARY OF CONGRESS CATALOGING-IN-PUBLICATION DATA

Hake, Kelly Eileen.
  The bride blunder / by Kelly Eileen Hake. — Large print ed.
    p. cm. — (Prairie promises series ; no. 3) (Thorndike Press large print Christian historical fiction)
  ISBN-13: 978-1-4104-2132-6 (alk. paper)
  ISBN-10: 1-4104-2132-5 (alk. paper)
  1. Large type books. I. Title.
PS3608.A54545B76 2010
813'.6—dc22   2009049344

Published in 2010 by arrangement with Barbour Publishing, Inc.

DEDICATION/
ACKNOWLEDGMENT

For the Lord, who gave me the words to write and the precious friends who encouraged me to do it!

For Aaron, a wonderful editor and exacting historian, without whom this book wouldn't be what it is.

And, most of all, for Steve, who wrote alongside me hour by hour when I thought I had nothing left to say. This book wouldn't exist at all without you. . . .

CHAPTER 1

Baltimore, Maryland 1859

"No." Marge Chandler shook her head, wishing it were so easy to shake away the sudden image springing to life in her mind. "No more bows, Daisy."

"Well . . ." Her cousin nibbled on the edge of her naturally rosy lower lip and fingered the velvet trimmings before her. "Perhaps you're right."

"Nonsense, darling — it's your wedding dress!" Daisy's mother, the aunt who'd raised them both since Marge's parents didn't survive the crossing to America, bustled over and snatched up the ribbons. "Besides, you know better than to ask Marge her opinion on matters of fashion."

True. Daisy should know better by now. A wry smile tilted Marge's lips. *Aunt Verlata will always override me.* Not that it mattered — Daisy could wear a rainbow of gaudy velvet bows and still entrance any audience.

Her smile turned rueful as Marge caught a glimpse of her own reflection in the dressmaker's looking glass. Aunt Verlata's sense of style didn't hamper Daisy's charm, but somehow Marge couldn't manage to carry off the same fussy furbelows with any panache. While feminine touches showcased Daisy's graceful build, her own more generous frame made such flourishes conspicuous. And never before had her relatives indulged in so many fripperies as for Daisy's much-anticipated wedding. Marge's gown for the affair — a light blue silk that had done nothing to deserve such treatment — drooped toward the ground, overburdened with tiers of ruffles.

"They are lovely," she soothed her aunt's ruffled feathers. "But the Belgian lace is so exquisite, I can't imagine drawing attention away from it." *Not to mention the flounces and crystal beading . . .*

"Well, there's truth in that." The older woman snatched her fingers away from the bows as though they'd attempted to scald her. "It might look overdone."

"There's a possibility of that." Ruthlessly strangling the smile that threatened at her aunt's comment, Marge moved to take the ribbons away. Far, far away.

"Wait!" Daisy surveyed the ribbons then

cast a speculative glance at Marge.

Oh no. Closing her eyes couldn't halt the inevitable. She'd learned that when she was six — and they buried Mama and Papa at sea — and kept relearning it every time something came along she desperately wanted to change.

Like Daisy's marriage. Her beautiful, vibrant, loving cousin — the woman who could wed any man in town — had chosen Mr. Dillard. *Trouston* Dillard. The Third. Marge wrinkled her nose. She'd cover every garment she owned in bows if her cousin would choose a man who cared more about Daisy than himself, but she had a sickening suspicion she'd only get the bows.

"Mama, don't you think Margie's dress could do with a few bows? The things she usually wears are so very plain."

"It's foolish for a teacher to dress up, Daisy. My clothes are serviceable, as is appropriate." It was a wonder her cousin didn't mouth the words along with her, the discussion had been so oft repeated.

"Yes, but my wedding will be a good opportunity for you to . . ." A delicate shrug completed the thought.

"To . . . ?" This wasn't something to let pass by. Daisy never censored herself, so something left unspoken made alarm bells chime.

"Dress up and . . ." Oh dear, there she went quiet again. This had to be bad.

"And?" Marge didn't miss the furtive glance between mother and daughter.

"And show to advantage, dear." Aunt Verlata lifted one of the bows out of its case and held it up to Marge's bodice. "With Daisy getting married, your time will come soon enough."

"I see." She blinked against a stinging dryness in her eyes. *Now that Daisy's unavailable, the men will have to settle. I have the chance to be someone's second choice.* "In that case, Auntie, by all means, add those bows." *Anything to chase away my cousin's old suitors!*

Buttonwood, Nebraska Territory
"It's smoking, son." Grandma Ermintrude's raspy chortle made Gavin Miller pull his hand away from his pocket in a hurry. "You ought to just post it already."

"Next time I'm at the mercantile, I'll pass it on to Reed." He finished his eggs and pushed away from the table. "It's not a pressing matter."

"Men don't bother writing letters if it's not something important, boy. Fact you got an unnatural attachment to this one makes

10

it even more suspicious. Now, drink your coffee before you leave the table." She tapped a gnarled finger on the smoothed wooden surface. "I'm not going to drink it, and no grandson of mine is coward enough to run from breakfast and a few questions."

Gavin raised his mug and scowled into brew bitter enough to strip whitewash. Grandma made her coffee the same way she made her conversation.

And that's a blessing, he reminded himself. If his father's mother weren't such a strong personality, his mother's father wouldn't have sponsored his move west to set up his own mill. Gavin and Grandma Ermintrude got along tolerably well most days, so bringing her along worked out well — most days.

He set down the mug only to have her refill it lickety-split.

"So, who's the gal?"

"What gal?"

"Don't play dumb with me — that's the question I asked you." Her eyes narrowed, the lines spidering around them deepening to webs. "Marguerite."

"Marguerite?" For a fraction of a second, Gavin didn't place the name he'd written on the envelope.

"What'd I tell you about playing dumb? I saw your scrawl on there plain as day —

Marguerite. No skin off my nose you've swapped sweethearts from that Daisy you used to mention." The things the old woman tucked away in her memory never ceased to amaze him. How many times had he mentioned the woman he'd left back in Baltimore? Twice?

"Marguerite is French for *daisy,*" he explained to forestall any more coffee. "She has her grandmother's name, but no one calls her by it."

"Fancy." She lifted her pinky just so as she took a sip of milk. "And just like youngsters these days to disregard the better choice. Goes by Daisy instead — she must be a plain one, your gal."

"Anything but." Not that he planned to wax poetic about Daisy's fine looks. Grandma would turn right around and accuse him of being blinded by beauty. She did things like that — latched on and poked until she moved things to go her way. Which made as good a reason as any to post the letter today. She'd nettle him about it until he took care of the thing.

"Oh?" When one lifted brow failed to elicit a reaction, the other winged its way upward. "Mouse brown hair, straight as a pin, most likely."

"Black ringlets." *That bob when she walks*

or tosses her head to laugh. Her easy laughter had attracted him in the first place.

"Dull, dishwater gray eyes?"

"Green."

A martial glint lit Grandma's eye as she flung more challenges. "Too tall for a woman, I'll wager."

"Petite." The brims of her fanciful hats only reached his shoulder.

"Ungainly shape, lurches when she walks." A smirk brought the closest thing to a smile Gavin typically saw on his grandmother's face as he shook his head. Looked like she was enjoying herself. "Teeth browned and breath foul?"

He couldn't hold back a guffaw at her hopeful tone and the contrast of his memory to the portrait Grandma painted with her words.

"A widow saddled with squalling brats?"

"She's never been wed and is young."

"You're certain about all this?" Her merriment sharpened to a thin edge of a smile at his agreement. "In that case — you have no reason not to send the letter."

Lifting his mug, Gavin took a swig of coffee in admiration of how she sprang her trap shut with the type of precision he prided himself on with his mill. "True."

"Now you're thinking straight." Belying

her earlier words, Grandma poured a hefty measure of coffee into the splash of milk covering the bottom of her cup. "After all, besides her saying no, what's the worst that could happen?"

"Daisy, I picked up the post while I was out." Marge tilted her head toward the study as they passed each other on the stairs. "You'll find a few late responses to your wedding invitations on the writing desk, when you find a moment to take a look."

"Thank you, Margie." Daisy gave her cousin a quick hug before continuing down the steps, making a side trip to the dainty escritoire she favored by the study window.

Settling herself on the matching chair, its seat upholstered in her favorite shade of green — to match her eyes, though she would never admit it — she caught sight of a tidy stack of letters. The sight brought a smile to her lips, not only for the basic joy of receiving mail but also for how thoroughly Marge-ish the orderly pile seemed.

Largest letters lay at the bottom, smallest resting atop them, with all the corners squared to make straight lines. Marge supplied a system for everything, created order out of chaos, and made the world make sense down to the tiniest detail. Daisy didn't know quite how her cousin managed these feats, but she long ago accepted it as fact and determined what it meant in life.

Firstly, no matter how hard she tried, Daisy would never be half so capable as her slightly older cousin. Not so clever, not so useful, not so good at making things work the way they should. As her letter opener sliced through the first missive with a satisfying tear, Daisy remembered the time she'd wasted trying to measure up — back when it bothered her that she couldn't seem to be as practical as Marge.

Another acceptance to the wedding. How lovely. I'll have to adjust the reception numbers. . . . She set it aside and reached for the next, allowing her thoughts free rein. Eventually, that whole setup had led to her second realization: So long as Marge made things run smoothly, Daisy didn't need to. Things got done better when Marge did them, and they were both happy enough so long as Daisy did her job — which was, of course, to drag Marge into some sort of social life.

Oh, regrets . . . She set that one off to the other side of the desk and continued going through the letters, putting them into whatever mound seemed appropriate as she thought of all the fun her friends who couldn't attend her wedding would miss out on.

Because, of course, that's what Daisy excelled at. Fun! Always ready to laugh, she loved the social swirl. Her duty, in return for Marge allowing her this carefree sort of life, was to make sure Marge didn't give in entirely to her serious side and experienced some enjoyment of life.

But with Daisy's upcoming marriage, a third realization plagued her. She'd failed her cousin. Daisy would waltz off into a merry marriage with Trouston, whose stolen kisses grew more insistent by the day, and leave Marge behind to a life without laughter or passion. Their whole lives, since Marge's parents didn't survive the crossing to America, Mama had tried to hide the fact Daisy, as her true daughter, was her favorite.

And Daisy had tried to make up for the fact that Mama made a hash of trying to hide something so obvious. She knew her cousin better than anyone alive, and Marge needed a family to call her very own. But if Daisy couldn't find something — and soon — Marge would sink into the role of spinster schoolmarm for the rest of her born days.

With a deep sigh, she sliced open the final letter — addressed ever so formally to

"Marguerite." Which must have been why Marge put it in Daisy's pile — wedding responses might be more formal than everyday letters, when most people spoke and wrote to either of them as either Daisy or Marge. It made it less confusing, since they shared their grandmother's name.

Her eyes widened as she read the message. A proposal! From Gavin Miller . . . But Daisy was affianced. And surely Gavin knew. . . . The banns were posted, notices sent. Good heavens, she winged wedding invitations to just about every person she'd ever met. Surely the son of Baltimore's richest miller, who'd been a good friend to both her and Marge, had received one?

She'd kept a list somewhere. . . . A search of all the drawers and cubbies of the escritoire finally yielded the list. Sure enough, Gavin Miller's name appeared. He'd received an invitation to her wedding.

Daisy gasped and jumped to her feet. That meant this letter had to be for —

CHAPTER 2

"Marge!" Her cousin's unladylike bellow brought Marge running full tilt down the stairs at speeds the railroad would be hard pressed to match. "Marge, come quick!"

She almost crashed into her aunt, who rushed toward the hallway coming from the study with a panicked look Marge was sure matched her own. Daisy *never* hollered. Something had to be horribly, dreadfully, unprecedentedly wrong.

Aunt Verlata sailed through the door a scant second before Marge — and only because Marge knew she'd never hear the end of it if she infringed on a mother's right. *No matter that Daisy yelled for* me *at the top of her lungs.* She squashed the thought. It didn't matter once she realized her cousin, far from lying broken or bereaved upon the plush throw rug blanketing most of the study's hardwood floors, was bouncing — yes, *bouncing* — toward them. Daisy was the only woman Marge ever witnessed who could actually bounce as a means of transportation.

"Marge!" Daisy didn't adjust her volume as she launched herself into a smothering hug. "I'm so happy for you!"

Why? Marge winced from the volume, but her hackles raised for an entirely different reason. She'd love to be able to say her Fruit of the Spirit had ripened to such a degree she never begrudged another person any joy. But she and the Holy Spirit knew full well that wasn't the case.

Generally, she'd give just about anything to keep a smile on Daisy's face. But she'd learned the hard way that whenever Daisy felt happy *for* her, trouble loomed. Simply put, the things Daisy felt ought to make Marge happiest bore the uncanny ability to make Marge miserable. Tiers of ruffles and rows of bows on fancy dresses were a minor example.

"Darling, I've never heard you . . ." Obviously Aunt Verlata groped for a term to describe Daisy's earsplitting screeches. "*Yelp* . . . in such a manner. You caused no small amount of alarm. Marge and I both thought you were in some pain."

"Far from it." Daisy unwound from about Marge, her more sedate tone underscored by an odd crinkling that hadn't been notice-able before. "It's just so exciting!"

"What is?" For the first time, Marge noticed Daisy held a letter — now abused and rumpled — tight to her chest. She instantly surmised this to be the instigator of Daisy's outburst.

"He's on the list!" Her cousin thrust another paper, this one clutched in her hand, toward Marge. "Gavin Miller."

"Gavin . . ." Marge's breath caught at the mention of her old friend who'd gone westward. She and Daisy hadn't heard from him since he left — a niggling source of upset she'd refused to acknowledge. After all, she'd pinned no hopes upon the hand-some, determined, talented man who'd actually taken the time to speak with her as well as Daisy.

Liar. Her conscience pinged at her attempt at self-deception as she smoothed what she now recognized as part of Daisy's pages-long list of invited wedding attendees.

"Here!" Her cousin's perfectly coiffed curls blocked her view for a moment before a buffed nail tapped the paper just above Gavin's name. "See? He's on the list, Marge!"

"So he is." *Of course he is. I put him there, hoping he'd show up.* Marge blushed as the first hint of excitement welled up. Perhaps Daisy knew of her little infatuation for their friend? "Did he respond? Is he coming for the wedding?"

"No–o–o–o." The drawn-out response doused Marge's newfound anticipation until Daisy thrust the second sheet of paper — the one she'd cradled against her chest — into her hands. "Better! Read this, Marge!"

Marge accepted the note, slipped her spectacles onto her nose from where they hung on a slender silver chain around her neck, and could practically feel the breath of her aunt upon the page as she set to read. On the pretext of wanting more light, she moved toward the window, making certain to turn slightly to provide more privacy.

Smoothing the crinkles, her fingertips brushed over the lines Gavin wrote, the teacher in her noticing the thick strokes of his penmanship, the ink-filled hollows of his vowels, the friendly way his words leaned to the right. She allowed herself a small smile before she scanned the greeting.

Dear Marguerite,

"This isn't for me, Daisy." She whirled back toward her cousin. It says 'Marguerite.' No one calls me that."

21

"No one calls *me* that either." A truculent expression set her features. "And it *can't* be for me. Keep reading."

She turned back to the window, shoulders rigid, and read once more.

Dear Marguerite,

I know no one calls you by your Christian name, but a man only does this once in a lifetime — I hope — and I want to do it properly. We've been friends for years, and it can come as no surprise I've admired you during that time but wanted to prove myself before coming forward. I think fondly of our conversations about the adventure of making a life out west.

Marge's vision blurred for a moment, her head dizzy with a sudden hope that could never be. She closed her eyes until she felt steady, one palm flat against the warmth of the sunbaked windowpane. The heat calmed her, enabling her to read on.

Now my mill is running well, I make a good living, and I'm in the position to provide well for a wife on my own terms. Would you do me the honor of becoming my bride? If so, my father will see to your travel arrangements to join me in Buttonwood.

Hopefully yours,
Gavin Miller

Marge read it again before resting her forehead against the heat of the window. *It can't be. He must mean Daisy.*

"Marge?" The weight of her aunt's hand descended upon her shoulder, concern evident in her voice. "Are you all right, dear?"

"It's for Daisy." Marge straightened and thrust the letter toward Aunt Verlata. "Not me." She couldn't even look at her cousin, lest her disappointment spill into bitterness.

"No, it isn't." Daisy edged toward her with far more hesitation and tapped her list. "Gavin knows I'm affianced, Marge. He received a wedding invitation."

A pure, sweet note of hope rang in her heart. "Did he respond?"

"Well, no . . ."

"Bachelors seldom do, unless their mothers do so for them." Aunt Verlata passed back the letter. "Mr. Miller has no mother to do so. And what is this mention of conversing about westward adventures?"

"That was you, Marge." Daisy's subdued reminder, so different from her natural exuberance, gave it more credence.

"We spoke of it, but Daisy was there."

"I nodded, but I was bored. You were the one talking about homesteads and townships and articles you'd read and making history." Daisy wrinkled her nose. "I like *shops,* Marge. They don't have those in the wilderness. Everyone knows that!"

"That is" — Marge paused — "true." *And logical. What has happened that Daisy is being the logical one?* Her mouth went dry as a desert. "You remembered the conversations about westward expansion, and *that's* why you looked up the list, isn't it?" Her cousin never looked anything up. But she'd deemed this important. *Because she knew I wouldn't believe Gavin meant me.*

"Yes." Daisy waved the list. "And it's right here!"

"Thank you." Marge buried her in a hug. *Gavin asked* me *to marry him. He wants* me, *not Daisy.*

"So" — Aunt Verlata slid her arms around them both, making it a group hug as she joined in — "you know what this means, don't you?" If the other two women hadn't been holding her, Marge held a strange certainty she'd float.

"Yes," Marge and Daisy chorused.

I'm getting married! Marge would have

24

shouted her answer aloud, but Daisy beat her to the punch.

"Now we need to buy *two* trousseaus!"

He spotted her doing it again. Midge Collins headed his way, bonnet forgotten as usual, sun bringing out the red tones in her mahogany hair, only to change course as soon as she caught sight of him. This time, she darted behind the smithy.

Amos didn't plan to let her get away with it. Moving around the far side, behind the attached stables, he could cut off her get-away route. Stepping around the corner, that's exactly what he did. With one shoulder rested against the structure and the bulk of him leaning in her way, he made her pull up short in a hurry. And not just because she was a petite little thing.

He got the impression most folks forgot what an undersized woman she really made, because the rest of her came out so big. Some folks had that way — a smile, a sharp wit, a way of holding themselves that made them ten times their natural sizes. They learned it out of necessity, though — and that was just one more mystery to add to the pile that made up Midge.

"Miss Collins." He tipped his hat.

"Mr. Geer." Her nostrils flared at being

thwarted, making some of those freckles dance. Cute. "If you'll excuse me, I —"

"Nope." He crossed one booted foot over the other and got comfortable. Time to enjoy himself.

"What?" Her brows came together in obvious frustration, not going upward in astonishment as she begged his pardon, like most ladies would do. He liked that.

"I said, 'Nope.' I'm not of a mind to excuse you, Miss Collins." Amos unleashed his grin. "See, we need to have a discussion on why you've been avoiding me."

"Who says I've been avoiding you?"

"No one says it. And no one else has noticed. But I have, and I want to know why."

She looked at him for a long moment, as though measuring him. "You know, if you keep asking questions, you might run across an answer you don't like."

"Try me."

"All right, how's this?" She leaned closer, close enough for him to catch some sort of light, flowery scent. "You want to know why I avoid you?"

He took his shoulder off the wall and leaned closer to hear her lowered tones. "Yep."

"Well, Mr. Geer . . ." Quick as a deer, she

26

slipped between him and the wall and scampered off, calling out her answer, "You can't always get what you want."

Amos chuckled as he watched the edge of her skirts swish around the building. *We'll just have to see about that.*

CHAPTER 3

"Your pacing won't make the stage get here any sooner." Grandma Ermintrude's amusement came through loud and clear.

"It'll come this afternoon," Gavin conceded. "And Daisy will be on it. . . ." He walked faster.

"So you want to wear a hole in the floor to welcome her?"

"You want to change your mind about coming to the café for dinner and waiting on the stage?"

"To sit and twiddle my thumbs until her highness arrives and I can *ooh* and *aah* like a yokel?" No one could snort like Grandma. "If I don't like her, do you plan on sending her packing?"

"Daisy's easy to like." He pushed aside a pinch of misgiving. Grandma wasn't so easy to get along with, but Daisy charmed everyone. People got along like millstones — too much distance didn't do any good. Too

28

close, and everything jammed. In time, they'd find the right balance.

"Just the same, I'll wait until you bring her here. No sense making the private into a public matter. You two are wise to spend some time before having the ceremony." She jerked her head toward the mill. "Did you set up your bunk?"

"All set." Gavin had decided not to whisk Daisy to the altar immediately upon her arrival in Buttonwood, thinking it best for her to get some rest and settle into town life first. With Grandma to make it proper, he'd bed down in the mill for a few nights until Daisy knew for sure she'd be willing to make a life in the Nebraska Territory. "If you're staying, I'm heading on to town."

Daisy grew up sheltered, surrounded by fine things. Her romantic outlook of the West might not last long enough for her to make a go of it. Lovely and lively though she may be, Gavin didn't intend to chain her to him and a way of living she'd resent. Best to think things through and not collect regrets.

The wagon ride to town did nothing to clear his thoughts or siphon away his energy. Easy enough to figure out why . . . if he were man enough to admit it. This restlessness didn't come purely from excitement. No, an underlying nervousness picked at him. Questions about whether Daisy would be happy to see him, if she'd like the town, if the house he'd built near his mill were good enough — they swirled together in his brain to form a mass of unknowns.

Lord, I prayed to You before coming out here, and You gave me peace. I prayed before writing the letter, and You gave me peace. I prayed before sending the letter, and that very morning Ermintrude gave me the kick in the pants to move things along. So, no matter what happens when she steps off that stage, please help give me the peace to know it is Your will.

"Mr. Miller!" The warm greeting of Mrs. Grogan stopped him in front of the mercantile. With a toddler on one hip and another child obviously on the way, Opal Grogan seemed a woman who'd taken well to motherhood. "Good to see you."

"Miller." Her husband, Adam, gave a friendly nod. Adam was one of the most prosperous farmers in the area, the Grogans having been in Buttonwood since the town began in one of the rare fertile pockets alongside the Platte.

"Today's the big day." Another feminine voice had Gavin angling so he didn't block Mrs. Reed, who'd come up behind him.

"Stage ought to be in soon."

"That's right." Midge Collins joined them, shaking her head. "So let's hope the rest of the town is a tad more subtle about their intent to watch for a glimpse of Mr. Miller's bride-to-be."

"We like to be welcoming," someone — Gavin couldn't tell who — protested. "Good to be friendly and introduce ourselves."

"Well, Grandma Ermintrude wasn't feeling up to making the trip to town, and I'm sure after a long stage ride, my bride-to-be, as you put it, will be worn out." Gavin silently blessed Grandma for her wisdom in avoiding a spectacle. "So the introductions will have to wait a little while."

"Sounds like a glimpse is all you'll get." Miss Collins sounded amused, but Gavin didn't mind. She'd been helpful, pointing out something he was now determined to avoid.

"Everyone knows the wedding isn't today." Adam Grogan made a show of male support. "And he's right to take her to get to know his grandmother before making the town rounds."

"Glad you understand." Gavin decided on the spot to charge Adam only half rate for the next load the farmer brought to his mill. You couldn't put a price on easing a man's

31

way, but you could show gratitude. "When the time is right, you'll all be glad to have her as part of the town."

"There's bound to be curiosity about her." Mrs. Reed's pale green eyes danced with it even as she spoke. "But it's not bad. We don't let any of the gossips grumble about her staying with your grandmother until you wed. It's known you've made arrangements to sleep elsewhere."

"Miss Chandler won't be looked down on," Mrs. Grogan chimed in, and for the first time, Gavin realized he was catching a peek into the power structure of the women of the town. How things ran. It seemed Opal Grogan, Clara Reed, and even young Midge Collins carried considerable weight.

It made sense, considering their connections. Mrs. Grogan linked two previously feuding farms — Specks and Grogans, the two most powerful properties in town. Mrs. Reed and Miss Collins were related to the town doctor and owner of the only mercantile. Not to mention they were all young and friendly.

Daisy would do well to make friends of them. She'd feel more at home with companions her age, and they'd ease her way.

"Thank you. She has a real heart for others, and it will do her good to know she already has friends in Buttonwood." That did the trick. The married women beamed at him, and Miss Collins quirked a brow in acknowledgement. Gavin felt his first smile of the day tug on the corners of his mouth.

"If you'd like, we could make up a small dinner party," Mrs. Reed offered. "Myself, Saul, Midge, Opal and Adam, and, of course, Josiah and Doreen." She listed everyone present, plus the owner of the mercantile and his wife. "Something private to ease her into things before church on Sunday perhaps?"

"That's a wonderful idea!" Mrs. Grogan chimed in. "Or even afterward, to get to know her better. Whenever she's comfortable."

"We'd like that." Gavin barely got the acceptance out before he spotted what looked like a brown cloud on the horizon. The stage was coming — an hour early.

Now, Midge wasn't a great believer in the loving-kindness of the Almighty, but she didn't question His existence. And she'd hatched a few theories of her own over the years.

One of them was that every single person got a gift at birth. Not the myrrh or frankincense or gold mentioned in the Bible for baby Jesus — although gold *would* have been nice, mind — but a different sort of gift. A talent, perhaps. Whatever gifts people received got pointed to the sort of things they'd think were important.

Midge even extended her theory to the realm of matchmaking. People's talents had to match up — not be the same, but they had to mesh right or a couple wouldn't work out. Adam and Opal — both peacemakers, but neither of them weak enough to be walked over. That worked. Clara loved on people once they got close. She matched up with Saul, the healer who provided a different sort of care. Doreen, who could say the right thing, went well with Josiah, who had the uncanny way of knowing what someone needed at what time.

As for her, Midge's flair was for observation. She watched, she listened, she *noticed*. In short, she spotted things people didn't want others to guess at. She read expressions, registered changes in stances or gestures, wondered about things that were none of her business because she learned long ago that a girl never knew when something might *become* her business.

It pays off to pay attention.

And right now, from her vantage point a few paces away — out of sight of Mr. Amos

Geer — Midge couldn't help but frown. Mr. Miller seemed like he was holding back his excitement before, but now that the stage arrived — the top loaded down with more luggage than she could've dreamed up even with her considerable imagination — his posture tattled of surprise.

He'd reached up to help down a woman, smiled in a friendly but not loving way at her, and asked something to make her shake her head slightly. Why was he glancing back in the coach? And there . . . the stiffening of his shoulders as he signaled for the luggage to be brought down.

Mr. Miller didn't look excited anymore. His smile stretched tight instead of wide, his movements went jerky, like a body's does when doing something under protest.

Midge looked at the new lady, Miss Chandler, who seemed vaguely uncertain and massively overdressed. *No . . . something is wrong here.*

She watched Mr. Miller take Miss Chandler's elbow — touching her as little as possible as he helped her into his wagon. *Very wrong, indeed.*

All too aware of the town's scrutiny as the stage pulled up, Gavin took a deep breath. It didn't matter what anyone else thought

— although Daisy's charm and looks would win over the stodgiest grump in no time flat. But it did matter if she felt uncomfortable the moment she stepped foot in town.

The stage stopped a few feet in front of him, making him walk to meet them. He pulled down the folding steps as the dust settled then straightened up to open the curved door. A mass of lavender skirts floofed into view before one dainty hand, clad in soft tan leather, reached toward him.

Daisy. He enfolded her tiny hand in his, stepping back as one small foot extended toward the steps, offering a glimpse of polished black boots whose endless buttons encased tantalizingly trim ankles. She descended, gaze lowered to watch her step, her hat blocking her face until they moved a short distance from the coach. It was only when she raised her head to smile at him Gavin recognized the woman before him.

"Marge?" He clasped her hand in both of his for a moment. Unexpected it might be, but it was a pleasure to see his old friend. Daisy should have told him she'd brought her cousin for companionship on the journey. "So good to see you!"

"Wonderful to see you as well" — a faint blush colored her cheeks before she added — "Gavin." Her use of his given name sent an odd, though not unpleasant, clench to his midsection, but he brushed it off. They were soon to be family, after all.

He peered past her. "Where is Daisy?"

"She couldn't accompany me, I'm afraid." Marge lifted her chin. "With her wedding date so near, she couldn't leave, and Aunt Verlata and I determined it wouldn't be overly improper for an affianced woman to travel alone." A teasing smile tilted her lips. "Daisy told me to be sure and mention how put out she is that you didn't RSVP to her invitation."

"The invitation . . ." The echo came out choked as the stagecoach driver began tossing down Marge's luggage. *Daisy is to be married . . . but why is Marge here? Marge . . .* All at once, the missing memory slammed into place with the finality of a nail in a coffin. Marge . . . named for her grandmother, just like Daisy.

I got the wrong Marguerite!

CHAPTER 4

Marge perched atop the wagon seat, right hand curled around the rough board to help keep her balance as they rolled toward Gavin's mill. After days on end in the stagecoach, jouncing along rutted dirt prairie roads was nothing new. Her backside could attest to that. No matter. The journey paled in comparison to what she found at its end.

Gavin. . . . She snuck a sideways peek at his profile, gaze traveling from the sweep of his sable hair to the firm set of his jaw. Back home, the family encouraged friends and close acquaintances to call her Marge, and Daisy by her favored nickname. Having two "Miss Chandlers" created far too much confusion. So Gavin had been using her given name for quite some time, but today marked her first use of his. He'd seemed surprised, though not displeased — a reaction that reassured her of her new place in his life.

He hadn't said much, but Marge found that reassuring as well. What words Gavin did give were enough. *"So good to see you!"* Simple, warm, and welcoming — genuine. Her fiancé remained the man of her memories, which meant they'd have a good marriage. Solid. Comfortable.

Marge peeped through her lashes at him once more, drinking in the way hard work beneath the sun had bronzed his skin since last she saw him. His lips formed an almost-straight line, swallowing the slight fullness she remembered. It looked as though he was thinking. . . .

As though sensing her perusal, he turned his head. His dark brown gaze searched her face as if seeking answers to some unspoken question.

The sudden intensity of it warmed her cheeks in what she knew to be a blush . . . although Marge wasn't in the habit of blushing. Blushing, she'd always maintained, was for two types of girls: silly wigeons who didn't realize that it was whomever spouted the drivel who should be embarrassed, or those naturally charming women like Daisy whose blushes meant she was enjoying herself. Marge didn't fit either category.

Which meant Gavin's scrutiny had turned her into a temporary wigeon.

She silently blamed Daisy even as she offered him a smile and he returned his attention to the road. *This behavior is all Daisy's fault! Nattering on and on about how romantic it was that Gavin nursed an affection for me but never spoke up until the time was right, then brings me across the country to be by his side . . .*

All right. Perhaps it wasn't *entirely* Daisy's fault. Marge thought the same things, let the knowledge fill her with delight until it seemed nothing and no one could make her frown. What she could — and would — lay at Daisy's door were the ridiculous fantasies she'd indulged in throughout the long journey. If her cousin hadn't filled her head with ludicrous scenarios of her grand reunion with Gavin, she wouldn't feel self-conscious now.

But truly, she'd known full well there'd be no overblown display of passion. She hadn't expected him to sweep her into his strong arms the moment she stepped off the stage and declare how very much he'd longed for her arrival. Such behavior wouldn't be in keeping with the reliable, steady nature she so valued in her groom-to-be.

Marge Chandler wasn't a woman who

expected or even sought a grand passion. Such theatrics wore thin over time and flaked away to reveal the tawdry substance beneath. Like gilding atop plaster — it wouldn't last. No, she looked for something simpler and sturdier, and Gavin Miller provided exactly what she'd always dreamed of.

He chose me.

A gentle breeze pushed away the last lingering bit of warmth from her blush as the mill came into view. It didn't seem to be running, but she hadn't expected it to be, with Gavin not there to attend it. The slightest shift or stress in the workings could set off a reaction to ruin the entire operation, so a mill required constant vigilance.

Much like a classroom.

She smiled at the connection until a small twinge of regret chased it away. Married women weren't permitted to teach, and she'd miss it sorely. But now wasn't the time to think of the students she'd left behind or the injustice of how men could work and support families and women weren't allowed to teach. . . . No, now was the time to begin her new life. As a bride. As a wife.

She stifled a groan of frustration as the blush returned. *Wigeondom awaits.*

Instead of dwelling on the thought, she

41

inspected the structure before them. Three stories high, the stone building reached toward the sky like a beacon, breaking the relentlessly flat stretch of prairie, despite the manufactured hill built behind it for the millpond. The source of the mill's power looked placid but slightly murky — typical for water of the Platte River. A thick millrace connected the pond to the waterwheel standing upright alongside the building, easily reaching the second story.

"It's beautiful — easily as fine as any big-city mill." She craned her neck as they rode by toward a modest, two-story, whitewashed house beyond.

"I like to think so." Pride colored his voice as Gavin hopped down and came around to lift her out of the wagon. Broad hands closed around her waist, sending heat skittering up her spine until he set her on the ground. "After I put Smoose in the barn, I need to start her up. Would you like to see?"

Smoose? Marge eyed the massive draft horse, decided it did rather resemble a moose in horse form, and gave an enthusiastic nod. "I couldn't tell whether the overshot wheel had buckets or paddles."

"Paddles. Buckets don't keep the pace as steady, in my opinion, and paddles are simpler to replace." His appreciative glance made her glad she'd read up on gristmills. A short walk to the small stable and they headed onward to the mill.

The manufactured hillside made easy access into the second story, where the millstones and housing dominated the center of the floor. A wooden grain chute slid from the ceiling to just above the large receptacle above the stones.

"This is the hopper." Gavin pulled a lever and the chute opened, allowing grain to fill the hopper. When he was satisfied with the amount, he closed the chute. "The grain will funnel down through the hole in the top stone and be crushed beneath and come out here." He touched various parts of the machine as he spoke, and Marge could see the loving familiarity even as she knew he was giving an oversimplified explanation.

"The gears are housed on the bottom floor and have to be turned by the wheel — which you noticed earlier. Now that there's grain to be ground, we're ready to get her running." Marge followed Gavin to a door at the far end, which opened to a wooden walkway of sorts above the end of the millrace.

"The sluice gate" — he crouched and gestured to the mechanism as he spoke — "adjusts to different heights, depending on the amount of water speed and pressure needed to turn the wheel at any particular time." He raised the gate, releasing a gush of water that steadily streamed down to hit the flat paddles of the overshot wheel, pushing them downward until the wheel caught the momentum in a constant, smooth turn.

"It seems so simple, but it's not at all. So much thought and time and precision to make it run . . ." When he smiled at her musings, Marge decided to make a request. "Sometime, after I meet your grandmother, I'd like to see the gears and learn more."

"I'd like that." He took her arm and led her back outside. The pleasure of showing his mill faded from his expression. "Let me tell Grandma Ermintrude you're here then bring you to her." With that, he released her arm and hurried into the house ahead of her.

Blinking at the sudden change and odd behavior, Marge followed at a slower pace. Why wouldn't he simply walk her inside and introduce them when the old woman knew she would arrive today? A jumble of voices, a sound of exasperation — surely that came from Gavin — began to raise doubts.

"*Marge.*" She heard him stress her name but didn't catch the lady's reply. Unwilling to eavesdrop, she halted a few feet away and tried to calm the tumult suddenly arising in her stomach. Something didn't feel right. . . .

Somehow, Gavin had to figure out what he was going to do before the gnawing numbness wore off. Shock, folks called it. Sure, it'd seen him through a cursory round of introductions in town, loading up the wagon, and the ride home. He'd even managed to put it all aside for a few moments because she seemed so interested in the mill. But now he had to take her to the house.

And Grandma Ermintrude.

Shock couldn't save him there. Everyone else only knew his bride-to-be's name as Marguerite Chandler, as was proper. Grandma, on the other hand, would immediately try to gain the upper hand by calling her Daisy. *And then the secret would be out — that I sent away for a bride and got her cousin by mistake. My mistake.* He winced.

The farce unfolded without him knowing until it was too late to prevent disaster. He forgot Daisy and Marge were *both* Marguerites when he wrote the proposal. They received it, knew he'd been sent an invitation to Daisy's wedding, and logically assumed he'd been sending for Marge. So

45

here he sat, driving the wrong bride back to his home — and she had no idea about any of it. This was the sort of situation that could drive anyone to abandon civilization and make like a mountain man.

But he couldn't do that. He had Grandma — and now Marge — to think of. *No Daisy.* That hit him hard. If she'd refused the proposal, he could've taken it. But thinking she'd consented to be his bride and he'd have the wife he wanted for the rest of his days, only to be disillusioned later?

Lord, I prayed over this and trusted in Your will . . . and You sent me Marge? Now I know how Jacob felt when he got Leah instead of Rachel. A dry swallow didn't make the knowledge go down any easier. *Except Jacob still got Rachel after a few years, and I'll never have a chance with Daisy. The only way I can figure is to marry Marge and never let her know of the mix-up. I sure as shooting can't tell her she's the wrong one. . . . Besides, I sent for Marguerite Chandler as my bride, she arrived, and I need to follow through on that commitment.*

It didn't make doing the right thing any easier though.

With a mishmash of half-formed thoughts clashing in his mind, he told Marge something about telling Grandma she was here

46

and rushed off. It didn't come across as gentlemanly, but when a man had no options, he couldn't be choosy.

"Grandma." He burst through the door and plowed into the parlor. "Marguerite is here."

"I would hope so. Not at all good manners to leave your bride in town." She raised her head slightly, in the manner of a fox trying to catch the scent of new prey. "Don't leave her outside. Bring her to me."

"In a moment." His mind raced madly. Telling Grandma Ermintrude about the mix-up would be the fast way to ensure Marge got beat over the head with it. Gavin wouldn't allow that. So, the only thing left was to say, "I made a mistake." *Did I ever.* "She goes by Marge now. Don't call her Daisy."

"Not Daisy?"

"Marge." He waited for her nod before dashing back out the door to fetch his bride.

And face his future.

47

CHAPTER 5

"She's ready." Gavin emerged from the house with a smile stretching his face — but that's exactly how it looked. Like a painful stretch.

Marge's stomach clenched still more tightly. *Just how difficult could one old woman be?* She straightened her shoulders. *No more difficult than a room full of students. God brought me here. He'll see me through whatever lies ahead.* She accepted Gavin's hand and returned his strained smile as they walked inside her new home.

Grandma Ermintrude waited in the parlor, posture ramrod straight, back not conceding to so much as touch the back of the settee. Steel gray hair trapped in a bun topped a face etched with a hardness to rival that of any metal. Eyes narrowed, lips thinned, hands folded and clenching the top of a cane — Grandma Ermintrude could easily have descended from a Gorgon.

So Marge did what every brave woman did in the face of imminent threat — resorted to pleasantries. "Lovely to meet you, Mrs. Miller."

The woman didn't respond at first beyond a further narrowing of the eyes and what Marge could only deem an indulgent harrumphing. And quite a harrumphing it was. Ermintrude Miller made it not only a sound, but a physical expression of disdain, as her shoulders raised and her chest puffed in indignation before finding relief in that not-so-genteel snort.

"We'll see about that." One wizened hand lifted from atop her cane in an imperious motion. "Come over here so I can get a good look at you."

Gavin seemed reluctant to release her, a sign Marge couldn't read as positive or dreadful, but she moved to stand before her would-be grandmother-in-law.

"Take off that hat. My eyes aren't what they used to be."

Somehow, Marge had a feeling that the woman before her remained as sharp as ever, but kept her tongue between her teeth. She untied her hat and slid it from her hair, resisting the urge to smooth back any wisps that might have escaped. Preening would be a mistake — and a useless one, at that.

Another harrumph. "You're not what I expected, girl." The inspection shifted from her hair, to her eyes, then swept down to the tips of her toes. "Taller, for one thing."

"To be fair, you aren't what I expected either." Marge imbued her shrug with a nonchalance she was far from feeling. "Although you didn't ask, my journey went well and I'm pleased to be here. I trust your day has been pleasant so far."

"Well, she has a mind." A cackle accompanied the comment directed at Gavin. "That's better than I hoped, although she's not as pretty as I pictured."

Marge sucked in a breath at that but held on. "Pretty is as pretty does, they say. I always say you can judge a person based on his or her decisions."

"Interesting." Two eyes sharpened upon her like knifepoints. "And you've made quite a few decisions recently."

"Yes." She smiled at Gavin, although his face could have been etched from the same stone he'd used to build his mill. "And I stand by them."

"So tell me, Miss Chandler . . . when did you decide to stop going by Daisy?"

"Grandma, don't —" A sort of fear flashed across her fiancé's face at the evidence of his grandmother's lapse. Men never dealt well with seeing weakness in their loved ones. Marge had seen it before.

"It's all right." Marge put a hand on Gavin's forearm when he moved forward. "It's easy enough to get confused, and Grandma Miller never met both of us, after all."

"No." Gavin shook off her hand and looked severely at the older woman. "She needs to remember herself."

"I haven't forgotten." A smile multiplied the grooves bracketing her mouth as she ignored her grandson. "*Both* of you, you say?"

"Yes, ma'am." Marge struggled to reconcile Gavin's harshness with her image of him, choosing instead to focus on Ermintrude's turnaround. "Daisy is my cousin, you see."

"Is she, now? Marge — short for Marguerite, yes?" A raspy laugh greeted her nod of acknowledgement. "Would this cousin of yours happen to be . . . oh, at a guess . . . a petite, green-eyed charmer with black ringlets?"

"Does it matter?" The angry burst from Gavin sent the fine hairs on the back of Marge's neck prickling.

"I'm not sure." Suddenly, it felt as though Marge were watching herself speak from

51

over in the corner. "Why did you ask me where Daisy was after I got off the stage? I assumed you thought she'd accompany me, but that's not the reason, is it?"

The look on his face provided all the answer she needed. Shame, disappointment, anger — they chased one another across his features until they burrowed their way into her heart.

"I did say she had a mind." Ermintrude's voice bore into the descending blackness. "I'll bet Marge here is a better choice than that Daisy you wanted in the first place."

"Marge!" Gavin slid one arm around her surprisingly slim waist and cupped her too-pale cheek with his free hand. At Grandma's words, she'd closed her eyes and swayed slightly.

"Ooh." A small moan, almost a whimper, broke through her lips — lips that bore the only color in her face aside from the dark fans of her lashes.

"Don't faint." He put the words to the panic gripping his chest. What would he do with a fainting female?

Her eyes flew open, two small palms pressed to his chest, and she pushed him away with a strength belying her sudden pallor. "I am not," she seethed, "the type of ninny who faints."

"Bravo!" Grandma Ermintrude thumped her cane in a show of approval. "I've seen enough ninnies to last a lifetime."

"Well, the world has seen enough liars." Hazel eyes suspiciously bright, Marge made as though to push past him and out the door.

"Where are you going?" He caught her elbow to bring her up short. It wasn't as though she could just flounce out of his sight and march back home.

"I need some time." She jerked her arm away. "To think."

"That's the one problem with those gals who have minds. They think on things." Grandma's delighted commentary made a muscle in Gavin's jaw twitch.

If the old bat had kept her mouth shut, I wouldn't have this problem.

"There's nothing to think about. We'll get married as soon as you're ready."

"Ready?" Her eyes grew even brighter as a strange, flat laugh hitched from deep inside her. "You'll have a long wait for that."

"You changed your mind?" The hot sting of wounded pride whipped around his throat, making the words tight.

"You change yours?" She tossed the challenge over her shoulder as she sailed out the front door.

"No." He stalked after her, anger fueling his steps so that he caught up to her just outside the mill. "I set out to marry Marguerite Chandler, and that's what I intend to do." He snagged her wrist this time, and the force of her halted momentum made her turn to face him.

"You set out to marry *Daisy* Chandler." Those long eyelashes of hers had gotten darker — and belatedly Gavin registered they were damp. Her eyes went so shiny because she held back *tears*.

The breath left him as fast and painful as if he'd been kicked in the gut. *I made her cry.*

Hurt angled her brows as she whispered her question. "And you weren't even going to tell me about the mistake?"

"Marge . . ." He wanted to say something to make it better but couldn't. "I didn't want you to know."

"You would have made me live a lie!" Fury blazed away the tears — a welcome change from where Gavin stood. Anger, he could deal with.

"I —" The loud groan of stressed oak poured through the mill windows, warning of calamity. "Stay here. I'll be right back." He sprinted to close the sluice gate, reaching it just as a great, splintering *crack* rent the air.

The water flow trickled to a stop, the wheel halted its turning, and all sounds of the running mill ceased. Somewhere down below, on the ground floor, he'd find a broken runner on a gear wheel. But now wasn't the time to inspect it. He had a bride to take care of.

Hustling back, he turned the corner to where he'd left Marge . . . and found no one.

His bride had vanished.

Amos Geer had been staring at her again. Midge shivered and picked up the pace, heading for the spot that never failed to calm her down.

When Gavin Miller and his new woman drove off, she'd stopped concentrating on figuring out what seemed a bit askew between those two and had looked down to gather her thoughts. Then she looked up to find a pair of blue eyes, so dark they seemed stormy, peering directly at her from behind a shaggy lock of corn-colored hair in desperate need of a trim.

Looked like she'd found a fellow watcher.

Not good.

Even worse, it looked like he'd found

her . . . first.

Midge let loose a huff as she pressed onward. Living in Buttonwood for the past four years must've made her turn soft. She'd have to work on that with another watcher around. The last thing she needed was someone paying close attention to the life she'd built in this small — although much larger than when she'd arrived — town.

She remembered the week before, when Amos blocked her escape behind the smithy. Yes, she'd been avoiding him since he first showed up in her town. It'd taken no more than a minute to sum up that the man was too confident, too perceptive, and too curious to be anything but trouble. But when he confirmed that he watched her as closely as she watched everyone else, she'd sealed her verdict regarding the tall newcomer.

Dangerous. He'd turned that considerable curiosity on the mystery of Midge Collins — and she'd spent years guarding those secrets. Nothing could persuade her to leave it to chance that Amos would not remember their encounter from four years before.

The more distance she put between them, the better she felt. Just as she went around the millpond, the point where she breathed easier knowing the apiary lay not too far ahead, something snagged her.

The sound of boots thudding against earth, still audible despite the muffling layer of thick prairie grass, gained urgency as someone came up fast from the left. Midge whirled around, instinctively crouching in a defensive stance, making her vitals less accessible to any attacker.

A flash of violet through the scrawny scrub oaks caught her attention just before Mr. Miller's bride-to-be came tearing full tilt around the millpond. Skirts streaming behind her, chignon bobbing precariously without the covering of any hat, Miss Chandler presented a picture of panic.

"Marge!" A deep yell from around the other side of the mill provided all Midge needed to know. Somehow, Mr. Miller scared this woman — and men who frightened women didn't deserve them.

Women on the run from such men, however, unquestionably deserved her help. Midge burst into a sprint, helping close the short distance between them, and grabbed Marge's hand. The other woman raised glistening eyes to meet her gaze but only faltered for a moment when Midge matched her stride.

They dashed past the scrub oak, past the border of Miller's land, and didn't stop running until Midge found the familiar grove of black walnut trees bordering Opal's apiary on Grogan grounds. Marge matched her pace — an impressive feat, and something more to respect in a woman who had enough sense to find the road when a man found his temper.

Neither of them spoke for a few moments, both too preoccupied with drinking in great gulps of fresh air laced with the faintest hint of honey. As their breathing calmed, the merry *buzz* of hundreds of worker bees busily zooming in and out of the dozens of wooden movable-frame hives in the meadow before them became discernable.

At least Midge could make it out in between the hitched, sniffle-laden, quickly-stifled breaths of her companion. Miss Chandler dabbed at her eyes and nose with a pressed linen handkerchief, tucking it into a pocket in her skirts before looking up. The mop-up job hadn't done much to hide the fact she'd gone on a crying jag. Red nose and watery eyes tattled on both her upset and her inability to play a good damsel in distress. That made her more likeable in Midge's book.

"You don't have to go back," she piped up once the other woman seemed ready to hear her out. "We'll get you taken care of. Now, what did he do?"

"It's a mistake." Miss Chandler's lips moved almost too slowly for the words she spoke. "A terrible mistake."

"Don't you worry." Midge reached over to give her a soothing pat on the back. "We'll make sure you get home again, safe and sound. No woman need put up with a man who done her wrong." She heard her molars grind in the silence as she waited for her new project to confide in her.

But this woman managed a rare feat — she kept her lips buttoned and her thoughts sewn up. She simply looked to the right, off to the distance, as though trying to make a plan, and periodically shook her head as though to clear it.

"Did he hit you?" Midge couldn't see any marks.

"No! Gavin would never do such a thing. How could you say that?" In an instant, the sorrow and uncertainty gave way to bristling indignation. "He's a good man."

"If you're so fond of him, I don't know why you were dead set on running away from him. I suppose that's your business, but seeing as how I thought he'd done you wrong and tried to lend a hand" — Midge worked what scant angles she could — "maybe you could see your way clear to explaining why you don't want to marry the man?"

"If only it were that easy." The tears came back. "I'd rather no one saw me like that, but I needed some time to think on my own."

Obviously this would take some additional needling to get any useful information. Midge used another tactic. "Understood. I'll just wait here while you finish thinking about the reasons you don't want to marry such a fine man."

"Simple. He doesn't want to marry *me*."

CHAPTER 6

If she had her "I'd rathers," or *druthers,* as Aunt Verlata termed them, Marge wouldn't be confiding in this piquant girl who'd whisked her away from the mill. Proclaiming aloud that Gavin didn't want her did nothing to ease the heart-hollowing impact of its truth and only served to broadcast her shame.

Contrary to what she'd told Gavin's grandmother, she'd done an excellent ninny impression when she hied off like that. Fainting ninnies, at least, held no control over their unfortunate reactions. Unless, of course, they were that vile breed of fake-fainting ninny, whose real classification became far less pleasant.

Marge would have said she didn't believe in fleeing one's troubles but rather standing one's ground and confronting them head-on. Putting off an issue didn't make it go away, after all. Yet when things became unbearable and granted her a moment to make a bid for freedom, she ran.

She ran away from going back in the house to face Awful Ermintrude. She ran from seeing the man she'd rejoiced to marry tell her he didn't want her but would take her on as an obligation. Most of all, she'd run until her heart had no room to feel anything other than the threat of bursting through her corset in overexertion.

What she hadn't expected was running into the woman before her. A woman who'd seen her, upset and fleeing, and not wasted time asking questions but rather taken her hand and led her to what must be a safe place. A woman who now thought the worst of Gavin . . . because of Marge.

"Not to be combative," the younger — she looked younger, at least — girl began, signaling an oncoming disagreement.

"Wait." Marge held up one hand, palm outward. "Whenever someone says they don't intend to be combative, or argumentative, or disagreeable, or any such thing, it is a sure sign they are about to be. So I will restate that the cause of my distress lies in a mistake and nothing more, in the hopes you will not question my word when I say that Gavin does not want to marry me."

"Ah." The other woman, who Marge suddenly noticed wasn't wearing a bonnet or hat any more than she was, seemed to be fighting a silent battle. Her lips twitched. "Easy to see you don't know me. I'm Midge Collins."

"Marge Chandler." She barely caught herself before adding how lovely it was to meet her — entirely inappropriate in this situation.

"I know." Miss Collins lost the battle and a wide smile won out. "I also know that Mr. Miller wrote, sent for, and brought you here to be his wife. So I doubt you have any cause to worry about him wanting to marry you."

"You think me a lackwit, and I can't say I blame you. What bride, newly reunited with her groom-to-be, runs from him as though chased by the hounds of hell?" Marge pinched the bridge of her nose, hoping to ease some of the tension throbbing behind it. "But a terrible mistake has been made, and I am not the bride Mr. Miller hoped for."

"Hogwash. You're Marguerite — Marge, if you prefer — Chandler. The woman he's told everyone he's going to marry. The woman he picked up at the stage and brought home to his grandmother. There is no mistaking that." All merriment faded from her features. "If he's threatened or harmed you, don't try to protect him. It will only get worse."

"You almost have it right, Miss Collins." Marge could see there was no recourse but to tell this woman of the mix-up. Otherwise, Gavin's reputation would be forfeit. "I am Marguerite Chandler, who goes by Marge. Gavin Miller did set out to marry Marguerite Chandler. The problem, you see, is that he wanted my cousin. We're both named after our grandmother, but she goes by Daisy."

"You're putting me on." Suspicion slid into the set of the other girl's jaw. "Two Marguerite Chandlers, and you're the wrong one?"

"Precisely." Despite her best efforts, the hot salt of tears pricked her eyes, and her breath hitched once more. Marge fumbled for her handkerchief, barely registering as her newfound confidant flomped onto the shady bit of grass before them.

"Well, that's about as crooked as a snake in a cactus patch. Oh, and it's Midge. Any woman who can keep up when I'm racing down the plains earns that right."

"Thank you, Midge." The unspoken offer of friendship eased some degree of the isolation that washed over her in encroaching waves. "Please call me Marge."

"Do you know," her companion offered, drumming her fingers against one knee as she thought aloud, "I never did like daisies. They look nice, but I can't say I care for the smell."

The random nature of the comment did the trick, forcing a chuckle despite the circumstances. "Marguerite is French for *daisy,* and my cousin always smells very nice."

"I'm sure she does, but this situation you're in puts off an awful stench — and Ermintrude Miller isn't going to make things any sweeter." Her friend stopped drumming her fingers. "You can stay with my family until you go home, if you like."

"Go home . . ." Her knees suddenly shaky, Marge decided to sit before the ground rose up to meet her.

Oh, Lord . . . give me strength. If I go home, everyone will know. Half of Baltimore knows of my engagement to Gavin, and none of them will be surprised to learn he wanted Daisy instead. I'll be a laughing-stock. Daisy will be wracked with guilt. Aunt Verlata will pity me and trot me in front of prospective suitors until my eyes cross. . . .

"No." The horror of such a future flashed before her with such agonizing clarity,

Marge's stomach lurched. "I can't go back."

"That gums up the works." Midge chewed on her inner lip. It was clear as fine crystal that it would do no good to ask why her new friend didn't want to go home.

Because that's the way reality stood. Marge blanched when she thought it over, but the fact she thought it over at all meant returning to Baltimore — if memory served, and memory always served Midge — remained a possibility. An unattractive possibility, judging by how pale the other woman had gone, but that could be due to any number of things. Like pride. Best tread lightly on that one.

"If it were me, I wouldn't be in a hurry to let everyone know either. How much time do you reckon you have? Can you stay until Daisy arrives?"

"Daisy won't marry Gavin. She's to be wed this very month's end — Gavin's father didn't take that into account when he purchased my stage tickets and couldn't transfer them." A gasp of mirthless laughter escaped Marge. "Otherwise I would have waited a little longer before coming here. As it stands, I'll miss my cousin's wedding and have none of my own."

"Little wonder you two thought he proposed to the Marguerite without a fiancé." The words came out with a wince hard on their heels. *Could've been more sensitive there.*

"We'd even sent him an invitation to Daisy's wedding." The beleaguered bride-to-be busied herself trying to find a dry spot on her handkerchief. "I feel such a fool!"

"You are not." Midge rummaged around in her own pockets until she found a rumpled but serviceable linen square and passed it over. "Proposing via letter to Marguerite without clarifying which one seems a numskull thing to do though. Since we're assuming he thought you were both unattached."

"A mere oversight . . ." The rest of the mumble went to the handkerchief.

"A whopping great oversight, if you ask me. More to the point, when he realized what happened, he shouldn't have told you."

For this, at the root, is what had her hackles in a rage. No matter Gavin Miller got the wrong woman, his trap should have stayed shut. He sent for a Marguerite, he received a Marguerite, and he had no business making her feel unwanted. Real men followed through on their commitments. Just look how much he'd hurt poor Marge.

"He didn't tell me." A delicate blow

punctuated the confession. "Grandma Miller asked why I didn't go by Daisy anymore, and I figured it out."

"Then he plans to marry you anyway?" *Well, a point to the miller then. At least he had the right idea, even if he didn't carry it out well.*

"That's what he says." A slightly less delicate blow.

"I take it you're less than thrilled."

"You could say that." A downright honk.

"Bully for you. Women aren't interchangeable, and I wouldn't give him the satisfaction of my hand when he didn't bother asking for it properly in the first place either." Midge leaned back. "He's going to have to court you now."

Marge's hiccup of laughter didn't bode well. "Gavin doesn't want to marry *me,* and he won't. At best, he doesn't want word to get out that he's stuck with the wrong bride." She groaned. "Folks around here will find out soon enough. Is there an inn nearby? I need a place to stay until I can sort out a plan."

"No inn, but you're more than welcome at the Reed house — which is my family. I'm adopted, in case you're wondering." Midge hopped to her feet and dusted off her backside. "What sort of plan do you think you'll come up with, a single woman on her own?"

"Surely I can find work as a teacher out west. I have experience and letters of reference." Her new friend followed suit in brushing dust from her skirts. "Never thought I'd need those letters, but I always feel it's best to be prepared. It pays off."

"You're a teacher?" Midge barely held back a whoop. The town council had been looking for someone to take on the local children as soon as they finished building the schoolhouse, and one too many of them had broached the subject with her lately. If they didn't scrape together enough sense to see she'd make a poor schoolmarm, she'd have to find another solution. "Looks like you're an answer to prayer, Marge. Buttonwood needs a teacher."

"That would be . . . ideal." Hazel eyes blinked in disbelief. "Do you think the town council would consider a woman for the position, or are they solely looking for a schoolmaster?"

"No need to worry about that." Midge started trekking back toward the mill. "My adopted father and grandpa are on the council. So is the husband of a close friend. None of them would look down on a woman, and all of them would support you on my say-so — especially once Clara and Opal weigh in."

"I met them briefly before Gavin and I left town."

"Yes, you would have. They like to meet everyone new. Clara would be the green-eyed blond, Opal the blue-eyed redhead. Clara is married to Dr. Reed, the man who took me in."

She hurried, pleased when Marge increased her speed to match. Midge did so as much to gloss over the topic of her informal adoption as to get to the mill faster. Much as she liked to ask questions, answering them didn't sit well.

As they rounded the millpond, Marge's steps slowed. "Gavin should be relieved to be well rid of me." A forced smile accompanied wistful words.

Midge shook her head. "If I'm any judge of men and their mettle — and of this there is no doubt, although you don't know it yet — Gavin will not let you leave him so easily."

"He cannot stop me from teaching."

"I did not say he could or would." She caught sight of her friend's fake fiancé as he rounded the mill like a charging bull. "But, at a guess, I'd say you underestimate his determination to wed you."

CHAPTER 7

Gavin circled the mill. He searched inside the mill — all three stories. Twice. The barn yielded no sign of a bride on the run either. No woman of sense would go back in the house with Grandma Ermintrude, and Marge always struck him as the practical Marguerite, so he resorted to hollering like a madman.

No results.

In scant moments, his bride-to-be had become a bride-already-gone. With nowhere to run, what strange thoughts crashed in her mind? The most illogical option — returning to the house to throw him off — brought him nose to nose with Grandma.

"Never got the bride you wanted and already lost the one you found?" Sounded like she'd been waiting for him since he'd bellowed for Marge. "You've got a real touch with the ladies."

"I take it she didn't come back here then."

"Told you that one had brains to rattle betwixt her ears. No woman with sense or pride stays where she's unwanted if she has the slightest choice." Grandma Ermintrude cocked her head. "Not that this one has a choice. She just needs time enough to think it through and she'll be back."

"I *told* you not to call her Daisy." Gavin gave vent to the ire that continued to mount, swelling with each moment he couldn't look after Marge. "Why couldn't you leave well enough alone?"

"Why couldn't you tell me the truth?"

"You would've used it against her." She wanted truth? He'd give it to her.

"Never." A long-buried pain rose from the depths of her gaze. Grandma's voice went soft. "I'd never do that to another woman."

"Grandma?"

"Now *you* . . ." Her customary sharpness returned in an instant. "*You* I would've taunted with it, and that's a fact."

"Then don't ask why I didn't spill the whole story with her waiting out front." Anger at himself for how he'd handled things and at her for how her quarrelsome ways influenced him made his tone harsh. "You gave me cause to doubt the way you'd react."

"Blaming others for your mistakes makes

72

for more mistakes to come."

"I'm sure there will be." With that, he headed back to the mill. Until Marge returned, he'd busy himself repairing the gearwheel mechanism that gave way earlier. He set to work, restless in the silence. No turning wheels, no sounds of water churning, gears turning, and grain grinding accompanied him this afternoon. No cheerful *tap* of the damsel against the shoe as grain worked down the hopper between the millstones. Only stillness.

He stopped every so often to go upstairs and outside, checking to see if she'd returned. No such luck. Three times he repeated the process, but it wasn't until he'd replaced the splintered tooth entirely and did several test runs to assure himself of the integrity of the piece that he spotted someone approaching.

No, not *someone. Two* women skirted around the millpond toward him. One wore the purplish color Marge arrived in, so Gavin abandoned his post and hustled to meet them. When he drew closer, he identified her companion as none other than Midge Collins — one of the women he'd hoped Daisy would befriend.

Relief at Marge's safe return crashed against rage that she'd ever left. Regret joined the other two emotions when he saw her reddened nose. *Has she been crying this whole time?*

"Marge — we were worried about you." Somehow it didn't sound like the reprimand he'd intended or the half apology he almost felt appropriate. He sounded stiff.

"Were you?" Miss Collins noticed his voice sounded off. Her very posture spoke of disapproval and suspicion.

"Thoughtless of me to disappear like that." The mumble hardly sounded like Marge. "But in times of trouble, I find it best to collect one's thoughts and determine a course of action." This last sounded more like her.

"I already determined what we'd do." He kept it vague, uncertain how much Marge told Miss Collins. The less anyone else knew about the problem, the better.

He could already hear the gossip if word got out. *"There's our town miller — such a fine head on his shoulders he can't even propose to the right girl!"*

"Your plan is unacceptable." The red all but left her nose. "Thankfully, I ran into Miss Collins here, and we've devised a better one."

"This is none of Miss Collins's affair." With great effort, Gavin kept from shouting. "You are my bride. This is a matter between us."

"Ah, but that's just the problem, isn't it, Mr. Miller?" Miss Collins stepped forward. "Marge is *not* your bride."

"She will be." Gavin's jaw thrust forward in an expression of such determination Marge could almost have believed he wanted to marry her.

Almost.

She opened her mouth to reply, but another voice sounded.

"Would you all get inside this house" — Grandma Miller's caterwaul belied her age — "so an old woman can hear what's going on?" Standing on the front stoop, cane planted in the dirt one step down, she glowered at them all from a good distance away. Such a distance, it was a wonder she'd managed to know there was anything going on at all — particularly with the sound of the mill running.

"*Another* watcher." Midge's mutter made absolutely no sense, and Marge didn't bother asking. "Do you know, I always thought of her as a cantankerous woman, but I'm starting to think she's got spunk. Why don't we all go inside?"

Because you were closer to the truth

75

with cantankerous? She bit her tongue, instead admiring the way Midge managed to work her way inside the house in spite of Gavin's obvious discomfort. All three of them trouped in to follow the old woman's command — although Midge was the only one to manage some semblance of enthusiasm.

Grandma Miller inclined her head in a manner fit for royalty. "Miss Collins, how do you come to join us this afternoon?"

"I ran . . . across" — Midge's choice of words would have amused Marge at any other time — "Marge as she sought some time for private reflection. I'm afraid I drew some faulty conclusions regarding Mr. Miller." Here, her gaze flicked to Gavin. "So Marge explained your predicament to make it clear he'd done her no wrong."

"Thank you for not letting the townspeople of Buttonwood think I chased you off." Gavin's dry tone strengthened Marge's resolve.

"So you should thank the gal." Grandma Miller chose to speak up on her behalf. "If she let Miss Collins think you sent her running off like that for any reason other than the truth, you'd sorely regret it. As it stands, this couldn't have been an easy thing for Marge to divulge. It doesn't reflect well on either one of you."

"It's hardly Marge's fault, from where I sit." Midge demonstrated a friend's loyalty already. "But broadcasting she wasn't the woman your grandson wanted will hardly enhance her standing — or her options — in Buttonwood."

"Options?" The word came out as a muted roar. "What options? Marge will marry me, as planned."

"I most certainly will not." She didn't even care that she sounded waspish. "As I said, Midge and I made other plans."

"Have you?" An old woman's head truly ought not swivel so swiftly nor so far as Grandma Miller's managed during this conversation. "Things grow more interesting by the minute."

"No, they haven't."

"Yes, we have. Marge mentioned she's a teacher," Midge cut in, refuting Gavin's denial. "Buttonwood needs a schoolmistress, and I'm willing to speak on her behalf. It all works out."

"You see?" A hard swallow cleared her throat enough to allow the words through. "I don't have to marry you."

"You don't have to marry me, but you will." Gavin crossed his arms over his chest. "As planned."

"You didn't plan on wedding me, so it's moot."

He took three large steps closer and peered down at her. "I plan on it now. I planned on it since you alighted from the stage and I knew why'd you'd come. Make no mistake, *Marguerite* Chandler, before long, you will be Marguerite Miller."

His stressing of her formal name, far from driving home the point or underscoring any commitment, incensed her afresh. "Marge." She poked a finger into his chest with each word she ground out. "Call — me — Marge."

"Good point. If you'd called Daisy, well, Daisy, she wouldn't be here in the first place." Midge made herself comfortable in a wing-backed chair. "Although I, for one, am quite glad Marge came to Buttonwood. We need her."

Suddenly, Marge realized she'd just prodded a man. Who wasn't her fiancé. In public. She felt the blush heat her cheeks even as she balled her hands into fists and pushed them deep into the pockets of her lilac traveling ensemble. *Running like a hoyden, confiding in strangers, putting my hands on a man . . . what am I coming to?*

"You mistake me. I said *Marguerite* because I proposed to her as such, and she accepted that proposal. We are bound by that agreement, and she needs reminding."

"Fools don't grow on my family tree. He gets that from his mother's blood. My son didn't pass on the type of addled thinking that would make a man keep mentioning he didn't specify which woman he was proposing to." Grandma Miller made this general announcement while Marge headed straight for her reticule, opened it, and withdrew what she sought.

"Reminding everyone that this whole mess is all his fault won't do him a lick of good." Midge sided with the old woman. "Marge, what are you up to over there?"

"Here." She moved to Gavin's side and slapped the money onto his palm, folding his fingers over it. "You did not propose to me. You proposed to Daisy. A misinterpretation doesn't bind me to you, although I do owe you something. This is for the stage fare."

"I don't want your money." He made as though to return it, but she backed away. "I want your hand."

"Do you?" Someone else spoke the question on Marge's heart, and it took her a moment to realize it was Midge.

Lord, I already know the answer. Please give me strength to move forward. I trust it's

*Your will for me to teach the children here —
that there is a reason and a purpose for this
horrible misunderstanding.* Otherwise, it
would simply be too cruel to leave her
standing here, staring at the man she'd been
so delighted to marry, waiting for him to
say — again — he didn't want her.

Gavin didn't answer immediately, a blessing and curse, in that it showed he was taking time to truly consider the question. His
perusal took her in from the top of her head
to the tips of her toes before he uttered one
word. "Yes."

Air became unbreathable for an instant.
Until she saw him open his mouth and
knew the next words would somehow ruin
it.

"She is mine."

Something primal rippled up her spine,
but her mind and heart rejected it. "I don't
belong to you, Gavin Miller."

"He already said he wanted her." Seemed
like Grandma Miller, along with Midge, was
enjoying the show. "What more is she after?"

"Tell him, Marge." Midge cheered her on.
"Tell him what he has to do if he wants
you."

"I won't play out this farce." Her nose
prickled, signaling another onslaught of
tears.

"Marge . . ." Gavin's request cut through her confusion. "Tell me."

"All right." *The worst that can happen is he doesn't do it, and that's already where I stand.* "If you want to marry me, Gavin Miller, you're going to have to do one thing."

"Which is?"

"Prove it."

Chapter 8

"Prove it?" Gavin echoed the challenge she'd thrown down like a gauntlet. "Doesn't me saying so and asking repeatedly do that?"

"His mother's side, I tell you." Grandma Ermintrude couldn't seem to hold it in. "If he only took after my son, he'd cotton on far quicker."

"I'm inclined to believe you, Mrs. Miller." How he'd ever thought that Collins girl would be helpful stumped Gavin at the moment. It must have shown, because she addressed her next comment to him. "From where I sit — quite comfortably, I might add — you have a lot of proving to do. For one thing, I haven't heard you ask Marge to marry you on one single occasion. You do, however, demonstrate a distinct talent for giving orders."

"Now *that* he gets from me." Leave it to Grandma Ermintrude to make a man proud.

"You're both wrong. I didn't issue orders. I stated facts." If he had to stand trial, he'd provide a solid defense. "Marge will marry me. It's the obvious decision based on what she's already done."

"Forgive me for failing to see how my refusals would make marriage a foregone conclusion."

"A man proposes to be sure a woman wants to marry him." Gavin didn't know how women managed to get these things so twisted around, but he'd straighten them out. "I know Marge wants to marry me. She wouldn't be here otherwise."

"You think . . . that's why . . . ooh. Wrong!" The woman he'd just proclaimed wanted to marry him spluttered the most vehement denial he'd ever heard.

"If you didn't want to marry me, you wouldn't have left your home and family and come here as my fiancée." He could be patient, even understand that her position made her vulnerable. But the woman had to see reason. "I'm not wrong."

"That proposal theory of yours was." Grandma Ermintrude shook her head. "A man doesn't only ask a woman to wed him to see whether or not she wants to."

Miss Collins simply glowered at him. "Her wanting to is only half of it. A man proposes

83

to demonstrate to his woman how much he values her."

"The mere act of asking implies that." Three women in the house were two too many. Possibly three too many, but that wouldn't help Gavin win a bride.

"And you haven't asked." Marge recovered her ability to speak. "You asked Daisy. You've proven that you want to marry *my cousin*."

All of a sudden, the problem became clear. *Easy enough to get that bee out of her bonnet so we can get married and move on. Marge will be a good wife, and no one need ever know things weren't planned this way.*

He closed the short distance between them, dropped to one knee, and took one of her hands in both of his. Looking up into hazel eyes wide with surprise, Gavin gave his future wife the one thing that would make all the mistakes better — a proposal. Better yet, a proposal before witnesses.

"Marge Chandler, will you marry me?"

Her lips parted, her eyes searching his, she held perfectly still for one spellbound moment. Then she snatched her hand from his grasp and backed away. "No!"

"What do you mean, 'No'?" He lurched to his feet and tracked her. "You said prove it." She scuttled farther back when he came within reaching distance. "You said a man proposed to demonstrate how much he valued his woman."

Their deranged dance continued — his stalking closer, her scooting backward around the room in a bid to avoid him. "I proposed. I proved I valued you." With his final point, he backed her into a corner. Literally.

"I mean, 'No, I will not marry you.' " She lifted her chin, defiant despite being caught. "Or, if you like, 'No, you have most certainly not proven yourself.' "

"I don't like it." He leaned closer, deliberately placing one palm against the wall. "You can't change the rules."

"Don't accuse me of cheating." Sparks of green blazed in the honey brown of her stare — he'd never noticed that before. "Yes, a man proposes to show he values his woman." She reached up and pushed on his elbow. When it didn't give way, she ducked beneath it and made an escape. "But the problem is you can't skip the steps that come before."

"You made no mention of other steps." He looked at the space where she'd been so neatly sandwiched a scant moment before. A faint scent of something . . . clean . . . lingered. He liked it. "What other steps?"

"I'm not *your* woman." She'd taken refuge between Miss Collins and Grandma Ermintrude, of all people.

"You will be as soon as we're wed." Confound her circular logic.

"Wrong way around." The ever-helpful Miss Collins poked her nose in again.

"I didn't have to prove she was my woman when she first came. Why now?" *And how?*

"Before, everyone thought she was the woman of your choice. That was enough." An exasperated *thump* of Grandma's cane sounded. "Think, boy. How do you win a woman?"

Gavin swallowed a groan as the answer hit him like a pebble between the eyes . . . with enough force to fell a lesser man. "You three are saying I have to court my own mail-order bride."

"I think it's best you stay here with Grandma Miller while you teach" — Miss Collins directed the statement to Marge — "rather than come home with me, after all. Seems only fair to allow Mr. Miller the opportunity to" — she turned to give him a meaningful look — "get to work."

Hard work was to be met head-on. *"And whatsoever ye do, do it heartily, as to the Lord, and not unto men. . . ."* Amos considered the verse in Colossians a daily challenge. Fulfilling it meant food on the table for Mother and his six siblings, a sense of satisfaction in a job well done, and a well-earned night's rest.

It also, he reflected as he sat on a church pew on Wednesday morning, brought with it the benefits of clean living. The Geers hadn't set up in Buttonwood for much more than a month, as of yet, and already people took notice of a solid work ethic. With the mill finished — though he'd only been around to help put on the final touches — the town council contracted him to build a schoolhouse.

Perfect timing, since he and the family arrived too late for spring planting on the homestead and a paying job came as nothing short of a blessing. Amos went ahead and stretched his boots beneath the pew ahead of his. Might as well get comfortable — his presence was more of a formality than anything else.

It wasn't as though he had much to say in the hiring of a new schoolmarm. He hadn't been in town long enough to bear any right to vote on anything so important. No, Parson Carter and Josiah Reed — minister and mayor, or Field Mouse and Fox, as Amos privately dubbed them — requested his presence so that they could all discuss the progress on the schoolhouse. Ostensibly, if they hired on the new woman, she might make some requests and such forth.

No matter. He'd adjust whatever they liked. Today's meeting caught his interest for a few reasons — that he had four school-aged brothers and sisters didn't even make the top two. A few questions rustled around in the files of his mind, so Amos made sure to show up early. Good call.

The council filed in and took chairs at the front of the church. Then in walked the two points of interest. Amos stopped slumping and sat up straight as Midge Collins strolled in alongside Mr. Miller's new bride.

Just as I suspected. Only one new woman got off that stagecoach — but married women don't teach. Here then lay an entire collection of questions waiting to be answered. Amos couldn't help but notice Mr. Miller didn't join his bride-to-be for the interview this morning. *Never a dull moment when one pays attention.*

Especially when Midge Collins made an appearance. Amos's focus slid to her and stayed put — with good reason. Now there was a woman to work for. She knew it, too. Had half the pups in town sniffing after her skirts but knew better than to go twitching them at anyone. Every man alive heard of women who played hard to get. Well, here he'd found a woman who meant it.

He never could resist a worthwhile challenge, and it didn't hurt that this one came wrapped in a petite package with that saucy smile and a few freckles. *Always had a soft spot for freckles.*

But the one girl Amos fixed on talking to went to extreme lengths to avoid him. *I wonder if she remembers our encounter four years ago. How long can she hold it against me for "manhandling" her?*

He'd find out soon enough. Until then, Amos fully intended to enjoy the view. So he watched and listened as Midge explained to the council how Miss Chandler came to them highly qualified, with letters of reference, and would like to help them set up the Buttonwood school.

More importantly, he listened to what Midge avoided saying. No mention of how it'd been rumored she herself was to be given the post. Not a word about Mr. Miller and Miss Chandler's impending marriage. The unsaid attracted more and more attention.

"Miss Chandler, your references exceed expectation and your experience speaks to your ability." Saul Reed gave a satisfied nod and fell silent amidst nods of agreement.

"There is an issue left to address." Frank Fosset, a short, jovial man who sold and traded oxen to wagon trains heading to Oregon, apparently hadn't gotten the same information as others on the council. "Miss Chandler, it is my understanding you came to Buttonwood to be Mr. Miller's bride. As you know, married women find themselves carrying many responsibilities that preclude them from teaching. I apologize for asking a personal question, but it seems the council has forgotten to look into this matter of your marital plans. Are you getting married or not?"

"Eventually." Marge refused to slouch. "I plan to marry in the future, but Mr. Miller and I have yet to determine absolute compatibility and set a date."

Despite Midge's efforts on her behalf, Marge knew there'd be questions. This council meeting would only be the beginning of the queries, speculation, and downright gossip about her and Gavin.

Gavin. Strange how she couldn't re-erect the barrier of his name in her mind. After calling him "Gavin" in her mind for when she claimed him as her fiancé, then for a scant hour in person, she couldn't convince her head or heart to reclassify him as "Mr. Miller," as was proper. Oh, when she spoke to others she could adhere to social convention easily enough. But in private . . .

They always say you're at your truest when no one else is watching. Marge didn't want to think about the things she hid within, the things she allowed no one to see. *What does that say about who I am?*

"The Grogans, my son, and I are aware of the . . . uncertainty regarding Miss Chandler's arrangements with Mr. Miller." Josiah — at least she thought that was his name — Reed, owner of the mercantile and mayor of Buttonwood weighed in. "Until such a time as the matter is settled, we understand she is to live with Ermintrude Miller, while Gavin takes up temporary residence within the mill itself."

"While Miss Chandler and Mr. Miller go about reacquainting themselves," Dr. Reed — Midge's adoptive father — added his voice, "she is applying for the position of schoolmistress. Should she wed, obviously another candidate would be needed."

"Which would leave us in the lurch." Mr. Fosset seemed unlikely to cave to popular opinion. "We need some sort of stability or contingency plan if we're to take on such a poor risk." He belatedly realized how that sounded as he added, "No offense, Miss Chandler."

"None taken." *Though I'm not half so poor a risk as you might think. Have they not noticed Gavin didn't bother to accompany me this morning? In all likelihood, I'll be a school-marm until I can no longer remember the subjects I teach.*

"We'd be no worse off than before." The farmer, Mr. Grogan, held true to Midge's prediction.

"No. I remember us discussing Miss Collins as a possible candidate for the position."

Marge held back a sigh. Normally she didn't like to judge. But to her understanding, Mr. Fosset dealt in oxen. Perhaps that was the source of his bullish obstinacy?

"I don't believe I'd make a good candidate." Midge didn't mince words. "Besides having no experience, patience isn't my strongest suit. Everyone knows that."

Guffaws met her admission.

"What if we compromise?" Parson Carter leaned forward. "Hire Miss Chandler to help set up the school and keep her on so long as is possible, but with an added provision."

Hope, vibrant and welcome after the flat-tening revelations of the day before, fluttered to life. "What provision?"

"Miss Collins trains alongside you as your successor." The parson couldn't look more pleased as the rest of the council nodded in agreement.

Marge stood in no position to protest, although one look at her friend's face told that Midge felt just as she had when she realized Gavin didn't want her.

Trapped.

Chapter 9

Peace and quiet. That's all Midge really wanted. Complete silence. A place with no one and nothing but utter stillness. So she could shatter it by shrieking.

Instead, she got a guided tour of the new schoolhouse-in-progress. Led by none other than Amos Geer. Amos. Geer. The very reason — aside from her total lack of patience and inability to remain still indoors for any significant length of time — she balked at becoming a teacher.

The moment they contracted Amos Geer to construct the school, Midge decided to have nothing to do with it. Folks were always saying to "listen to her gut," and that man made hers grumble. Not in a sour milk sort of way, but in a keep-your-distance type of warning.

A warning she'd done her level best to heed until a scheming town outmaneuvered her. All because she'd tried to do the right thing for a fellow outsider. *The old adage is true — no good deed goes unpunished.*

She scarcely refrained from aiming a kick at the stray rock in her path — that would have been childish. Instead, she played a little game as the three of them trouped toward the building. A game of how-many-things-about-Amos-are-unattractive. Midge prepared to create a long list.

Four years ago, that incident at Fort Bridger, for one thing. He most likely didn't even remember it. *But I do.*

Then there was the sad matter of his overconfidence. His walk alone should be a source of shame. That stride, legs swallowing the distance as though it was nothing, shoulders relaxed as though completely at ease.

Why couldn't he slouch, stoop, strut, swagger, or go stiff in the neck like every other man in town? Those men had the sense God gave a goat and knew full well that everybody had something to cause a hitch in their get-alongs. Any man unaware of his flaws made for a fool.

And any man who could hide his so well became a threat.

"Here we are." An obvious statement — and another thing to add to her list of things to dislike, since people who said obvious things lacked ingenuity, as Amos gestured to the already-laid foundation of the schoolhouse. "You can see it'll be a good size, but plan for the walls to be thick."

"It's larger than the schoolroom I managed in Baltimore." Marge seemed pleased, at least. "Why will the walls be so thick, I wonder?"

"Council batted around a few ideas when I came up with the building materials' cost. Wood's scarce around these parts, so we'd have to ship in whatever we used. It's not the best insulator against weather. Would need steady upkeep and repainting, too. But the main argument against it seemed to center around the issue of safety."

"Fire." Midge fought to keep from going pale. Amos would notice — and it made her freckles stand out.

"Yep." His nod didn't seem to notice anything unusual. "Some folks saw a wooden schoolhouse full of boisterous children and a stove as a catastrophe waiting to happen."

"Not worth the risk." She let them both know she agreed with that opinion. "Brick is a better choice."

"Expensive." Marge frowned. "Wouldn't the money be better spent on books, slates, ink, and paper for the children to use?"

"They balked at the high freight cost, but I found a substitution." He made his way behind a cornerstone and lifted a piece of canvas to reveal an orangish red block far larger than a normal brick. "This is made from a type of red clay found not too far from here. It holds up well to wind and water, and the thickness of the blocks will keep the building sturdy enough to withstand the worst storms."

In spite of herself, Midge crouched, stripped off a glove, and ran a hand over the block. A fine layer of soft reddish grit dusted her fingertips. She rubbed them together. "Little red prairie schoolhouse — not brick and doesn't have to be painted. Ingenious."

"I can see now why the walls will be so thick," Marge commented. "We'll be glad of it in the heat of summer."

"This will make the place dark." The very thought of it — forced to stay cooped up inside in a dim room with thick walls — made Midge's toes twitch with the need for a quick escape.

"We've ordered a total of six windows." Amos pointed first to the length then to the breadth of the foundation. "Each side will have two, so you'll get light in morning and afternoon. The third pair is slightly smaller, to bracket the entrance."

"Glad to hear it." Her toes stopped twitching, at least. Well . . . mostly.

"Will I need to speak with the council about ordering a blackboard, desks, and supplies?" It seemed Midge wasn't the only one who made mental lists, as Marge began rattling off things like primers and hornbooks. "Or has that been seen to?"

"The blackboard and desks, they're ordered. I couldn't speak as to the rest." Amos stepped up onto the foundation, walking to the very center. "This is where we planned to put the stove so it'd heat most evenly come winter. If you ladies approve that, then there's not much else to discuss."

"I approve." *Time to leave Mr. Geer behind . . . far, far behind. So I don't have to consult with him again.* Midge looked expectantly at Marge.

"The council mentioned a bell?" Her friend's question may have been reasonable, but Midge didn't appreciate it all the same.

Especially when they all walked back to the general store and Amos Geer pointed up a narrow flight of stairs. "It's up there. You can't miss it."

Marge started up without a moment's hesitation. Midge, however, balked when Amos stepped back to let her go ahead.

"I've already seen it, thank you." It would take far more than a bell to make her waltz up those stairs, knowing her rump would be straight in his sight line.

"Good." A wide smile revealed that the slight gap between his front teeth hadn't completely closed in the past four years. He moved in such a way to block the stairs. "Now you can explain why you've been avoiding me."

Amos didn't bother to hide his amusement as his quarry looked to the left then right for avenues of escape. Let her look. He'd chosen well — with Josiah Reed at the far end of the counter, clear at the other end of the mercantile with another customer, Midge couldn't pawn him off on anyone.

At the same time, if she tried to go out the door, the bell would jangle to catch everyone's attention. He already blocked the staircase, and good manners dictated she wouldn't abandon Miss Chandler in any event. All he needed was time.

"Miss Chandler?" He pitched his voice to carry up the stairs but not across the store.

"Yes, Mr. Geer?" The miller's would-be-wife peeped over the top of the stairwell. "Will I not be able to find it?"

"I'm sure you will. It's to the left." A smile

would reassure her — and concern Midge — so he flashed one. "Mr. Reed might have mentioned a crate of primers up there, if you'd like to look for a moment." He heard a quick exhalation from the woman at his side, the type of sound that could only be called a huff. His grin grew.

"He mentioned no such thing," Midge spoke through gritted teeth. How anyone could call her something so stuffy as Miss Collins escaped Amos's understanding.

"I said he *might* have."

"We both know better."

"Then tell me something I don't know." He really shouldn't be enjoying this so much. "What did I do to set up your back?"

"What makes you think you're of any concern to me?" The imperiously raised brow could have fooled someone who hadn't watched her systematic avoidance over the course of weeks.

"Speak plainly. Are you in a sulk because you think I don't remember you?" He deliberately provoked her, intent to see whether she knew what he meant.

"Sulk?" She latched on to the word and ignored the question. "Grown women don't indulge in sulks."

"A girl I met once did — at Fort Bridger." Amos saw the flash of recognition in her eyes and felt a surge of satisfaction. *She remembers.*

"Did she? If I had to make a guess, I'd say you deserved whatever she threw at you." Her studied nonchalance missed its mark only because it was a shade *too* studied. "For amusement's sake, why don't you tell me about this so-called sulk."

She wants to know how much I remember. That boded well. For the first time, he caught a glimpse of the curiosity she kept contained around him. The curiosity that shone from her whenever she spoke with just about any other soul in Buttonwood — only to shutter when she glanced his way. *Why?*

"Scrawny gal." He saw her eyes narrow at that. *Good.* "Thought her to be about eleven when I first caught sight of her poking her pretty little nose where it didn't belong. Not time enough to shout a warning and be sure she'd hear me — much less heed it if she did — I ran up and pulled her away from the door."

Midge opened her mouth, obviously fixing to interrupt, but he held up a hand to stop her. She'd asked him to tell the story, and he'd finish his version before she got her say.

"You see, my brother Billy almost died in

101

that room just a few days before, and it hadn't been cleaned out. That nosy little girl could've died if I hadn't saved her. But did she thank me for my troubles?" Amos shook his head mournfully as Midge's glower grew still more fierce.

"No. Instead, she stomped on my foot, elbowed me in the ribs, and threatened me with a bloody nose. That little girl sure lucked out that I had a soft spot for freckles."

"You grabbed me from behind with half the force of a freight train and no word of warning!" she burst out in rebuttal the moment he stopped. "Then had the nerve to tell me it wasn't manhandling. Any male who sneaks up on a woman deserves whatever he gets — including that bloody nose you escaped." Midge drew a breath, still visibly livid. "And you're wrong. I did thank you."

"But you didn't apologize." Suddenly he recalled that she had thanked him after he explained about Billy.

"Did so."

"Only for stomping on my foot — not for elbowing me in the ribs. Now that I know you remember Fort Bridger," he said, shifting closer and lowering his voice, "you still owe me an apology."

"You won't get it."

"Looks like you're lucky." Amos heard the unmistakable sound of feminine footsteps on stairs and got in the last word. "I *still* like freckles."

CHAPTER 10

Gavin dipped his hand in the half-full sack of flour, knowing by the feel of it in his palm it was wrong. *Wrong, wrong, wrong.* Everything he'd turned out that morning either went to scrap feed or had to be put through again with exacting adjustments to fix what should have been right the first time.

Lord, is this Your way of telling me I should have gone to the town meeting with Marge? Part of wooing a woman is supposedly being supportive, but how does it help my cause to support her means of being independent? To encourage her to push farther and farther away from me?

To be sure, although he already knew exactly what he'd find, he rubbed the forefinger of one hand in the small mound of flour covering the opposite palm. Small grits tattled of stones set a hair's breadth too far apart. He let it fall back into the sack with a dismal pale *poof* and went to shut the sluice gate. If a miller lost his touch, he lost everything.

Same could be said of a man and his temper. In fact, that's where Gavin suspected the real problem lay. If he looked hard enough, he wouldn't find the flaw in the grain, or the gears, or in his knowledge or finely cultivated instinct for grinding and tending the mill. He would admit it came from his sudden sense of dissatisfaction.

If idle hands did the devil's work, distracted ones opened the doors. With a mind full of Marguerites, precious little focus remained for the mundane. Not when at that very moment, Marge stood before the town council, revealing that she most certainly did not plan to marry him.

An impossible situation. Go, and appear to endorse her decision to refuse him. Or stay, and seem to sulk at her defection. Either way, he'd be the butt of every joke in town until he got her stubborn self to the altar — *where she belongs.*

How to get the job done presented a problem. Particularly when he wanted to ask the woman what in tarnation she was about, broadcasting their business to everybody like this. Tempers didn't tempt anyone, so he'd have to keep a lid on his.

He could do that. Anger provided a poor

way of life, and Gavin didn't hold grudges. However, holding grudges didn't match up with bearing responsibility — and he didn't hold all of it in this situation. *Marge needs to meet me halfway.*

"I came all the way to Buttonwood." A surprised voice behind him made him realize he'd spoken aloud . . . and Marge had returned. "That's more than halfway."

"Not what I meant." He kept the exasperation from his tone and turned to find her silhouetted in the doorway. For the first time, Gavin looked at her as the woman he would wed — the woman who would stand and sleep alongside him for the rest of his life.

With strong shoulders for a woman, trim waist, hips round enough to bear a man several sons, Marge wasn't a woman he would have overlooked had she been standing beside anyone other than her cousin. Better yet, right now, she looked amused.

"This morning I came back to the house from town, and when Grandma Miller said you were here, I met you at the mill." Was that a teasing glint in her eye? Had Marge ever teased him before?

"Come a little closer," he invited. To his recollection, Daisy was the cousin with a ready smile and easy laugh.

"Said the spider to the fly?" She finished the first line of the nursery rhyme and shook her head, bonnet bobbing. The motion carried subtly through the lines of her body, making her skirts sway.

"I thought the spider said, 'Step into my parlor'?" At her nod, he held up a finger. "You forfeit a penalty then. One step."

"Mills have no parlors." She still gave him one step and held up two fingers. "Your penalty."

"So be it." He liked this side of her. "Now give me another, as a toll for entering my mill."

"You wouldn't demand such a thing!" Her overdone gasp amused him. "Besides, the miller himself bid me enter."

"That he did. He wanted his toll."

"Very well." She slid forward a few inches. "But the forfeit for churlishness is three full steps."

"Woman!" Three steps brought him far closer, but he managed to drum up a scowl. "You cannot penalize a miller for seeking his due! Three steps for impertinence!" Her three steps would have made but one of his, and they both knew it. His scowl lost some of its pretense.

"He overcharged." The merriment left her face. "Four steps from the man who asks too much."

"Then I'll grant two, for I seek what's right." His footfalls sounded heavy. "And take two from a woman who gives too little and then fines the miller for wanting more."

"I'll give no more until he proves himself worthy but penalize him further for the way he believes he's entitled to what he wants." Her eyes blazed with indignation. "Remember that, Gavin."

"So long as *you* remember I'm willing to pay for what I want." He gestured to the now-scant distance between them. "In time, I'll earn my prize."

"Prize, indeed," Marge muttered to herself as she made her way toward the house. "Consolation prize, more like."

"Hmph." The pronounced snort warned her of Grandma Miller's presence too late for her to keep her thoughts where they belonged — inside her head. The old woman seemed to be on her way back from the necessary. "Airing woes, are we, missy?"

"No, ma'am." She held the door open for her companion and followed her inside. "Just repeating something your grandson mentioned." *And adding the part he left unsaid, to remind myself of the true state of things.*

Just because Gavin grinned in appreciation at her good mood and little game didn't mean he truly enjoyed her company or wanted a lifetime of it. He'd made his choice — although he'd not received it. Now Marge made hers. If she didn't keep a tight hold on her emotions and plans, she'd unravel.

"You can peel those potatoes while you tell me all about it." Grandma plunked herself down at the table and began making short work of a mound of turnips and carrots. Venison already roasted in the stewpot atop the fancy modern stove Gavin had ordered for his wilderness home.

The stove he planned to have Daisy fix him meals on for the rest of their lives. A smile tickled the edges of her mouth at that thought. No matter how modern, a stove couldn't work miracles and cook for her cousin. Gavin might be disappointed to know Daisy couldn't so much as boil water. . . .

But no. It served no purpose to mention such a thing. And Marge wasn't so vain as to point out her cousin's lack of skill in hopes Gavin would appreciate the woman who'd come to Buttonwood to wed him. That would be folly.

"We lose folks to lots of things — time,

sickness, heat, drowning, animal attacks, wars . . ." The slightly croaky voice of her companion pulled Marge's attention away from her musings. "With all those dangers, seems pure foolishness to lose yourself in thought."

"If people thought more, many tragedies could be avoided." She set down a peeled potato and reached for the next in the pile. "I daresay fewer would be caused in the first place." *Like misbegotten, accidental proposals that seem cheery and full of hope but snatch away everything just because no one stopped to truly think about what was going on!*

"Unpleasant situations like proposal letters gone awry?"

Thunk. Her blade chopped off a large hunk of the potato she'd been peeling. It seemed rather pointless to feign nonchalance after that telltale move, but Marge gave it her best. "Perhaps."

"Perhaps a thoughtless mistake will turn out for the best. Sounded to me like that cousin of yours was all smiles with no spirit to back it up."

"Daisy is full of spirit." The knife met the table as she lost her concentration again. "My cousin is a force unto herself — something no one who's not met her can possibly appreciate. And there's no one who doesn't like a good smile."

"True. Maybe you'd best stop scowling."

"I'm not scowling!" Marge glared at the mangled potato before her for a moment before realizing it. A grudging chuckle escaped her at her own ridiculousness.

Grandma Miller added an approving cackle. "Good to see you have a sense of humor. I started to wonder. More to the point, you'll need it if you're going to wed that grandson of mine."

"Oh, but I'm not going to wed your grandson." Slow, careful strokes of the steel knife sent peels curling toward the table. "I'm going to teach here in Buttonwood. Eventually things will be settled enough I'll not stay here any longer, and Gavin can find a new bride." *One he wants.*

"He already has Daisy's replacement. Why would he need anyone else?"

"It's not a matter of need." Another perfect, methodically peeled potato joined the pile. "It's a matter of what your grandson wants in a wife. I am most assuredly not that woman."

"A man wants a woman. Plain and simple." For all the bluntness of the words, the older woman's gaze stayed fixed to the table. "One who'll put supper on the table and babies in his nursery. You'll do quite well."

"No, I won't." *A man has to choose that woman.* "I won't be second choice to my cousin."

"I can understand that. Maybe even respect it. But if you think half as much as you seem to, take some advice from an old woman." Grandma Miller raised her chin, eyes blazing with some old ember of memory. "No one wants to be second choice to another woman. But it's worse to be a slave to your own pride."

CHAPTER 11

"Don't you love me?" Trouston looked up from where he'd been nibbling — in slightly slobbery fashion — behind her ear.

"You know I do, darling." Daisy gave one of his perfect curls a playful tug in hopes the gesture would distract him. Of late their stolen moments seemed to become more and more awkward. And if Trouston's urgings were anything to judge by, it was a good thing they'd be married before week's end.

"Sweetikins, we've discussed this." He drew back, cupping a protective hand over the back of his skull. His glower told her the petty gambit worked beautifully in shifting his attention. "You know it takes Richards far too long to see my hair properly done. I won't have you messing it up."

"Sorry." She tried to look penitent even as she shifted forward from the half-reclining position he'd pressed her into on the settee. "Your valet does work wonders." She suppressed a disloyal spurt of amusement at her fiancé's vanity. Valets for men had gone out of fashion decades before, after all.

"Where are you going? There's no rush, my dear. Your mother won't expect me to bring you back for hours yet."

"Mmm . . ." She sought a reason for her conspicuous movement. "Suddenly I'm parched. With no servants here, I meant to go find a glass of water." A bright smile hopefully covered her sudden discomfort.

Leaving the Brodington musicale a bit early under pretext of a headache seemed a fine idea when Trouston whispered it to her after that dreadful performance by one of their daughters. No misgivings fluttered in her stomach when he drove her to the two-story townhome he'd purchased upon their engagement, telling her he wanted to give her a private tour before the servants took up residence the next day.

But now . . . now the faint chimes of muffled good sense thumped unpleasantly in the back of her mind. Proper young ladies simply did not disappear into empty houses with a man.

Even an engagement didn't excuse such laxness.

"Allow me." Without a moment's hesitation, Trouston left the room, his lanky frame angling out the doorway as though eager to fulfill his mission.

That's my Trouston. At his show of devotion, the alarms stilled. After all, Trouston could be depended upon to uphold respectability. She trusted him with her hand, her heart, and her entire future — of course she could rest easy for an hour or so in his company! There'd be an entire lifetime of such evenings to look forward to.

She waited for the ballooning sense of elation to overtake her, as it always did at the thought of being Mrs. Trouston Dillard III. And waited . . . The usual ebullience escaped her, leaving an oddly deflated sort of feeling she most emphatically did not wish to dwell upon with scant days to go before her wedding.

"Darling! Thank you!" His return spared her from the uncertainty, giving her good reason to push away any doubts and glide across the room to meet him. She accepted the proffered glass and took a deep draught without bothering to so much as glance.

"Easy, sweetikins." His warning came too late, as the pungent brew burned its way down her throat, leaving her spluttering. "I thought we'd toast our upcoming wedding with some particularly fine Scotch."

"Trouston!" She coughed up his name,

wishing she could cough up the vile brew currently snaking its way down to her stomach, trailing a discomforting heat in its wake. "You know I don't imbibe!" Daisy blinked, trying to hide how her eyes watered — something he would surely disapprove of.

"I'm disappointed. This is one of the finer things in life, Daisy. I thought to share a sophisticated pleasure with you, and you cavil like a schoolgirl."

"No!"

"Give me the rest. I won't have you waste it." The sharp lines of his jaw seemed brittle as he nodded at her glass. "If you won't toast our happiness with me, I'll take it back."

The burning sensation faded, leaving a dull warmth at odds with the chill of his words. "Take what back?" *Our happiness?* Her fingers curled protectively around the sapphire ring he'd given her to mark their engagement. "No."

"You'll drink it?" Triumph gleamed in his eyes as he raised his own glass. "That's my girl. To my beautiful bride and all the happiness that awaits us."

"To us." Daisy lifted her own glass and took a tentative sip. This time, the heady mixture swirled against her tongue before sweeping its scalding path down her throat. She allowed only the smallest gasp to betray her discomfort.

Disapproval clouded Trouston's gaze when he saw how much still sloshed in her cup. "I've seen more enthusiasm from you over a new pair of gloves." He looked pointedly from his empty glass to hers. "You only ever get one husband."

"I'm overcome." Her laugh sounded shrill to her own ears, so she raised her glass once more, this time holding her breath for a deep swallow. It didn't burn so badly this time, although it still stung. Whatever the case, now so little swirled at the bottom of her glass — a heavy silver piece she knew was never typically used for spirits — Trouston couldn't scowl when she put it down. Which she did. Immediately.

"Come with me. I wish to show you the rest of the house." He took her arm, leading her through the places she'd already seen. Parlor, sitting room, breakfast room, formal dining room, kitchens, pantry, music room . . . and by then she couldn't quite remember why she'd ever been uneasy about spending time with her fiancé in their home.

A heady warmth suffused her stomach, her head felt light with hopes as they climbed the stairs and he showed her the nursery, the guest rooms, and, finally, the master bedroom. It was here he swept her into his arms and began pressing urgent, moist kisses on her lips and neck.

She giggled and wriggled away, spinning to look at the decor. The colors blurred a bit . . . cream and purple . . . "Lovely," she pronounced.

"Yes, you are." He guided her to the bed. "You seem a bit unsteady, sweetikins. Why don't you sit down?"

"Just a moment." She settled on the down mattress and gave an experimental bounce. "Comfortable."

"Yes, it is." He sat beside her, pulling her close for one of those deep kisses that always made her nervous and thrilled. He held her fast when she tried to tug away. "Easy, little one. Nothing to be afraid of. This is our home."

His smile coaxed one from her in return.

"Now, sweetie," he murmured, trailing a finger along the edge of her bodice as he spoke, "you're going to show me just how much you love me. . . ."

Marge stared at the sheet of paper before her in a mixture of rage and dismay. Another stage would come through town tomorrow . . . and folks back home would be expecting word from her about how things progressed.

Daisy would be waiting eagerly for news of Gavin's romantic tendencies. Descriptions of longing glances, fulsome words, and extravagant gestures the likes of which her cousin had been treated to since she first learned to bat her lashes at men. Somehow, a wry retelling of how Gavin's grandmother spilled the beans that Marge was the wrong woman wouldn't measure up.

On the other end of the scale, Aunt Verlata would be wearing a path in the carpets, fretting that something had gone awry and Marge hadn't made the splendid match they'd all gloated over. Her concern would be made up of one part horror at the idea of facing society should Marge have bungled things and become, in the eyes of civilized folk, a ruined woman with no prospects, and one part concern for Marge's safety.

Daisy may be the apple of Aunt Verlata's eye, but her aunt still cared for her a great deal. In truth, Marge only put concern for her safety as a secondary concern because she liked to think she'd proven herself to be highly capable. Capable enough to mitigate some of the worry that would plague her family if word about this little fiasco ever got out.

Which brought her back to the letter she needed to write. One page, filled with words to alleviate worry when, of course, anyone with a modicum of sense and the slightest inkling of the true state of things would be filled with misgivings. So Marge couldn't let them know. And she couldn't lie. That didn't leave much to say, and they'd know in an instant things weren't well if she didn't fill the entire sheet. Confound her hate of waste. Now they'd expect a page filled with news and descriptions of her new home.

Marge stared at the desk in front of her before finally standing up, walking over to the imposing collection of luggage dominating her room, and unearthing the trunk she sought. The sheer volume of bags, valises, trunks, and crates she'd dragged to this small town provided irrefutable proof of her foolishness. If hope sprang eternal, Marge had packed for it.

When she'd prepared a list of things to bring, she'd thought long and hard about what she'd need for a lifetime in a small frontier town. What her family would need, and since she'd always been a big believer in being prepared for anything, the list took on a life of its own. Now, as she dug her avel writing desk out of the trunk in question, Marge couldn't help but feel struck by the irony.

I prepared for everything except reality.

She couldn't muster even a tiny smile at that, no matter how she tried to appreciate the wry humor behind the situation. Instead, she took the wooden box over to the bed, plumped up the pillows, and settled herself comfortably. Only then did she unfold the box, on its well-oiled hinges, revealing a sloped writing surface inset with stiffened leather.

She lifted out the leather, withdrawing the smallest sheet of paper she could find before unstopping the small bottle of ink nestled snuggly in the carved-out niche of the corner. With her favorite mother-of-pearl dip pen in hand and a prayer on her lips, Marge set to work.

Dear Aunt Verlata and Daisy,

I trust this letter finds both of you doing wonderfully, as usual. As for myself, I'm very pleased to see the end of my journey westward. Days on end cramped inside a stagecoach wending its way over every rut along the Oregon Trail gave me a newfound appreciation for the everyday freedom of walking about on one's own feet, breathing in air that hasn't been mixed liberally with dust.

It's beautiful here in Buttonwood. Remember the time we spent trying to imagine what it would look like, Daisy? It's green, rolling grassland as far as the eye can see. I'm told as summer heats up, the green will turn golden, but for now it seems lush with wildflowers. The sky stretches almost endlessly above from horizon to horizon, largely un-marred by any buildings. No smoke fogs the air. The town itself is tiny, though with enough amenities to make it feel homey.

I've not yet had the chance to meet everyone — that will come on Sunday, after church. For now, I've made a friend of a young woman named Midge Col-lins. She's a lively sort and chosen to be Buttonwood's schoolmarm. I've been enlisted to step in and help set up the school as soon as the building is finished, which makes me feel like I'll be part of the town in no time.

Gavin is just as we remembered. Charming and handsome as ever, if a bit sun-bronzed, which looks quite well on him. His grandmother is a woman of great spirit and looks to make for some lively conversation, to say the least. The house and mill are beautiful and thoroughly modern, I must say. I'll go into detail in my next letter, as it seems I've quite run out of room and my candle begins to gutter. Tomorrow evening there is to be a dinner party of sorts to ease me into knowing some of the more prominent people in town, so I need to get a good night's rest and make the best impression possible!

All my love to you both,

Marge

If she pressed the nib of her pen particularly hard as she signed her name, she didn't think anyone could blame her. It was all she could do to leave it at "Marge." As it stood, though, they might suspect not all was as well as her letter portrayed if she added "Not Marguerite!" at the end of her signature. . . .

CHAPTER 12

Were it not for the sound of birds chirping a merry song, Gavin would have had no way of marking the arrival of morning. The bottom floor of the mill, built into the side of a man-made hill alongside the millpond, was designed to hold the gear housings and insulate against moisture.

He'd chosen to set up his temporary residence down here for practical purposes, not comfort. Customers saw the main floor and the storage area above it, where they placed the grain they brought for him to grind into flour. Gavin couldn't have a pallet and sundry items laying about the business. Tucked into the corner farthest from the gears down here, no one saw. The lack of light helped with that, of course.

Down here, no windows invited cheery rays of sunshine to brighten the darkness. Morning arrived unheralded by anything but the call of birds as they swooped around the millpond, scouting for insects and even fish. Normally Gavin loved that. Liked to think of it as just another way the gristmill served as a hub for the community and helped provide a steady food source.

This morning, the bird cries sounded shrill to his ears, as though determined to prey upon the unsuspecting. With the way the past two days had gone, he found himself missing the house more than ever. Waking up to a windowless, dank room seemed worth it when a man knew he'd have a bed — and a wife to share it with — in a matter of days.

Now that he could rest assured of neither wife nor bed in any foreseeable future, Gavin didn't have to guess why his outlook took a turn for the worse. A long stretch led to a series of not-unwelcome pops along his spine, loosening up his muscles for the day ahead.

Aside from a full day's work, he had that dinner party at the Reed place to look forward to this evening. Rolling over and punching his pillow did little to unleash the surge of outrage the thought provoked. Just before Marge stepped off the stage, he'd agreed to the meal as a sort of informal introduction to Buttonwood society — such as it was.

He'd thought it a chance to show Daisy a good time and show off his lovely bride-to-be in what would hopefully be the first of a string of social engagements befitting their status. Now, instead of bringing his prize, he brought an unending stream of questions. Even worse, a lot of those questions numbered as ones he couldn't answer.

Yet.

Gavin sprang out of bed. He didn't have much time. Questions demanded answers, and Marge needed to give him a few before the day began in earnest. More importantly, he needed to hear those answers before their plans that evening. He dressed hurriedly, sneaking into the house to wash up. No matter how skilled the man, anyone needed good light to shave.

By the time he got to the breakfast table, he saw Marge and Grandma Ermintrude putting platters of bacon and biscuits down. His stomach let loose a growl he could only hope neither of them heard. A rough night's sleep left him with a hearty appetite — and Gavin planned to eat enough to give him plenty of strength for what lay ahead.

Taking his place at the head of the table, he folded his hands and waited for the women to follow suit before asking a blessing over the meal. The warm, doughy scent of the biscuits rose beneath the heavier smell of fresh bacon and pungent coffee. Gavin waited for his stomach to still so as not to have his attention divided.

"Dear Lord, we come before You this morning and thank You for the food on our table and the company at it." He ignored Grandma Ermintrude's amused snort and kept on, "We ask Your guidance as we move forward, putting the past behind us and fixing our eyes upon the future You've placed before us. Amen."

"Amen." Marge didn't meet his gaze as she passed the biscuits — perhaps a sign that she was considering putting past mistakes behind them?

Gavin grabbed three and handed the basket over to Grandma, helping himself to a hearty rasher of bacon. His fork split the first biscuit without any difficulty, letting him spread a large gob of butter across the surface with ease. *I wonder whether Grandma made these or if Marge did?* He couldn't recall whether or not his bride-to-be knew how to cook.

That's the sort of thing a man should know about the woman he intends to make his wife. A big, buttery bite went a long way toward soothing his discomfort. *Although, I can be forgiven for not knowing whether or not Marge can cook. Originally it was Daisy I proposed to.*

He pushed away the sudden realization that he had no idea whether or not Daisy could cook. All women should be able to — and Daisy, always the epitome of everything feminine, surely wouldn't disappoint. Marge, however, with her more practical, bookish nature might have overlooked the domestic skill.

"Mmm." He decided a compliment might be the fastest — and most diplomatic — way to discover the truth. He polished off the first biscuit and began slathering another as he spoke. "This is delicious."

"I'm glad you like it." Grandma Ermintrude's amusement didn't help him one bit. "Been awhile since you've been so enthusiastic about breakfast. I wonder why that is?"

"Flattery?" When her eyes widened, he could see more of the green flecks livening the amber. Marge's lips twitched slightly — only once, as though holding back a smile. "Are you assuming I baked the biscuits, Gavin?"

"As a matter of fact, I am." Well and truly caught, he had no choice but to brave it out. His hopes for a response came to nothing as both women looked at him in amused silence. "Am I wrong?"

"Often." Marge's pert reply let loose the smile she'd been holding back. "Though I doubt that's the answer you seek."

A chuckle escaped him. "Hardly."

"Does he know whether or not you can cook? Or is he fishing to find what skills his surprise bride brings to the table — or doesn't, if it turns out that I made the biscuits?"

"I don't believe your grandson and I ever discussed my culinary skills, Mrs. Miller."

"Ermintrude." Grandma's bark took Gavin aback — the old woman rarely gave anyone permission to use her Christian name. "If all goes well, you'll be the next Mrs. Miller."

"That remains to be seen." The smile fled Marge's face at the first outright mention of the marriage question that morning. "Although I did bake the biscuits."

Is the thought of wedding me so awful? His food lost its flavor at the strength of her reaction. *I'm the same man she came all the way out here for. What am I supposed to change to make her want to be my wife again?*

"How are things going?" Midge darted around the corner of the house and whisked Marge aside before she so much as reached the door. "Tell me everything!"

"Not much to tell." Her shrug should, she felt, say it all.

"Pishposh. You can tell me what he said when you came home from the meeting yesterday and told him you'd be teaching, for starters." Her friend's eyes glowed with expectation.

The memory of their little game in the mill brought warmth to Marge's cheeks. She'd been playful with him — at a time when she should have been telling Gavin that she'd successfully received the teaching post and he wouldn't be stuck with her.

"You're blushing."

"Nonsense." Marge scowled. "Actually, Gavin and I didn't discuss it. He seemed to take it for granted that I'd be given the position and didn't so much as ask me how it had gone." A spurt of indignation overtook her. "He could have at least pretended some interest!"

"No, it seems that's not his way. Mr. Miller is pretending the teaching position is a whim — a sidelight, something that won't truly get in the way of what he wants." The younger girl rocked back on her heels. "Good. That means he does want you. Otherwise, he'd be anxious to hear all about the arrangements you made, when they'd take effect, and so on."

"Considering the schoolhouse isn't yet up, his asking about those sorts of things would seem overeager." The good mood that had buoyed her spirits on the walk to town abandoned her now. "Gavin's always been polite."

"Don't you think it would have been polite to escort you to the meeting and show his support of your ability?" Midge gave voice to one of the doubts that pestered Marge. "Or at least show some interest in how it went once you returned? No . . . if he's ignoring the whole thing, that's as good as trying to wish it away. He doesn't like the idea that you have options other than marrying him."

"Some men like to exert control. Gavin always seemed the type to have a good grasp on what went on around him." Marge shifted her sewing kit from one hand to the other. "Which must make this entire situation even more distasteful to him." *Makes me even more distasteful to him. A man used to making his own decisions and ordering his life just so — and he gets me instead of the woman he's handpicked as his perfect bride.* She indulged in a small sigh.

"Don't tell me you're going to be melodramatic or make a bid for martyrdom." Her friend's eyes narrowed. "You didn't strike me as the 'oh, woe is me' type. I've never liked that type, to tell you the truth."

Nettled, Marge lifted her chin. "Neither have I, though I've inclined slightly toward the mopes since I found out my groom isn't really mine at all. Difficulty deserves recognition just as do the kinder things in life. I won't pretend I'm pleased with the way things turned out."

"Mmm-hmm. Thought so." Midge made a show of walking behind Marge. "Yes, there it is. A bona fide spine. I'm glad to see you're making use of it again."

A short burst of laughter escaped her. "You'll make a far better teacher than you give yourself credit for, Midge Collins. Some people are born with a knack for passing out lessons."

"Not all of us have the patience to plan them."

"You strike me as the type to always have a plan or two. Speaking of which," Marge continued, lowering her voice, "was it your idea to invite me for a sewing circle this afternoon before the dinner party . . . or do I have someone else to thank for that?"

"Not my idea. That would be Clara — and she plans to sniff out why the miller's bride petitioned to become the schoolmarm. A few hours of cozy time with nothing but women, tea, and sewing would be enough to make anyone crack."

"It stands to reason they have questions." *No way to avoid that.*

"Questions abound." Midge gave the deep, satisfying sigh Marge held back. "But it's the answers that always cause trouble."

CHAPTER 13

Trouble walked through the door just after Mr. Miller and just before dinner. Midge stopped a very pleasant round of self-congratulation — a brief, private celebration that she and Marge managed to get through the sewing circle that afternoon without giving away too many personal details about her sticky situation — to gape.

Her mouth, like the door, hung open for a moment in what promised to be a highly unattractive manner. She snapped it shut as Amos Geer strode into the parlor, looking for all the world as though he'd been invited to join everyone for dinner. As Clara took his coat, the suspicion sneaked over Midge that that's precisely what had happened.

When did Amos Geer wrangle an invitation into her home? And when had she become so lax in her watching that she'd not noticed until it was far, far too late to stop or even minimize the damage? Such thoughts screeched to a halt as she painted a pleasant smile onto her face. After all, he was doing the very thing that made her want to avoid him at all costs. . . .

Amos Geer was watching Midge. Again. With an intensity she could scarcely believe went unnoticed by her family. Although, if she thought about the matter, she most emphatically did not want them noticing his interest. So that was for the best. For a brief moment, she considered how nice it would be if she didn't notice him either.

Him watching me. She shook her head once to clear it. *If I didn't notice the way his eyes follow me around, I wouldn't have to deal with him at all.* Flawed logic, but it did seem that the more she attempted to avoid him, the more determined the man became to catch her off guard. Midge rather hoped after the interrogation he sprang on her the day before he'd become bored. Now that he knew she remembered him — she quelled a spurt of satisfaction at how well he remembered her — he could stop wondering and move along.

Except he was moving along into the parlor. Straight toward her. Midge fancied he could hear her molars grinding, and that brought the ridiculously warm smile to his face. *Contrary man. Well, if cornering me makes the game fun for him, I'll take away the thrill.*

"Why, Mr. Geer!" She came forward to meet him, her smile growing as his faltered. "I didn't know you were joining us this evening." A swift, accusatory glance at Clara got her nowhere. Her adopted "mother" busied herself trying to coax information from Mr. Miller — who Midge believed would be no more forthcoming than herself or Marge.

"Miss Collins." He gave a shallow, almost imperceptible bow. "Mrs. Reed invited me. When I heard of the plans for a small, intimate dinner among friends, I couldn't resist getting to know some of the most fascinating people of Buttonwood a bit better."

"A wise choice." She kept her smile in place and didn't kick him, although she noticed the faint emphasis he'd placed on the word *intimate.* "I do wonder what other . . . surprises . . . Clara has in store for us this evening." She made a show of looking at the door as though hoping for additional guests.

Amos surveyed the rest of the party, seeming to take some sort of head count. "Traditionally, the hostess makes sure numbers are rounded out." A wolfish gleam lit his gaze. "I do believe I'm intended to be your dinner companion."

The nervous burble of laughter died as Midge looked around. Aunt Doreen and Uncle Josiah. Saul and Clara. Adam and Opal. Mr. Miller and Marge. *He's right.* She stifled a groan. *Clara did invite him to even out the numbers — the perfect reason for him to stick to me like a barnacle for the entire evening!*

"Excuse me; I need to check on the food." More accurately, she needed to check on the stove, but she certainly didn't plan on explaining that to Amos. As things stood, she beat a hasty retreat and headed for the kitchen without waiting for his response. He'd have to find some way to amuse himself other than pestering her with his laughing gaze and knowing grin.

Midge couldn't help but notice the differing reactions on the faces of her loved ones as she made her way through — an approving nod from Saul, the welling of compassion in Opal's gaze . . . though she wouldn't admit to it, a shrug of acceptance lifting Aunt Doreen's shoulders, and the exasperated shake of Clara's blond curls. This last caused a twinge in her breastbone — Midge knew full well Clara thought her preoccupation with the kitchen wasn't healthy.

But of all the people in the house, Clara should be the one who most understood. To be really fair about things, Clara ought to be the one most concerned about another fire. She'd been the one to live through the first one, after all. She should be at least as vigilant as Midge about making sure it never happened again.

Instead, Clara chalked it up to God's will — that classic Christian catchall that seemed to Midge a sort of spiritual "oh, well." Seemed to her that God got a pretty nice deal — praise for anything good and respect for anything unpleasant. She paused in the kitchen doorway, scanning for signs of any sparks or small, telltale curls of smoke anywhere they didn't belong. First glance showed nothing out of the ordinary.

An enormous pot of stew simmered on the stove — any larger and Midge would call it a vat. Whorls of fragrant steam rose from within, but no smoke. She ventured over and opened the oven, which kept an already-cooked beef roast tantalizingly warm. The baking compartment groaned with its load of corn bread — three pans stacked atop each other to retain their heat until serving. Seemed as though all was as it should be.

Just the same, Midge took a towel and ran

it around the farthest edges of the stove to clear away any bits of food that might spark later. Then she noticed someone had left the broom leaning on the wall a bit too close. She returned it to the corner, where it belonged. Finally satisfied no sudden blaze would consume the house and everyone inside it on her watch, Midge turned around . . . to find Amos Geer loitering in the doorway.

"How long have you been there?" She sounded snappish, but then, she felt snappish.

"Pretty much since you checked the stew." He braced one broad shoulder against the doorframe in what Midge was swiftly coming to recognize as a favorite posture of his. "Long enough to know you didn't hear me say I'd like to see the kitchen."

"You followed me." *Again.*

"Yes. I planned to see more of the house — I've an appreciation for architecture." That made sense, considering he'd helped build the gristmill and now worked on the schoolhouse. That might have put Midge at ease, if he weren't looking her up and down and still talking. "Turns out, I got to see far more than I planned on."

Amos watched her fight the flush rising on

the crests of her cheeks. The rosy glow somehow made her freckles brighter. He liked that. He also liked the way he managed to discomfit her — the girl was obviously far too used to being the one with the upper hand. It'd do her good to have that turned around.

"You saw me straightening things up and checking on supper." Her nonchalant tone warred with the flush she finally wrestled under control. "Nothing interesting about that."

"I beg to differ." Not that he planned to mention just how interesting he'd found the view when she leaned down to peer inside the oven.

Her spurt of laughter caught him off guard. "Odd. You don't strike me as the sort of man to beg for much." With that, her mask fell back into place. Gone was the flush, the flash of hesitance in her gaze that let him know he got under her skin. Before him stood the composed, confident woman with a mischievous streak that promised to liven up the dullest days.

But he already knew that Midge. Everyone knew that Midge. Amos wanted to see more of the woman she kept hidden so well — plumb the depths of the tiny cracks in her fearless facade. For now, it didn't matter why he wanted to. He just did. "You're right — I don't beg. But I do differ."

"Differ as much as you please. I still say there's nothing of interest in spying on me doing my chores."

"Spying?" He noted the way her eyes narrowed infinitesimally for a scant moment, an accidental acknowledgement that she'd revealed more than she intended. *She feels exposed . . . as though I've intruded on something. And she knows she just gave it away.*

"Spying, lurking — whatever term you prefer." An airy gesture to brush away her discomfort. "Truly, Mr. Geer, you should find a new hobby."

"And if I like lurking?" He allowed his amusement to show.

"It still doesn't get you very far."

"I'm not planning on going anywhere, so that's not a problem."

"You should plan on rejoining the others."

"We will." He didn't budge an inch. "As soon as you tell me what made you so afraid of fires."

Her mouth opened and closed twice before she managed a single word. "What?"

"At first, I assumed you wanted a reason to avoid my company." Amos ignored the

141

slight inclination of her head at that statement. "Because your aunt Doreen had just come from this direction a few moments before you took off. Now I know better."

"I'm glad to hear you acknowledge that I didn't lie. Now that we have that settled, we can get back to the party." She took a step forward — the first time she'd ever voluntarily moved toward him. Obviously she wanted this conversation to end.

Which made him want to pursue it all the more. "Either you're excessively neat and overly conscientious — which strikes me as out of character — or you're afraid of a fire."

"I hope I'm not excessively anything."

"Oh, you are." *Suspicious, for one thing. Secretive. Clever. Appealing . . .* "But that's a topic for another time. Right now, I want to know why everyone seemed to expect you to go to the kitchen almost as soon as your aunt left. Why you stopped in the doorway and looked over the room as though searching for something. Why you checked every nook and cranny of that stove and oven then cleaned it and inched back a broom that was several feet away to begin with."

A succession of emotions flickered across her gaze. Anger, fear, and longing dazzled him with their swift intensity before she schooled her features to reveal nothing. She didn't say a word — didn't acknowledge his observations.

"I'm right." He left the doorway to stand before her as something else fell into place. "You're afraid of fire. You're the reason the council decided to make the schoolhouse out of brick, aren't you?"

"It's a wise decision." The protective glint stayed long enough for him to truly appreciate it this time. "One I support wholeheartedly."

"You more than supported it." Another step closer. "You insisted. Admit it."

"There's nothing in the world I could insist on that would make a difference if the men in town leaned another direction." Evasive and overly modest, the answer struck a false chord. "Insisting doesn't make much of a difference in anything." That statement rang true.

"Fair enough. You're too clever to outright insist on something, but you suggested and persuaded until you got your way." *No wonder, with those big eyes . . . A man would have to be made of stone to hear her pleading about her worries over a schoolhouse fire and not do what he could to alleviate them.*

"I like to think logic holds sway when presented properly."

"Indeed? Then surely you know I will

persist in my questions until you explain the reasoning behind your impressive vigilance against any wayward sparks in the kitchen." Ah, but he enjoyed matching wits with her. Not only did he relish the thrill of the challenge — and such challenges came by only too rarely — he reaped the additional reward of seeing her discomfiture as he undermined all her arguments.

"Persist as you please. It will do no good."

A pretty face and a sharp mind made for an intriguing combination. Add in some mystery, and Amos saw opportunity for entertainment long into the future.

"Oh, I don't know about that, Miss Collins." He let her step around him toward the door. "You're right — lurking becomes tedious. I should thank you."

She stopped and looked over her shoulder. "For what?"

"Don't you know?" A grin spread across his face. "For providing me with a new hobby. This one should be far more interesting. . . ."

CHAPTER 14

"Oh no, you won't catch me tagging along to a dinner party." Grandma shook her head. "Fodder for gossip is all anyone will want. The conversation cuts through folks the same time the knives slice through the meat."

No matter how Gavin insisted she wouldn't be tagging along — or coaxed and even hinted that surely Grandma could more than hold her own in any discussion — he wound up heading over to the Reed household alone. Not that it came as a surprise. Grandma refused the day before, and he'd had to mention to Dr. Reed that the old woman wasn't feeling overly sociable these days.

Not that Gavin could call to mind a time when Grandma ever seemed overly sociable, but the point still stood. Well . . . maybe that afternoon when Marge arrived, ran off, and returned with Midge Collins in tow.

Grandma Ermintrude seemed downright gregarious when surrounded with so much conflict. Though she may just have seemed more companionable than Marge, who bristled so pointedly at him once she'd learned of the mix-up.

He wouldn't have minded having his relative along this evening to help monitor the conversation and put in place any noses that started poking about in his business. Honestly, Gavin wondered if it wouldn't do Grandma good to get out and about more. If some friends wouldn't improve her outlook and give her something to look forward to beyond sneaking in those little barbs whenever they spoke.

Not that he could manipulate her into coming. He'd thought perhaps the lure of Miss Collins's company, along with witnessing firsthand how he and Marge handled their foray into town life, might convince her. With that failing, he had no choice but to arrive on the doorstep with nothing but staunchly suppressed concerns about how much Marge mentioned during the sewing circle she'd attended that afternoon.

"Mr. Miller!" Clara Reed opened the door and took his coat, peering behind him as though expecting someone else.

"Grandma didn't feel up to coming — I

mentioned to Saul that might be the case."
It seemed an explanation was needed.

"Oh, Saul told me." She still held the door
open. "Mr. Geer, welcome!"

"Thank you, Mrs. Reed." Amos appeared
in the entrance right behind him, making
Gavin marvel at how silently the other man
moved. "Glad to be here."

"Good to see you, Geer." He nodded in
acknowledgement as Mrs. Reed took their
coats to some closet or another.

"And you." The other man's gaze
skimmed the room, coming to rest on where
Marge and Miss Collins stood chatting. A
slow smile spread across his face. "I met
Miss Chandler the other day. Buttonwood
has a lot to thank you for."

"No thanks required." Gavin didn't like
the way Amos Geer peered in the direction
of his woman. Nor the way he addressed
Marge — not "your fiancée" or "your bride-
to-be" or even "your Miss Chandler," as
would have been appropriate. No, Geer left
it at a simple "miss," as though Marge might
still be available. Gavin forced a chuckle.
"My reasons for bringing her here are
entirely selfish, after all. Excuse me."

Without waiting for a response, he headed
straight for Marge. "Good evening, my
dear." He cupped her elbow in his hand and

angled close. Almost immediately, he felt calmer.

"If you'll excuse me . . ." Miss Collins murmured some pretext for politely making herself scarce. Her thoughtfulness raised his opinion of her a notch — though it would take a lot more for him to be glad of her budding friendship with Marge.

"Gavin, how was your day?" She must not have realized she used his first name — no blush stained her cheeks.

He wouldn't mention it. If she continued the familiarity, he'd have good reason to call her Marge as he was used to — a clear signal to any upstarts who thought "Miss Chandler" might not be firmly attached. Besides, he liked the sound of his name on her lips.

"Well enough, though much improved now that I can enjoy your company." Ah . . . here came the first faint stirrings of that blush. Excellent.

"I see you're continuing where we left off this morning." Her pause didn't elicit the reaction she sought, because she clarified. "More flattery?"

"You insult me." He steered her over to a sofa and sat down next to her. "Flattery means you think the statement false."

"Perhaps not false . . . but certainly

overdone." She scooted away a little bit. "Thank you, all the same."

"You're more than welcome." Under the pretext of making himself comfortable, he sprawled more — taking up every inch of space she'd just put between them. "I think you underestimate how much it means to a man to have something to look forward to at the end of a long day's work."

"Mrs. Reed will be delighted to hear you think so highly of her dinner party." Her smile brightened as Opal and Adam Grogan approached them.

Gavin sat in silence for a moment before exchanging greetings with the Grogans. They took a few chairs nearby and began the meaningless chitchat always present at such occasions — the sort of conversation that encouraged a man's mind to wander. Particularly when he had a lot to think about.

He watched Marge smile and speak, noticing how animated she was — the way she used her hands and leaned toward whomever she spoke with. His bride-to-be really was an engaging little thing, but she wasn't proving easy to catch. The ease with which she deflected compliments created an unforeseen challenge. *Daisy always took them as her due. Why doesn't Marge?*

Gavin kept staring at her. The more she tried to ignore it, the more the awareness grew, until it curled up into a tight, nervous bundle of uncertainty ricocheting within her ribs.

Why is he staring? What is he looking for? Is he comparing me to Daisy? Is he looking for flaws? These she almost understood, but it was the last possibility that made her want to weep. *Is he trying too hard to find something he might like — to convince himself he hasn't made such a bad bargain if he marries the other cousin?*

The entire time she discussed modern farming methods with Opal's husband, she could scarcely concentrate on recalling all the facts from the journal articles she'd read. Honestly, while she realized how important developments in steam-driven threshing would be to agriculturalists, Marge's interests were taking a decidedly self-centered turn.

Am I boring him? Is he thinking how horrible looking and dull I am compared to Daisy? She shoved the doubts away and tried to focus on the conversation. After all, Mr. Grogan appeared fascinated by her comments.

150

Hopefully Gavin noticed that . . . and it pleased him.

Not that she set out to please him. Marge fell silent as the two men began discussing the relative merits of steam versus water power for various aspects of cultivation. *Daisy would be bored to tears.* Even Opal, who had the same vested interest in farming machinery as her husband, seemed less than entertained.

She gave the other woman an understanding smile. "That's a lovely brooch you're wearing, Opal."

"It belonged to my mother." Her hand fluttered up to touch the long, thin pin adorning her collar. Studded with seed pearls and the faceted shine of marcasites, it glimmered in the lamplight.

"She always wears it." Her husband slid his arm around her waist, pulling Opal — and the chair she sat in — closer. "Opal's very loyal to her family."

"Mama's brooch and my wedding band." His wife thumbed the thin circle of gold adorning the ring finger of her left hand.

"That's better than all the finery I saw in Boston." Marge leaned forward for a closer look. "What you have there are true treasures."

"Exactly." Opal's blue eyes shone with the

151

sparkle of joy. "I'm so glad you understand." Impulsively, she reached out and clasped Marge's hand. "And I'm glad you came to Buttonwood."

"So am I." Gavin's deep rumble spoke her thoughts before Marge so much as opened her mouth.

"Are you?" It took incredible effort to keep the words light and teasing, but Marge turned from the Grogans to search Gavin's expression while he answered. *Are you really?*

"Of course he is!" Mr. Grogan stepped in, but not before Marge caught the flash of uncertainty in Gavin's eyes. "He hardly spoke about anything but your arrival up until now!"

"I very much doubt that." Hopefully a gentle smile hid the sorrow behind her reply. *Because Gavin wasn't talking about me at all — he was talking about Daisy the whole time. Two days in my company won't have changed his choice.*

"Mr. Grogan exaggerates," her fake fiancé murmured.

"Somewhat," Opal admitted. "Though Mr. Miller did speak quite highly of you. It was plain to see how much he anticipated your arrival, Marge."

Clara bustled up. "Perhaps it's not the

best of manners to mention it, but it's easy to see Mr. Miller is pleased to have you here. He can scarcely keep his eyes off you!"

Ah ha! So it's not simply my imagination. Marge could feel the heat of a bright blush sweeping from her cheeks down her neck. *Gavin* is *staring.* Now the only question was why she seemed embarrassed by the fact when he was the guilty party?

"Why would I want to?" He lifted a brow. "She's so animated it's easy to get caught up in what she's saying."

"Isn't it though?" Clara perched on the last seat in the arrangement. "Forgive me for my absence; I was just checking on Maggie. But the important thing now is that I noticed the same thing earlier. Even with her hands busy sewing, Marge is an energetic speaker."

"Something her students will appreciate." Adam Grogan's words made Gavin stiffen beside her, but certainly no one else noticed. "I must admit, when Midge first came to us asking that we hire your Miss Chandler on to help start the school, I had my doubts. Now, I'm more and more pleased by the decision."

"Your Miss Chandler"? Marge's spine straightened to match Gavin's. The last thing he needed was for the townspeople

153

pressuring him into marrying her. True, Mr. Grogan didn't know the details of their situation, but those types of comments would steer Gavin down the aisle whether he wanted to go there with her or not. And Marge didn't see any way to stop it, short of confessing the whole sorry situation.

Which meant she and Gavin would continue to play this infernal game of cat and mouse, as he toyed with her before swallowing his pride and his hopes and settling for a poor imitation of what he'd really wanted. Unless she stayed strong and saw through his ploys long enough to set them both free from the entire tangle.

"Marge will be a wonderful asset as she helps set up the schoolhouse." Gavin placed an emphasis on "set up" that no one could mistake. "I understand Miss Collins is to be the regular schoolteacher, after the initial starting up period?"

"It's far too soon to discuss timetables." She somehow managed to keep from glaring at the man. "I'll very much enjoy working alongside Midge to implement a curriculum and workable schedule that best suits the needs of the children. Without the building and without having met the students, obviously it's impossible to judge what will be needed."

"You give yourself too little credit." Gavin's smile suddenly looked predatory. "I'm certain it won't take you long to have things in order."

"We'll see." Marge kept her tone noncommittal, but inside, she stewed. How dare he interfere with her livelihood in a bid to maneuver her in front of the altar? Had the man no sense at all?

Chapter 15

"Daisy, he's here!" Mama poked her head through the door.

"I'll be downstairs in just a moment." Daisy forced a smile until Mama shut the door again. Then the smile fell from her face. *I should be relieved. No . . . I should be excited.*

Yesterday had marked the first day since their engagement — and, if she were to truly think on the matter, long before even that — Trouston hadn't called upon her or escorted her to some event or another. An absence made all the more conspicuous considering what had happened the night before.

I don't want to think about that. She shook out her skirts then smoothed them nervously. Daisy didn't recall absolutely everything from that night, but any time she started to remember, she pushed the thoughts away. They were too shameful, too embarrassing, too . . . unpleasant. And now, for the first time, she didn't want to see Trouston.

Yes, you do want to see Trouston. She looked at her reflection, dismayed by how wan her cheeks seemed. Daisy gave them a quick pinch. *He's your fiancé, and you'll be wed before the month is out. Anything that happened isn't important because you'll be together.*

Except . . . except that she had the nagging sense it was important. That the way he insisted she drink the Scotch . . . how his hands went everywhere . . . the way he demanded things he didn't have a right to yet . . . Somehow, all of that did seem important. But it was too late now. No changing her mind, no changing the past, and no changing the fact that he was waiting for her downstairs.

She put an extra bounce in her step as she reached the small parlor — her favorite room in the house. Here, the lighting was best, the seats were coziest, and even the rug seemed most plush. It never failed to lift her spirits to entertain a close friend in this little jewel box of a room. Until today.

"Trouston?" Her step faltered at the look on his face.

"Miss Chandler." He gave a scarce inclination of his head.

"Why are you calling me that? You've called me Daisy for ages." She looked and saw a new hardness bracketing his mouth, a stiffness to his neck, a disdainful glint in the eyes that before had so openly adored her. Her heart fell to the toes of her embroidered slippers. "What's happened?"

"I think you know."

"You are . . . displeased with me." Her fingers curled around the back of a chair. *Shouldn't he be sweeping me into his arms, vowing his eternal love? Telling me how much my trust means to him, how sorry he is that he hurt me?*

"Oh no." His gaze raked her with an appraising leer she would have protested under any other circumstance. "You pleased me all too well, *Miss* Chandler."

The memories she'd stomped down welled to the surface, searing the back of her throat with the acid taste of bile. "I told you we shouldn't . . . that I wanted to wait."

"But you didn't. And, while I enjoyed the experience, I have to say it's not worth taking a strumpet to wife."

She recoiled as though he'd slapped her across the face. "What are you saying, Trouston?"

"That's Mr. Dillard to you." How had she

never before noticed how sinister his sneer was? "And obviously, I'm saying that I won't bind myself to soiled goods. You're no better than you should be, which makes you not good enough to be my wife."

"But you love me." She blinked back tears, but they spilled down her cheeks anyway as she walked up to him, hands outstretched. "I know you do. I'm your sweetikins."

"I enjoyed what you had to offer." Another smirk. "Now you can play 'sweetikins' to another man. You still look the part of the innocent, my dear. I'm certain you can trap some poor, unsuspecting clod before he realizes the truth."

Something inside her gave way the moment her slap cracked against his curled lip. "You insufferable —" Her voice broke before she could utter a word that should never come from a lady. She lifted her hand to strike again, blindly seeking to vent the rage and hurt he'd inflicted upon her.

"Easy now." He caught her hand with ease. "I'll allow the first one — it's little enough compared to what I took. Any more and you'll have me rethinking my decision to be generous with you." Trouston's fingers — cold, always so cold — clamped around her wrist in an ever-tightening vise.

"I don't want anything from you," she hissed, trying to yank free. Daisy bit back a cry when he wrenched her wrist in a cruel motion and tried to beat him off with her other hand.

"Oh, I think you do." He caught her other wrist and yanked her close, the reek of his cigars washing over her. His mouth clamped over hers, cutting off her breath in a slimy assault.

Struggling only brought her closer against him, so finally Daisy stilled, sensing somehow that's what he wanted.

"Good girl." He was breathing hard. "If I'd suspected you had such spirit, I wouldn't have ended things so swiftly." Trouston let go of her right hand, wrenching his family engagement ring from her left. "As it stands, you're too popular for me to enjoy anything more than what I've sampled."

"You'll get nothing more from me." She jerked away, retreating behind the settee. "Don't fool yourself."

"Don't fool yourself, Daisy." He lingered over her name, making a mockery of the way he'd wooed her. "If I chose, I could demand more of your delightful . . . company . . . in return for my silence regarding your wanton behavior."

Her gasp made him grin.

"As it stands, I'm giving you a choice. Either you cry off the engagement, giving the standard reason that you've decided we shall not suit, or I'll break it off publicly and you'll be ruined."

"No." Daisy's knees wobbled. "Miss Lindner?" A horrible certainty swamped her as she recalled the way Trouston's previous fiancée suddenly cried off their engagement, leaving him heartbroken and dashing when he started to court her. "You've done this before."

"A gentleman never tells, my dear." Trouston headed for the door, opening it, and looking back one last time. "Unless, of course, you make me."

"Don't make me ask what happened last night." Ermintrude pounced the moment Marge showed her face downstairs the next morning. "I won't ask, you know."

"You just did." She shook her head at the older woman's blatant attempt to extort all the details without making a request. "Leaving off the question mark doesn't make it less of a request, you know.

"I know no such thing, nor do I care to. What I do care to know is how you held up in the face of all that curiosity last night. It was the first time I felt tempted to attend

161

something other than church since we got here."

"Then why didn't you?" She led the way into the kitchen.

"The drawbacks outweighed the lure. As time passes and the disappointments of decades etch themselves into your mind and flesh, you'll learn to avoid as many as possible."

Marge halted, eyes fixed on the older woman as she bustled forward in a pointed show of ignoring any reaction to the words she'd just spoken. She noted the slight stoop to Ermintrude's back and suddenly wondered if it tattled of the weight of regrets. *How long has she lived this way — expecting so little that she makes no concessions for others?* Pity welled up, unbidden, at the idea. *And she expects I'll become the same?*

"I hope not."

"I know better." Ermintrude lifted her cane and poked it toward the pantry. "Fried ham and flapjacks this morning, missy." She moved to the shelves and picked out a large mixing bowl, bringing it over to the table. Setting it down heavily then settling herself before it, she waited for Marge to bring over the flour, sugar, crock of butter, and oiled eggs. "We'll need milk, so you can gather your thoughts and try to refute me when

162

you get back."

"Very well." Rolling up her sleeves both to prepare for battle and to draw up the large bucket dangling in the well, keeping the milk cool and fresh, Marge marshaled her arguments. She marched back to the kitchen with milk in one hand, a pail of water in the other, and plan of attack at the ready.

"Heh. You've got a fire in your eyes and a set to your jaw to tell me a good conversation is in the offing." Ermintrude cracked an egg on the edge of the bowl with a deftness that belied her age. "So tell me, Marge-not-Daisy, how is it you foresee so clearly that you won't seek to protect yourself from disappointments as years go by?"

She set down the bottle of milk with a *thud.* "A low blow, mentioning Daisy." Marge swallowed any hurt the reminder caused and focused on the injustice of her opponent's tactics. "To resort to such tricks so soon smacks of desperation."

"Not at all. You're a teacher — easy to see you'd be inclined to make any debate an academic one." She splashed milk into the batter. "Academics aren't my style, and you'd best be prepared to deal with the school of experience." Ermintrude thrust a wooden spoon and the mixing bowl toward Marge. "No one escapes it."

"Why escape it," Marge countered as she fit the mixing bowl into the crook of her left arm, "when you can shape it?"

"Quick. I like it." The gleam of appreciation gave way to discomfort as she lurched toward the stove to start water boiling for morning coffee. "Even if it is just like a teacher to think she can control what life hands to her or what other people do. It never works that way."

"It's foolish to think one can control another person." She plunged the spoon into the bowl and began mixing, her arm moving faster as the words came pouring out. "No matter how much we may wish we could order what other people want or think, it's impossible."

If it were possible, everything would be different. Gavin would want me for his wife, we'd be getting married tomorrow, and everyone would be happy.

"It's stirred enough." The older woman tugged the bowl away, making Marge realize she'd absentmindedly mixed the batter until bubbles were forming. "Avoiding disappointments is far easier than taking them out on flapjacks, Marge."

"You're focusing on the wrong thing, Ermintrude, by thinking only of the negative. I choose to focus on my response. And I choose not to pull away from everyone and everything because I'm afraid of being disappointed."

"Now we come down to the meat of it. The way a person has to respond to disappointments. Well, I hate to tell you this" — it didn't sound as though the older woman hated to tell her so at all — "but there's only one thing that people do consistently when they can't have what they want. The same thing you'll do once you set aside your pride."

"I'm not a proud woman." A twinge told her that might not be entirely true.

"That's why you'll do what I did — what Gavin is already willing to do."

In spite of the churning in her stomach warning her against it, Marge gave in to curiosity. "What's that?"

"Settle."

CHAPTER 16

"Seems a fine-looking woman," a voice Gavin couldn't quite place emerged from the smithy. All the Burn men sounded alike, and with three of them, all talented smiths, it made for some confusion unless a body stood right in front of whoever was speaking. "Can't have too many of those around."

A few appreciative guffaws competed with the heat of the forge to fill the air while Gavin stepped inside. The father, Kevin, and his younger son stood by the water barrel. "Afternoon." He spoke loud enough to let them know he was there.

"Your ears must be burning." Kevin sauntered over. "I just told Brett there that I looked forward to catching sight of your bride at church tomorrow." The grizzled blacksmith gave a broad wink. "Don't blame you for keeping her under wraps this week."

"I told Pa she's a fine-looking woman." Brett — Gavin would be sure to remember the name, since this was the unmarried brother — headed back toward his anvil. "Never enough of those to go around out here."

"So long as you remember Marge is spoken for." No sense taking any chances. "Just giving her time to settle in to Buttonwood before making her my wife."

"What brings you here today?" The older Burn wisely changed the topic. "Can't imagine anything we made for that mill of yours would be giving you problems already." A displeased frown at the idea of anything he or his sons worked on being below standard birthed a deep furrow between his brows.

"Not at all." Gavin disabused him of the notion immediately. "Though the mill's easily gone through half again as much work as it typically would. Lots of grain stored up in these parts, lots of need, lots of work, so there's a good bit more wear than I'd usually see."

"Stands to reason." Relief relaxed the other man's features. The Burns, like everyone Gavin dealt with in Buttonwood, took pride in their work. "What do you need?"

"Mill pick. The one I ordered from a catalog isn't balanced right, and my old one is too worn down to sharpen and keep using." He produced the old one, its wooden handle worn smooth from years of use. "I doubt you can affix a new metal chisel piece to this one — wood's already been soaked to swell around this one — else I would have brought it to you before."

Wordlessly, the master blacksmith extended a massive paw, palm up, to receive the implement. When Gavin handed it over, Kevin Burn didn't grasp it. Instead, he kept his palm flat, fingers open, and tested the heft of the tool. Then, with his right forefinger, he nudged the wooden handle so the pick pivoted on the worn metal head. He ran his fingers over the chisel piece then shifted and got a grip on the handle, his large hand dwarfing the piece.

Finally, he nodded. "You're right — trying to affix another head piece would weaken it or ruin the feel." He raised it to eye level. "For the new version, I assume you'd like the same style handle? I've not seen this type before, with the slight bend, but it makes for a more secure grip. I can see why you got so much use out of it."

"Yes, make it as similar as possible." That the blacksmith inspected it so thoroughly and noted its distinctive traits made Gavin rest easy. "It's obvious you appreciate quality."

"Of course we do." A mischievous smile lit Kevin's face as he tucked the pick into his work belt. "In tools and women. So why don't you tell me about this fiancée of yours?"

"Now I know why he's been so closed mouthed." The younger smith edged closer. "He didn't want any of the other men gearing up to swipe his bride-to-be before he got her down the aisle. I caught a glimpse when she stepped off the stage, and it's easy to see he has good reason to be worried."

Gavin's eyes narrowed at the threat. It might be spoken in jest, but it hit too close to home for his liking. "You don't know Marge. She's not the sort to flit from one man to another."

Daisy is. The sudden thought took him off guard, but he couldn't deny the truth of it. That's part of why he'd been so surprised and relieved when he thought she'd accepted his proposal — he'd gauged the chances of her having found another beau to be most likely. *And I was right.* His frown deepened. *No chance I'll let Marge slip through my fingers, too.*

"A steadfast woman's worth her weight in gold. If she wears a pretty face, so much the better."

"She wears a pretty face, and she was

wearin' pretty clothes to make a pretty li'l picture when I spotted her, Pa."

Little? Gavin paused to consider. *Daisy's the tiny one.* "Marge isn't overly petite, and you're in no position to judge how pretty she is." *Sure Marge is pretty. In a quiet sort of way someone has to get close to her before being able to appreciate it.* "You shouldn't be gawking at a woman from across the street and deciding she's to your liking." *You shouldn't be looking at all.*

"I don't see the appeal of doll-like females. There should be enough to a woman for a man to appreciate." Brett let loose a wolfish grin. "Everyone will get a close enough gander after church tomorrow to see that I'm right about her looks."

"Remember yourself, Burn." Gavin took a step forward. "More than one look and we might tangle."

"I'll remember." The burly young blacksmith crossed his arms and waggled his brows. "But you remember something, too, Miller. Spoken for ain't the same as taken."

Midge woke up early — even for herself — that Sunday.

Usually, the darkness around the edges of her window curled back beneath the insistence of morning light before she arose.

170

Even then, by the time she washed and dressed and pulled back the window sash, the town buildings just began to glow with the rosy oranges of sunrise.

Today, she scarcely knew she'd opened her eyes. To be sure, she shut them, noted that, yes, everything did get darker, and opened them again. This time she could make out the hazy, indistinct borders of her window, where the very first blush of light barely began to appear. She lay there, watching it take on more space, more dimension.

Most folks she knew said darkness grew deeper and light grew lighter. Midge held the opinion that light had every bit the depth of dark — more, as a matter of fact, as it possessed the power to plumb every crevice and make anything visible. To her way of thinking, the world needed more light.

But they weren't going to find it in church.

She groaned and let her head fall back on the pillow. *Today's Sunday.* Which meant hours stuck indoors, sitting on hard pews, listening to that Parson Carter drone on and on about the light no one could see. *So how does it do anyone any good?*

Unable to remain still for another second, she rolled out of bed and tromped over to her water basin. Mind churning over other things and eyes having to navigate more shadows than usual, she knocked her shin on the small wooden trunk beside her washstand. Hard.

Amazed the resounding *thud* hadn't woken anyone else, Midge perched atop that self-same trunk, hiked her nightgown around her knees, and poked at her bruised shin to determine how badly she'd gotten it. Starting where she figured it'd be a good distance from the main bruise, she still sucked in a breath. Yep — it'd be a good one. Probing closer to the bone, her fingers hit a warm wetness — blood.

She curled the stained fingers upward, swung that hand over, and gave it a good dunking in the washbasin. Then, making sure she held her nightclothes away from the injury, she lit an oil lamp on her dresser and peered down to get a better look. Crimson welled from a gash about four inches above her ankle, right where she'd made contact with the metal trunk latch.

Little red streams raced down her leg toward the bare wooden planks beyond the edge of the rug. Midge caught them with one swipe of a clean washrag, dabbing the cut and squinting to try and determine whether or not she'd have to tell Saul about the mishap. Having a doctor adopt you came in handy, but he also tended to over-react about minor scrapes, pulling out witch hazel and what-not at the slightest provocation.

Hmm . . . deep enough to consider bothering him but minor enough to manage on my own. She pressed the rag down hard, drawing in a hissing breath at the stinging sensation, but she kept pressing until she counted to one hundred. Cautiously, she lifted the rag. Sure enough, the bleeding slowed to almost nothing at all. She'd had worse.

A surge of memories made her drop the rag. The crushing pressure of having her hand caught in one of the mill machines when she was seven — she lost three fingernails and her thumb snapped before the foreman had it shut down. That's when Nancy stopped letting her work. Her hand healed, the throbbing ache replaced by hunger's gnawing insistence as she hid in her sister's room. Until the foreman found her and kicked them out.

Midge drew her knees to her chest. *My fault.* She'd accidentally caught her almost-healed hand in the drop-front desk and let out a small cry. Not much. Just enough for them to find her and fire Nancy. That's when they moved in with Rodney —

Nancy's beau. Midge began to rock back and forth.

The sharp pain of every breath after Rod-ney knocked me across the room for talking back to him that first week . . . what she now knew to be the symptom of a broken rib. The constant bruises she and her sister wore as they struggled to eke out a living, until Rodney put her sister on the streets as a common prostitute. Until the night he chose to end the life of the child Nancy had conceived and took both of theirs in the do-ing.

Her eyes fixed on the deep black-red of her own blood on the rag, remembering her sister's blood-soaked pallet. Remembering Nancy's waxen face as Saul Reed checked for signs of life and found none, telling Midge God had taken the last good thing from her life.

Her beautiful sister, so good and kind that she prayed even for the men who used her body and belittled her for the privilege, ripped from this world. Nancy could have none of the things Midge got to enjoy now — a fine bed, plenty of food, lovely clothes, friends who'd never know the things she'd done in the past. Everything Midge had, Nancy deserved — but Nancy was gone forever.

My fault. She stopped rocking and rested her forehead against her knees. *I'm as old as Nancy was when she died for what I did.* Midge stuffed half her fist in her mouth to muffle the broken sobs. *And nobody knows it but me.*

CHAPTER 17

The scrape of the straight razor may irritate some men, but Gavin found it calming. He peered in the mirror, lifted his chin a fraction of an inch, precisely positioned the blade, and used deft strokes to finish the job. When he concluded, he rinsed his instruments, put them away, patted his face dry, and gave himself one last look-over in the mirror.

Let that hulk of a blacksmith try to outdo me this morning. Gavin straightened his collar, knowing his Sunday best to be better made than most garments in town. Whistling, he headed down the stairs, only to pull up short at the vision awaiting him in the parlor.

Ermintrude had donned her most gaudy ensemble for the occasion — a burnt orange monstrosity he'd attempted to "lose" during the move out West, but somehow it always reappeared. Awful as that sight may be, it wasn't what made him stop. No, he reserved that honor for his fiancée.

Marge must have plotted with the older woman, for she looked some sort of fashion-plate apprentice in a peach-hued dress and fur-trimmed frock. If the color weren't objectionable enough, Gavin grappled with the fact she looked good in it. Downright delectable, if someone put him under oath.

He didn't like it one bit.

Somehow, the peachy tint brought out a becoming color in her cheeks he hadn't noticed before. The rosy pinks she'd worn alongside Daisy made her seem good and sallow. Back then, Marge had weighed down her outfits with layers of ruffles and poufy sleeves until a man could see her coming from a mile off. He'd sort of noticed since she came to Buttonwood that all the bows and flounces seemed to have vanished, but this morning he missed them. *She shouldn't look so slim and elegant.*

"He looks like he swallowed a porcupine." Grandma Ermintrude's gleeful observation told him he needed to better keep his thoughts from his countenance. "Told you he hated orange. I can't tell you how many times he tried to get rid of my favorite dress. Or how many times I thwarted him." She ran a loving hand along the line of her skirts.

"Surely you didn't try to throw away your grandmother's favorite dress?" Disbelief didn't quite conceal Marge's amusement. "Such a thing would be wasteful — and rude."

"I've offered to replace it thrice over."

"Style may change, and I wouldn't mind updating it, but I doubt I'd find the color twice."

Exactly. "Surely something would please you."

"We both know better." His grandmother's comment was thrown down like a gauntlet, but Gavin knew better than to remark upon it. When he simply walked over and offered an arm to each of them, she gave a resigned sigh. "Didn't rise to the bait."

"Nope."

"Wise move." Marge's laugh sounded suspiciously like a giggle, but Gavin had never heard her giggle before. "For what it's worth, I told her she should've taken you up on the offer. Three dresses in a variety of colors makes for a better deal."

"I thought so." He almost suggested she select a softer shade — like the one Marge showcased — but didn't want his fiancée to know he liked it. *The less she wears this one, the better. At least* — he allowed himself an appreciative glance — *until we're safely married.*

"Three times the opportunity to wear one-of-a-kind creations you'll disapprove of!" When she bit her lip, a dimple peeked from her left cheek. "So Ermintrude just might change her mind, after all, and your grandmother and I will shop."

"I am ever in your debt." Gavin replied as expected — with wry humor — but inwardly chuckled. Marge's smiles were worth the joke at his expense. Besides, no matter her threats, nothing they came up with could be as bilious as that vile burnt orange. Particularly considering Marge's newfound sophistication in her own dressing habits . . .

Which he had cause to deplore as they came within sight of the church. Or, more accurately, within sight of all the townsmen waiting to catch a glimpse of his intended bride.

The intended bride who he hadn't really intended to marry but now did — as soon as he convinced her to agree. The intended bride he couldn't truly lay claim to despite everyone's understanding of the situation. The intended bride who looked far too becoming in her simple peach dress this morning.

Gavin didn't miss the way Brett Burn's

eyes widened when he got a good, long look at Marge. Nor did he miss the way folks whispered and elbows burrowed into ribs. Looked like his fake fiancée was the roaring success he'd predicted Daisy would be . . . and she hadn't even uttered a word yet.

His spine stiffened as the Burn men broke away from the crowd and headed over, masculine appreciation written plain across their features.

Gavin glanced at Marge, who blushed becomingly at the certain knowledge she held everyone's attention.

He started plotting ways to get her back into fussy pink dresses — immediately.

She'd never been so thankful to slide onto an uncomfortable pew in all her born days. Marge stifled a sigh of relief at having made it through a throng of gawkers and well-wishers to take her seat in church. For the next few hours, at least, the attention would be where it belonged. On God.

After the service, she'd be in the midst of things once more, but she'd use the time to collect herself. Marge well knew she'd be nothing more than a nine days' wonder in Buttonwood. Once everyone discovered she didn't hide any deep, dark secrets or reveal any exciting talents, they'd lose interest.

Waiting for the newness to rub off would take only a little bit of time. So lost was she in the comforts of these thoughts, she missed the hymn the parson named for the start of service.

Yet as the familiar words rose around her, Marge swiftly recognized it. Not a hymn of lilting praise nor a slow acknowledgement of the suffering the Lord underwent on their behalf, this less-oft heard song struck a chord Marge would rather have left alone this morning.

"Father, whate'er of earthly bliss
Thy sovereign will denies,
Accepted at Thy throne, let this
My humble prayer, arise:
Give me a calm and thankful heart
From every murmur free;
The blessing of Thy grace impart,
And make me live to Thee."

Nevertheless, she joined in the singing of it, knowing the words to be true. Knowing that the very way her heart ached at speaking them meant she needed their message more than ever.

As the hymn continued and Marge sang along, she added a private prayer to the worship.

Lord, lately it seems as though You've tantalized me with certain promises, only to pull them away. It's not my place to question Your will, but I can't deny how my heart aches to know Gavin wanted Daisy. How Ermintrude's caution about settling rings in my ears every time he smiles at me. I care for him and always have — enough so that a part of me wants to marry him and take what happiness I can. Help me be strong and follow Your will, Lord, even if it denies me marriage and I am to teach for the rest of my days.

She blinked back tears as the hymn and her prayer came to an end, waiting to feel as calm and thankful as the song promised. But she didn't. Marge shifted on the wooden bench as Parson Carter prayed then began the introduction to his sermon for the morning.

"Today I'm delving into the book of the prophet Jeremiah, who I think really gets into the heart of the way we follow God." Parson Carter, a tall, spare man with spectacles and tufts of white hair over either ear, looked every inch the mild scholar. Even his skin had the look of aged parchment — at once tough but vulnerable to the wear of years of demands made upon it. "Chapter seventeen discusses more than the more common issue of what we do to follow Him.

Verses seven and eight, particularly, deal more with the *why* and *how.*"

Marge made an effort not to shift restlessly. Honestly, she was as bad as some of her former pupils! But the reason believers followed Christ was simply because He was God, and she expected more from a sermon than a restating of this. She needed a deeper understanding, something to take away from church that she didn't already know, or at the very least, a reminder of something she hadn't considered in a long time.

The parson's voice recaptured her attention as he began reading directly from the Word. " 'Blessed is the man that trusteth in the Lord, and whose hope the Lord is.' "

Oh. Shame washed over her at her arrogance. *I shouldn't have assumed I knew what the message would be. He's speaking of following the Lord in trust, not following facts.* She closed her eyes at her mistake. *Although . . . we do put trust in facts. We do trust Him because He is. So, in a way, I was right. But trust goes so much deeper — the heart can know what the head cannot.*

Her gaze slid to the man beside her, who listened intently as the parson kept reading, describing the man who trusted in God as a tree planted by a river, nourished and fruitful even in times of drought.

My heart tells me that Gavin is such a man. My head tells me I was a fool to ever imagine he wanted me.

She listened to the parson speak of the link between trust in God and putting one's hope in Him.

Did I put my hope in God when I came to be Gavin's bride? Was I hoping that He'd answered my prayers for a husband and trusting this was His path — or was I putting my hope in Gavin?

Marge didn't like the questions that were starting to spring up. Not the ones about what brought her to Buttonwood and not the more urgent ones she couldn't seem to stomp down as the parson talked about anticipation for the future. With supreme effort, she tore her gaze away from Gavin.

What is it you're hoping for now, Marge? God's will — or your own?

CHAPTER 18

Midge sat on an unlined pew, her back not touching the wood rest behind her, posture rigid as a poker stick as she listened to Parson Carter speak about trust and hope.

She chewed the inside of her lip until it made her wince, realized that would give her away, and forced herself to stop. Still the man kept yammering on and on, misleading the entire town as everyone around her sat there, lapping up the lies as though they were soul-saving truths. Midge switched to a new little game to keep herself from bursting out with her opinion and disgracing the family who'd done so much for her.

Not for all the satisfaction in the world would she embarrass — or worse, hurt — Saul, Clara, Doreen, and Josiah Reed. So instead, she listened to Parson Carter like she never had before. Tuning out everything else, she raised her boot heel and tapped the fresh cut on her leg every time he said "hope." It kept her grounded, gave her something to focus on. It wasn't until she felt a wet warmth around her toes she realized she'd opened it again . . . and that, perhaps, it was deeper than she'd originally thought.

No matter. Small wounds stung, bled, scabbed, and healed. It was the deeper ones a body had to watch out for. The ones that made people with sense want to cover their ears and race away when folks proclaimed how good and great God was. Only Midge knew He had her trapped now. So she went ahead and considered the problem that had plagued her since Dr. Saul Reed swept into her life.

Which one's worse — me or God? God, for knowing everything but not paying enough attention to listen to Nancy's prayers but granting mine when I begged for a different life? Or me, for forgetting to ask that Nancy could come with me?

The searing, dry, scratchy feeling clawed its way up the back of her throat to her eyelids until the heat of tears stung the dryness away. Midge willed the tears away, digging her fingernails into her palms in rhythmic squeezes until it seemed the series of red half-moons would never fade. They would. They always did.

But for now, the important thing was that they got rid of the tears so no one would know how much she hated sitting here. How much she hated pretending to belong next to the Reeds, how much she wanted to scream at them all to wake up — that they deserved better than a God who wouldn't come through for them when they most needed Him. Midge knew it — she'd lived it. Her sister lived it . . . then died from it. And all the pretty praise songs in the world wouldn't change it.

So she went back to the circle of questions she'd chased since she first realized they were chasing her back. *I'm worse — Nancy was my sister, and it was my fault we got kicked out of the textile mill and she fell in with Rodney. It fell to me to protect her, and when I couldn't do it in life, I absolutely could have in my prayers. I deserved to be punished for being so selfish.*

Only, there was a problem with this answer. The same problem she'd come up against for the past four years. Did Midge deserve to be punished? Without a doubt.

But Nancy didn't. Nancy deserved all the wonderful things in the world, and instead God gave her sorrow and pain and death. So either He wasn't paying close enough attention, because He got the wrong sister, or He knew hurting Nancy would hurt me most. She sucked in a sharp breath.

Because the cycle didn't end there. Four years ago, when she first came to Buttonwood, Midge had been convinced prayer didn't work. God either didn't hear them or didn't care. The reason why prayer proved ineffective didn't matter so much as the fact it was. Back then, Midge was still stuck on the fact she'd asked for a better life, and she hadn't realized she only assumed God would know that included Nancy.

At one point, Clara almost had her convinced she'd gotten it turned wrong way around and she needed to add more praise to her prayers and less requests. So after thinking on it, Midge decided to give it one last try — and thanked God for the one solid thing she couldn't help but be thankful for. She praised him for the fine house that kept her and the new people she cared about safe and happy.

The next day, it burned down — almost killing Clara and Opal in the process. As she looked at the ashes, Midge knew that something had gone wrong. Either she'd messed up her prayers somehow, or God had botched up again. Whichever way, it was a pattern she didn't plan on repeating.

But even as she sat on that stiff pew in the middle of church, vowing once again not to get caught up in that same problem, Midge couldn't help but make one small comment — and if God heard her, so be it.

All right, maybe we both messed up. But only one of us is supposed to be perfect. . . .

Amos sat beside his mother and the oldest of his younger brothers in church, enjoying what he found to be a first-rate sermon. Church was the one time Midge didn't command his attention — even though she always fidgeted the whole way through. But by the end of today's teaching, he'd cast more than a few concerned glances her way.

Her face — more tan than just about any other woman's he'd ever known, since she hardly ever wore her bonnet — went oddly white. It made her freckles stand out more, but for once Amos didn't find it entrancing. Something was wrong — and he wanted to know what it was.

No, he admitted to himself, *I want to take care of whatever the problem is and bring back her smile.* Not that he had any right. Or even that he should want to take such a role in her life. *But I do. Midge Collins caught my attention four years ago, and when I saw her again in Buttonwood, it seemed she'd never let go.*

So Amos had done a fair bit of praying, talked it over with Ma, and made his decision. His fascination with this woman hadn't ebbed — so it stood to reason God was pointing him in her direction. *She's running away from me just as fast, but it's been a steady pull, and the Lord will have His way with us both.*

At the conclusion of the service, while everyone clustered around the miller and Miss Chandler, Amos hunted down a few folks who wouldn't need today's introduction. It took a little doing, but with the right maneuvering, he managed to get Dr. Saul Reed, the doctor's father, Josiah, and both their wives on the far side of the church. Away from everyone else.

Not a one of them said a word — he wouldn't have if he were in their boots. All four looked at him expectantly — unblinking. If he didn't find it so amusing, it would be downright eerie. As it stood, he got the impression they already knew the general reason he'd snuck them over for a private conversation.

"Afternoon, Reeds." He gave a respectful nod — directed mostly toward the men. "I appreciate you coming over to talk with me on such short notice."

"So talk." From anyone else, the words might have sounded short, but Josiah Reed had a smile on his lips and a knowing look in his eye that told of a good nature.

"Don't rush the man, Josiah." His wife, an even better-natured woman by the name of Doreen, if Amos recalled rightly, shot her husband a warning glance before fixing her gaze on him once again. And again, forgetting how to blink.

"No rush at all. I want you to know I've taken my time about this, brought it before the Lord before bringing the matter to you." Approving nods — and restless fidgeting from Dr. Reed's wife — met this pronouncement. "Normally, I'd just speak with Dr. Reed about this matter, but your family is as close as mine, and that's something I respect. So I stand before all of you this afternoon, seeking your permission to court Miss Collins."

"I knew it!" Clara Reed burst out. "Knew it at the dinner party. You have my approval, Mr. Geer."

"Same here." Josiah added his two cents. "Now that you spit it out." A wink softened his gripe.

"Well, aren't you two quick to agree?" Dr. Reed raised his brows at his wife and father. "Traditionally, the man explains what he has to offer the girl and why he's interested."

"That's when he's asking permission to propose," his wife reminded. "Mr. Geer only asked about courting."

"I knew right off Clara was the match for you," Josiah reminded his son of a fact Amos hadn't even known. "Maybe someday you'll learn to trust my instincts."

"Midge trusts her own instincts." The elder Mrs. Reed's quiet voice cut through the chatter. "And she avoids Mr. Geer." Her brows drew together. "I'm not entirely certain that's a bad sign, but it's by no means something I assume to be good. So I'll leave it at this: You've my approval to spend as much time with Midge as she'll allow. If you're the right man, you'll convince her to see things your way."

"She avoids you?" The good doctor seemed to be tabulating something in his head.

"Yes." Bad as it sounded, Amos wouldn't lie. "I disconcert her. She seems rather used to getting her way and winning most battles of wit or will."

"You've answered my next question — whether you know her well enough to be sure you want to court her."

"Well enough to want to know more — though I've a question I'd like answered, if you wouldn't mind." Amos jumped on Dr. Reed's statement. "Something I surmised, but Midge won't admit or explain. I'd appreciate it if you'd shed some light on the topic."

Uneasy glances and surreptitious head shakes had him wondering what the Reeds feared he'd ask. "We'll try," seemed the best he could hope for.

"The night of the dinner party, I noticed Midge seemed unusually preoccupied with keeping order in the kitchen. I think she hides a fear of fire."

"No wonder she avoids you — you pay such close attention." Most people would have missed Doreen's comment beneath a flurry of explanations, but Amos heard it loud and clear.

That means Midge hides more than one secret. I wonder what they are? He tucked the intriguing question away to play with later.

For now, he listened as Clara Reed's voice won out and she started over again with an answer to his question. "Four years ago, we had a house fire. Opal Speck — Grogan, now — and I were inside, and we almost didn't make it out. Saul and Adam pulled us to safety. Ever since then, Midge has become very vigilant about keeping watch over the stove . . . even though it was a fireplace that caused the problem."

"I see. It makes sense now."

"She's very protective of those she loves." A smile spread across Dr. Reed's face. "Midge needs a strong man, and so far none in Buttonwood have been able to match her." He stuck out his hand for a firm shake. "It's settled. You have our blessing."

"Thank you." Amos moved along to shake Josiah's hand. "You won't regret it, I assure you."

"Of course not, Mr. Geer." The older man shook his head. "We just can't promise you the same thing."

CHAPTER 19

"Daisy, darling, I'm ever so sorry for you."
Cornelia Walthingham poked her snub nose
in the air and looked down it. "You must be
perfectly devastated that he's dropped you."

"She cried off, you silly goose." Alice
Porth, a girl Daisy privately used to consider
too plainspoken for her own good, came to
her defense. "He didn't drop her. No man
would!"

"I'd never say such a thing." Daisy managed a small, secretive smile, which dissolved the instant her teacup reached her
lips. *Not out of modesty, but because it's not
true. Cornelia has it right — Trouston dropped
me. And I was wrong about Alice.* She set
down her cup with an uncharacteristic *clink*.
She's perfectly lovely.

"Terribly conniving of you to suggest
otherwise, Cornelia. It smacks of jealousy."
Daphne Kessel joined the ranks of friends
supporting Daisy in her time of need.

"Particularly considering the way Trouston carries on about the whole thing."

Dread clutched her stomach, making Daisy reach for yet another pastry as she tried to seem carefree. "Whatever do you mean? I've not seen him, of course."

"Don't you know? He's crushed by your defection. Claims he'll never love another." Alice swiped the last cake from the tray, so Daisy rang for more. "He's gone so far as to don a black armband to signify that he's mourning your loss."

"Ridiculous." Suddenly she lost her appetite. The very idea Trouston made such sport over the way he'd used her and ended their relationship, making a show of himself to draw attention and pity, it created a swell of such rage, even shopping couldn't possibly cure it. "Pure theatrics. It's one of the reasons I came to see we wouldn't suit."

"He swears you'll come back to him." A jealous gleam lit Cornelia's gaze. "That no other woman can capture his attention and he won't leave off until you're his once more."

"Trouston will persist for precisely so long as it takes him to realize black armbands, when worn consistently, stain certain fabrics." Daisy knew she made her ex-fiancé sound petty, and perhaps sounded rather low herself, but she didn't care. "He's exceedingly conscientious about his appearance."

"Not so conscientious he wouldn't fight for you." Daphne gave a little sigh. "It's positively romantic the way he's threatened any man who so much as looks at you to a duel."

"What?" Daisy's posture, already held straight by her tightly laced corset, became even more rigid.

"Mr. Dillard says he simply can't abide the thought of you with another man, and thus he won't allow one anywhere near you." Alice leaned forward. "Haven't you wondered why none of your old beaus have come to renew their suits?"

"I presumed they were exercising judicious manners and allowing a respectful period of time to pass so as not to offend me or Mr. Dillard." Daisy delivered the line just as she'd rehearsed, for of course she'd wondered. *Though I assumed that somehow men possessed an uncanny ability to know when a woman had been despoiled and would no longer be of interest to them.* "It never occurred to me that Trouston was making threats to hold them at bay. Of all the nerve!"

"Every woman appreciates a man who

197

knows what he wants. When will you put him out of this miserable waiting period and take him back?"

"Yes, when?"

"Can you arrange for us to watch the reunion?" A flurry of exclamations greeted Mama's question.

"Mama, I already made it clear. I won't take Trouston back." *He doesn't want me to. It would ruin his scheme to play merry bachelor for the rest of his born days, leaving a string of heartbroken women in his wake.* The thought lent a very convincing sniff to her own performance.

"But you must! You simply must." The torrent of feminine cries blended into one shrill babble, making Daisy wince.

"It's so dashing, the way he's working to win you back." Alice, in particular, refused to drop the matter. "You'll seem a horrid, hard-hearted tease if you refuse him."

" *'Playtime is over, Daisy.'* "Trouston stopping her when she tried to ease some distance between them . . . " *'You belong to me, and no man likes a tease. . . .'* "Another piece of her murky memories from that night rose to the surface, making her gasp.

"I'm not a tease." Tears sprang to her eyes. *If I were, this wouldn't be happening. I'd still be engaged, not knowing what an awful man I*

198

chose, instead of sitting here in polite company, pretending to be one of them. Pretending I'm not base and ruined and not worth their time or friendship. "Excuse me, but I'm afraid I've come down with a megrim."

"You do look frightfully pale." Mama frowned. "Go rest for a while. I'll check on you in a bit."

Placing one hand to her temple, Daisy skirted around her friends and various pieces of furniture until she reached the hall. The moment she slipped from sight, she sagged against the wall, drawing in a ragged breath. *It's only a matter of time until they see what I've come to. Lord, I can't go back and fix it. I can't remake myself into what I was before I erred so badly . . . and all the wishes in the world can't make it better.* She swallowed a sob.

"She did not look well." The words were proper, but Cornelia's tone carried no concern. Instead, a malicious hint of satisfaction underscored her observation.

"Daisy simply hasn't been the same since she threw over Mr. Dillard." Daphne drummed her fingernails on the rim of her saucer as she always did when unsettled. "I worry for her."

"As we all do."

"If she doesn't recover her composure

soon, it may be too late for her to find someone else." The satisfaction sounded even more pronounced now, and Daisy determined to have nothing more to do with Cornelia. "If she's truly foolish enough to let a prize like Mr. Dillard slip away."

A prize he's not. She didn't want to hear any more. Placing one hand on the banister, Daisy headed up the stairs on silent slippers until she reached her room. *But slipping away . . . if only I could manage to. Everything would be better.*

Eschewing the bed, she reclined on the divan near her dressing room and thought of how much she wished her cousin were there. *Marge wouldn't have left me alone with Trouston. And Marge would know what to do, now, after . . .* The tears she'd held at bay rolled down the bridge of her nose. *I wish Marge were here, instead of out west. Or that we could change places and I could be far, far away from Trouston and all the mealy-mouthed misses still besotted with him.*

She sat bolt upright. *What am I thinking? I* can *be far away — it's the perfect solution.* Her first real smile in days tugged at the corners of her lips, and she gave in to an unladylike grin. *I'll surprise Marge with a visit!*

The way Gavin saw things, ladies liked

surprises. So long as they weren't creepy, crawly, slimy, dirty, or involving hard work, women couldn't get enough of the unexpected.

All right, if I'm going to be out here almost before the sun decides to rise, I may as well be blunt about the matter. Ladies don't like surprises — they like gifts.

Well, who didn't? Gifts showed a woman she was being thought of. Cared for. Appreciated. No souls on earth could deny wanting those things — not without lying through their teeth, at least. Presents made for tangible expressions of the things people had a hard time talking about.

In other words, a present made the perfect way to further his case with Marge and speed up this courting process. She wanted him to prove his desire to marry her — and asking didn't suffice. Showing her off to the whole town and laying claim seemed to backfire. Brett Burn hadn't been the only one whose eyes lingered too long. Nor had Gavin missed the way they all seemed to find reason to chat with her whenever he escorted her into town these days.

Gavin pulled his hat brim lower and squinted, trying to make out the different low-lying plants hidden by prairie grasses. He didn't make a habit out of hunting plants, but exceptions existed for every rule. It didn't matter if he had to tromp around for miles before he'd found and gathered enough of what he'd come looking for. Gavin didn't intend to show up at breakfast empty-handed this morning.

Prove it. Her challenge rang in his ears as he spied the first of his unofficial harvest and fell to with a vengeance. If words didn't prove it and standing beside her didn't prove it and respecting her wish to help set up the school didn't prove it, Gavin had one more weapon in his arsenal to show a woman that he valued her. He'd prove it with a strategy so well laid even Marge Chandler couldn't deny it.

And she'd like it.

With a resolute nod, Gavin stepped over the area he'd stripped bare and moved on. *More.* A handful wouldn't be enough, and a man only got one chance to pull off a grand gesture. Repeating a failed attempt just looked foolish — and he wasn't a man to play the fool. Nor was he typically a man to play the romantic, but Gavin had already lost one bride. If a little show of finer feeling netted him another, at least he'd keep his pride.

Show me a man who won't tromp over ten miles of prairie gathering wildflowers to sal-

vage his pride and earn a bride, and I'll show you a liar or a lout. Though not every man could put a personal twist on the exercise — a sweet sentiment designed to win a woman's heart.

Not only would he earn favor by presenting Marge with flowers, he upped the ante in several ways. First, by gathering them himself, which meant he put out effort, as opposed to the way things were done back in Baltimore where a man purchased such things. Then, he'd remembered her favorite color — purple — and only chosen flowers of that shade. *Good thing the strange breed blooms around here.* . . . As the crowning touch, he brought Marge a bouquet of no flower but wild daisies . . . same as her name.

This was the type of thing women went wild for. Romance, thoughtfulness, individuality, a creative flair — all told, he should have her consent to wed him before the week ended. They'd stand before Parson Carter, with the entire town looking on and wishing them well, next Sunday.

Three days is short notice. Best make it some day next week. I'll let Marge decide, to keep her happy. Good to make the little woman feel as though she's involved.

By the time he'd gathered a huge bouquet

and made his way back to the house, Gavin felt better than he had in over a week.

Time to win a wife!

CHAPTER 20

The days settled into an easy pattern. Too
easy. Marge awoke the following Thursday
feeling as though something had changed.
She lay perfectly still beneath the warm
weight of the bedclothes, trying to determine the difference. When she couldn't, she
closed her eyes. *Lord, what new thing awaits
me this morning? I try to put my trust in You
— though I'm afraid my hopes still lie with
Gavin. Whatever the day holds, help me trust
in You, and help me put my hope where it
belongs.*

Upon opening her eyes again, Marge suddenly knew. The icy misgivings that she'd
clenched around her heart since the moment Ermintrude first mentioned Daisy's
name now thawed. All the concern and hurt
and disappointment hadn't melted away,
but the unrelenting, pinching pressure of it
lessened. She pushed the covers aside and
hopped out of bed, eager to get downstairs

for her morning debate with Ermintrude as they prepared breakfast.

I'm trying, Lord. Thank You for seeing that and helping.

She tackled her long mane of hair, amazed to find her brush sliding easily through the thick strands. Since her first night in Buttonwood, she'd slept so restlessly it'd become a morning battle to untangle night's knots. As a result, she beat the older woman downstairs and had the milk and water already inside by the time Ermintrude showed up.

"Either you're rising earlier, or I'm sleeping later. I choose to believe it's the former."

"I agree."

"Now *there's* a pleasant surprise." Ermintrude's brows winged upward until they almost touched her hairline. "I take it you've grown tired of losing our little arguments every morning and decided to take the easy way out from now on?"

"Hardly. I enjoy our *discussions*." Marge emphasized the final word in that sentence. "Arguments indicate a sort of bitterness and a cyclical futility I don't believe describes the way we converse."

"That's more like it." She thumped her cane on the floor in approval. "Glad to see you've not lost your spirit."

"On the contrary, it grows stronger by the day."

"Then Buttonwood must be doing you some good." The deep timber of Gavin's voice in the doorway caused them both to turn around. He stood there, one arm behind his back, a broad smile brightening his face.

"You're early, too." Ermintrude's grumble sounded genuine, and Marge softened slightly at the idea the older woman felt cheated of their debate time.

"We'll continue our conversation later today. Don't think you've escaped." Her jest had the intended effect, making her opponent straighten up at once in anticipation.

"You'll be the one wanting to escape!"

"No." Gavin crooked a finger, still keeping one arm behind his back as he called to her, "Marge wants to come over here."

Instantly suspicious, she didn't budge. "We've played this game, Gavin. I said I'd give no more steps until you proved yourself worthy." It didn't help the situation that Ermintrude watched them both with avid curiosity.

"That's what I'm trying to do. We were far closer at the end of that round. Give me that, at least."

Against her better judgment, her curiosity guiding her, Marge shuffled until only a few feet separated them. "This is as far as I go." *Physically, at least.* Her heart and dreams drummed onward, until her hopes placed her firmly in his arms. *He says he's trying to prove himself — Lord, let him succeed! Please, please let this be the end of the difficulty and that be the reason I felt better this morning.*

"I told you I'd earn my prize." His stare caught her, held her fast. "You told me to prove myself. I've spoken the words, shown you before my peers and been proud to claim you, treated you well as the woman in my home." Here, he ignored a faint squawk from Ermintrude, though it sounded more like a reminder of her presence than any true protest. "I've proven myself in all the ways I know how, save the traditional courting gifts."

"Oh, Gavin." Shame flooded her even as something softened at his determination. Could it be that Gavin truly wanted to wed her for reasons beyond duty or guilt at his mistake? "No gifts. It was never my intent for you to purchase anything."

"They say the thought matters most." He pulled a massive bouquet from behind his back with a dramatic flourish. "I bring these to you and hope you read my thoughts and find all the proof you seek." He held the bunch of flowers in front of him, his expression gleefully expectant.

Marge stared at the overlarge clump of daisies he thrust toward her, mind working furiously. Smashed together, the blossoms wilted, bent, leaned at unnatural positions. Leaves trapped between the stalks poked through Gavin's thick fingers as though trying to escape confinement. All told, the flowers looked about as manipulated and abused as Marge felt.

"Thank you." Somehow she choked out the expected phrase. *He's trying. He brought you flowers. He picked them himself. They're even your favorite color — not that he remembers that. But he's trying, at least.* Some logical, optimistic part of her mind sent a litany of cheery thoughts in an attempt to mitigate the crashing disappointment, but it was no use.

Daisies. Daisy. The cousin he wanted but didn't get. He promises to show me his true heart and prove he wants me but brings the only thing he could possibly find to symbolize the bride he cannot have. Rigid cold spread its fingers through her chest once more, stretching their reach beyond where they'd dipped the first time she'd seen

Gavin's heart.

"Aren't you going to take them?" Two lines furrowed between Gavin's brows as he inspected his offering. "You seem overcome?"

The statement sounded like a question as Marge started to raise one hand to accept his gift then dropped it back to her side. "I can't accept these, Gavin." She took a step back — a larger step than normal, though she doubted he'd notice. "I appreciate what you're trying to say and the thoughtful manner you chose to do so. Thank you."

"If you don't like them I can pick something else." His grip tightened, forcing the poor plants into even more contorted positions. "Your cousin only likes violets and roses, but I thought you'd appreciate these."

"You still think of her often." Marge let loose a humorless rasp of laughter. It was either that or allow the parched ache in the back of her throat to bleed into dry sobs. "You can't have Daisy, so to tell me you've made your peace with your second choice, you bring me her namesake?"

"What?" Astonishment blanketed his features. "No. Marguerite means *daisy*. These are your namesake, Marge, every bit as much as your cousin's."

"I don't identify myself with the flowers."

"But . . ." Frustration brought his brows together entirely, and she could practically see him turning over her interpretation of his gift in his head, unable to argue with it. "Grandma, didn't you tell me these aren't even real daisies? They're Tahoka daisies — a sort of wild version. Different." He beamed as though that made everything better . . . instead of worse.

"Uu–u–g–g–h–h." A *thud* punctuated Ermintrude's moan.

Marge couldn't be certain, but she suspected the older woman dropped her head onto the table. Heavily. Which meant that Ermintrude, at least, saw the reason why Gavin should have kept this little fact to himself.

"I see." She stared at the increasingly bedraggled grouping as though it threatened to bite her. "So they're *fake* daisies?"

Marge saw the moment he realized where he'd gone wrong — he caught himself mid-nod and started shaking his head vehemently.

Too little, too late.

Where did it all go wrong? Gavin knew well and good he didn't have the time to hammer out when his scheme turned rotten, but the entire thing carried the flavor of an ambush. *When I realized she objected to the idea of my giving her daisies, I shouldn't have tried to soften it by backtracking on what sort of daisy they were.* That much, he should've seen coming.

Now, she'd stepped back from him. Not a small step, or even a series of hesitant shuffles, but one great big decisive step that showed he'd well and truly damaged his chances this time. Worse, no matter how fetching she looked with her eyes that bright, Marge seemed to be gaining more steam than she let off.

"Imposters, I suppose? Like myself?" Her voice rose with each question, gaining volume but losing fullness, as though getting louder somehow stretched it out.

"No. Absolutely not. Marge, that's not what I meant at all." He moved to close the distance she'd increased, but she backed away more with every move he made, until the kitchen table sat between them, with Ermintrude right smack in the center of it all. "You're taking this the wrong way."

"Since you asked me to read your thoughts by your gift and you brought fake daisies for the imposter who arrived in place of the Daisy you sought, I'm taking it rather well."

"If that's the way I meant it, you would be." Frustration started to seep through into his own tone. After all, he'd made a real effort here. *Even if I botched it.*

"Man finds himself in a hole, best thing to do" — Grandma poked him in the side with her cane to let him know she wasn't making a general observation, as though she ever just made general observations — "stop digging!"

"I thought you'd like them, so I went and got them for you. Being wrong about your reaction doesn't change the reason I did it." A muscle ticked in his jaw. "Purple is your favorite."

"You knew that?" His fiancée's stance relaxed slightly.

"Yes. You said so on the day you came to town — your dress was your favorite color." He scowled at the thought she implied he would lie about such a thing. "Easy enough to remember."

"But not everyone would." She softened a little more.

"I did. And I remembered that you're a flower every bit as much as your cousin. But when I picked you a bouquet, you looked at it like I insulted you." He stared down at the pitiful, if still enormous, lump of flowers in his hand. Suddenly he didn't want to be in the house anymore, standing in front of the woman who kept refusing him, holding a clump of mangled blossoms as though still hoping she'd accept them.

"Call when breakfast is ready." With that, he stalked outside, going a few paces before flinging the daisies into the dirt.

This is why men don't make grand gestures very often. When they fail, the blast knocks us back farther than we can afford. Now Gavin had to come up with a new plan.

Just as soon as he decided whether or not he really wanted to.

CHAPTER 21

I don't want to ask him. Midge grappled with the issue, livid at how well Amos had played his hand. Somehow, the man understood that the one thing she couldn't stand — aside from someone hurting any of her people, a depth to which Amos would never stoop no matter how badly he wanted her attention — was awareness of her own ignorance.

She took pride in knowing things no one else did — noticing what others didn't bother to look for reaped many rewards. So she didn't often find herself the last to know something. And it was driving her up the wall — or at least as close to it as physically possible.

The agitation provoked by Amos's secret, which everyone stayed cursedly closed lipped about, took her all over town. Clara beamed at her in the kitchen but wouldn't spill whatever Amos told them. So Midge hied off to Saul's office, waited for him to finish treating a patient, and launched into an interrogation he withstood with good humor — but no information.

Which took her to Josiah, in the general store. Midge made herself pleasant and useful, but her adopted grandfather didn't return the favor. He'd outright laughed at her attempts to nudge anything out of him and directed her to go ask Amos.

When Midge tracked down Aunt Doreen helping the Dunstalls with an afternoon of baking at the town café, she'd heard the same advice.

An exhausting day of fruitless attempts to coax anything from her loved ones brought Midge to the edge of becoming cranky. She squashed her irritation and made a fresh try the next day. And the next. Now, after a week of trying to wear down any of the adults in her makeshift family and failing to elicit anything but amusement, Midge needed a new strategy.

Pretending she didn't care wasted time. Not only did all the Reeds know better, Amos suspected her true reaction. If he didn't give her so much grief, Midge might even have given him some measure of respect for his clever scheme. She avoided him whenever he came near — so he'd thought up a way to make her come to him. A grudging appreciation for his shift in tactics didn't bring her any closer to thwarting him though.

She scowled. *If I could somehow let it go — not care about whatever he trumped up to manufacture a senseless conspiracy — that would show him how far above his silly games I am.* Midge gave a resolute sniff, turned on her heel, and headed back toward the house.

Or my apathy will provoke him to new heights. Her steps slowed. *I can't maintain the pretense of disinterest in the face of a continual onslaught. And the longer I hold out, the more humbling it will be when I finally ask him for something.* She halted in the middle of the street, debating.

Only a fool persisted in winning minor battles if it meant losing the larger war. *It's been five days — near enough to a week to show him he can't pull my strings so easily. If I wait longer, he'll know how much I fought against my curiosity.* Somehow, she'd almost arrived at the site of the schoolhouse before making the decision to go there. *So now is the best time to face him — beard the lion in his den, so to speak.*

Come to think of it, *lion* proved an apt association for him. The afternoon sun gleamed gold on his sandy hair, darkened at his temples from perspiration. As she drew closer, Midge watched him draw a large handkerchief from his back pocket, her gaze following the motion of his hand upward. Vaguely she noted that he wiped his brow, but Midge's attention caught on the breadth of his shoulders.

At some point during the day, as he shaped clay, straw, and water into the thick sun-baked bricks to build the reddish schoolhouse, he'd abandoned his coat. The loose white lawn of his shirt caught whatever scant breeze chanced by, the wind playing a happy game of hide-and-seek with his chest as it alternately pressed then lifted the fabric away. Dark suspenders outlined the broad V of his back as he mopped his neck and returned the bandanna to his pocket.

Midge sucked in a breath. No matter how devious his mind, there was no denying Amos Geer cut a fine figure of a man.

At least, he did until he turned to give her one of those slow, infuriating grins of his.

"Like what you see?"

His question made her throat go dry. "I suppose." Midge framed her answer cautiously. He'd snagged her staring, and it wouldn't do to pretend not to know what he meant. "Though the view improves with distance."

"Odd. The walls aren't tall enough to be seen from far off." His brows knit as though considering her words, and Midge realized her mistake.

"It's easier to imagine," she hastened to cover her mistake. *Amos didn't see me looking him over.* Relief tingled all the way to her toes.

"Now that's the first smile I've seen from you in a while." He tilted his hat back atop his head. "Pretty sight."

"I smile often." She stopped herself mid-glower and gave an overly sweet simper. "Interesting you see otherwise."

"Well, every minx needs some time to sharpen her tongue. I assume you credit me with the ability to withstand your practice."

Midge strangled a laugh at the quick brilliance of his riposte, instead focusing on her response. "Is it any wonder I lose my habitual good humor around you?"

"Wonders abound." His gaze grew more intense. "Although you don't seem the type to lose much."

"Oh?" *If only you knew.* "You might be surprised."

Amos watched the mirth fade from her features and could have kicked himself for whatever he'd said to provoke the signs of sorrow that stretched soul deep.

Fool. The Reeds took her in — obviously she's lost much. It was just too easy to forget that in the face of her vibrancy.

"What have you lost?" He wanted to step closer but sensed she'd see it as a violation. Instead, he held his ground.

"No less than anyone else." Sadness sifted into wariness. She must have realized too much of her thoughts showed.

Amos found himself torn between wanting her to stop throwing up barriers and donning cheerful masks and hating to see any glimpse of suffering in this indomitable woman. "Most likely, you've lost more than many."

"I do fancy myself to be exceptional, but in this case I'd gladly forfeit my status." An impish grin told him she'd recovered from whatever regrets tugged at her heart moments before. "Seems I'm doomed to lose many things."

"Such as?" He followed the prompt of her exaggerated sigh.

"Push buttons. I lose track of time when I'm enjoying myself. My temper, when I'm not." The grin grew shrewd. "But most of all, it seems I can't keep hold of my patience."

He burst out laughing at her display of wit. "So now we've come down to it — the reason for your unscheduled visit to the schoolhouse site?"

"You dance well, but I lack grace. Mr. Geer, you know full well why I've come here today."

"Ran out of the last drop of your limited supply of patience but have a surplus of curiosity?" Amos hazarded a guess and was rewarded with her grudging nod. "You held out longer than I'd anticipated."

"What? I wasn't holding anything."

It was almost too easy, but he couldn't resist prodding her. While she'd been refusing to come ask him what he'd spoken with her family about, he'd cooled his heels waiting on her pride. He raised his brows in a credible imitation of surprise. "Then you've lost more than your patience. What were those other things you listed — track of time? Must be the reason you've dawdled so long before coming to talk to me."

"Dawdled?" Scathing tones made the echo blister, but she hushed and didn't continue with whatever she'd almost set loose. Which, of course, made it all the more interesting.

Luckily, Amos knew well and good what she'd been up to for the past five days. Midge Collins didn't dawdle. She asked, interrogated, wheedled, and downright demanded information, but she'd kept busy trying to ferret out information for the entire week. Amos knew, because he'd kept himself entertained watching her venture all over town trying to run her family members into the ground. Apparently none of them had broken their promise not to reveal what he'd asked. Doreen even went so far as to commend his strategy.

"Your family wouldn't explain my request, I take it."

"Not so much as a peep." This was the closest thing to an admission of trying to discover what he'd said to them that Midge was likely to make. Yet she didn't come out and ask him.

"You're adorable when thwarted."

"I," she seethed at his compliment, "am *not* adorable."

"*Cute* describes children, and *pretty* is too common." He crossed his arms and made a show of looking her up and down. "We both know, Miss Collins, that you're anything but common."

"I'm many things." She looked somewhat mollified in spite of herself. Irritation turned to expectation, and she lifted a brow to prompt him. "Right now, I'm waiting."

"And I'm considering the minute possibil-

222

ity I was wrong."

"Of course you are." She shifted her weight from one foot to the other. "About what this time?"

This time. Ha. Her attempts to goad him affected him in exactly the opposite way. The more she opposed his attention, the more firmly he fixed it upon her. "If I am wrong in this instance, you bear the blame."

Triumph flashed in her eyes before wariness dampened it — she was too clever to think she'd won that easily. "How so?"

"If you aren't adorable, it's only because you won't let yourself be adored." He finally took the step he'd been denying himself, closing the distance between them. "*Now* tell me I'm wrong."

She stared at him in a silence that brought him more satisfaction than all the sparring he'd enjoyed before. "No."

"No?" He noticed she didn't step back. Whether she simply stood her ground out of stubbornness or didn't mind his nearness was hard to tell. Except he remembered their first meeting and knew Midge wouldn't put herself within arm's reach unless she felt good and comfortable there. "I want you to."

"But you're right. Adoration isn't for me. I don't look for it and I won't inspire it."

She tilted her head a notch to look him in the eye. "So for once, we agree."

"In that case" — Amos reached and tweaked a strand of hair that escaped her bun, fingering its softness before tucking it behind her ear — "I intend to prove us both wrong."

CHAPTER 22

Flummoxed. Midge could find only that single word to describe what Amos had done. She couldn't quite manage to get past it. And he knew it, too. The knowledge danced in his eyes and the slightly lopsided tilt to his smile.

He flummoxed me. She waited for a tart reply to spring to mind, but none did. Midge blinked. *Why? What is it about this man that he unsettles me?* She fixed on that lopsided tilt, refusing to look away but unable to meet his expectant stare. *Is it simply because he wants to?*

"Have you gone mad?" The very idea that Amos Geer succeeded in making sport of her brought Midge to her senses.

"Not at all."

She waited for an explanation, but it seemed she'd wait in vain. Meanwhile, his smile didn't diminish one bit. *He can't be serious. A man like Amos Geer, adoring a girl like me?* She didn't have to fake the snort of laughter that erupted from the very thought.

"What's so funny?"

"You." She took a savage satisfaction in watching his smile slip a notch. "You almost sounded serious."

"I am." Nothing in his face indicated otherwise. No laughter, no anger at hers — just an intensity that made her mirth dry up in an instant.

"You can't be." *Not me. Not the real Midge Collins.* She stared him down right back. *If you knew even a hint of the truth, you'd see why I laughed.* She took in a gulp of air. *And why I'm not laughing now.*

Truth be told, Midge knew as deep down as a body could that she wasn't a good woman. Oh, she tried to be. Four years with Saul and Clara taught her a lot about the way people should live and love, and she'd come a long way from the bitter child Dr. Reed plucked from a back alleyway. But lessons learned late in life only sank so deep. No one could wash away the sort of filth that seeped into a person's core early on.

Lucky thing of it was most folks didn't look that deep. Didn't care to and didn't know how. So Midge got by on being friendly and clever and following the rules. Well, most of them, anyway. Someday she'd marry a man who didn't look too closely and would never realize the taint she carried — and she'd make sure he was happy.

"Ask me what I spoke with your family about, Midge." The deep timbre of his voice caressed her name, luring her closer.

"What did you speak with my family about?" It didn't count as obeying orders, since she'd planned on asking him long before her feet brought her here.

"I wanted permission to court you." With that, he closed the door on any doubts about his sincerity.

But Amos Geer was a rare one. Before her stood a man who wouldn't just look into the heart of the woman he chose, he'd demand she give it to him entirely. If he glanced her way much longer, he'd see what she hid. Which, come to think of it, might be the easiest way to convince him he didn't want her.

Midge ignored a pang at the thought. Fact of the matter was she'd fought too hard to make it this long and still be Midge. She didn't plan to make a lot of changes or give up everything she'd built for the sake of a man — no matter how clever or handsome he may be.

"They approved." It wasn't a question. They both knew he wouldn't mention the matter if he hadn't received permission.

He nodded anyway.

"Well then" — she indulged in a sigh — "I suppose you'd best walk me home."

"I'd be delighted." His smile returned as he offered his arm, not in the least bit put off by her easy capitulation.

So he's not solely interested in a challenge. She watched him from the corner of her eye as they walked along in silence. *No matter. All I have to do is be myself and I'll chase him off in no time. It's for his own good — because spending time with Amos Geer doesn't appeal in the slightest.*

She kept walking, ignoring the silence. Ignoring the stares of the townspeople as they passed by. But most of all, ignoring the tiny voice in her head that got louder with every step.

Liar.

If she heard it again, Daisy very much feared she'd scream right there in the middle of the soiree. As things stood, she scarcely kept a hold on her temper. But truly, even the most well-bred of women had her limits.

"Daisy!" She didn't even see the woman's face before she found herself swept into a matronly hug. "I'm so sorry. . . ." Mrs.

228

Such-and-Such, whose name escaped Daisy at the moment, blathered on about broken hearts and their more horrifying counterpart — broken engagements.

She didn't really listen. The vibrations of her teeth grinding genteelly behind a grateful nod blocked out most of the speech. Not that it mattered — she'd already said *it*. The phrase Daisy now loathed with every fiber of her being. She'd heard people say often enough that no one wished to be pitied, but she'd never experienced the humbling nature of it before.

Outings used to be marked with smiles and laughter, chitchat and flattery, admiring glances and merriment. Now, that single, awful phrase eclipsed it all.

"I'm sorry. I'm so sorry. I'm *so* sorry. I'm so *sorry*." Even the overblown "I'm *so sorry*." All winged their way in an attack to make Grecian Harpies proud. No matter if and where the speaker placed the emphasis, the syllables remained the same. And so did their effect.

"I must go." With a cursory nod, she abandoned the mouthy matron in the midst of her monologue and took a turn about the room. *To Buttonwood, to be exact.*

She'd looked into taking the train, but as she should have remembered from earlier conversations with Marge, the train didn't go through that area. The stage wouldn't leave for a couple days and would take a frightfully long time — if Daisy were so foolish as to think she could manage traveling alone.

Marge handled such things with aplomb, but Daisy didn't. *Just look what happened the last time I was unchaperoned for any length of time.* She shoved the thought back to the dark recesses of her memory, back where she could almost convince herself it was forgotten.

Mama would stop her if she knew her plans — though Daisy fully intended to leave a reassuring note behind if her new scheme worked. She'd hatched it up upon arriving with Mama this evening and spotted Miss Lindner and her brother exiting their conveyance at almost the same time.

Mama insisted on following fashion, so the Chandlers rode about in a sprightly landau — only good for light town driving. The Lindners didn't seem to have time for fashion. To be honest, everyone seemed surprised when Trouston began calling on the quiet, bookish Elizabeth. Their very differences made them a striking couple, or so everyone exclaimed. She was pretty enough, with that black hair and pale skin — similarities Daisy ignored when Trouston came calling on her — but they shared no interests.

Daisy wished she'd paid more attention — now that she knew her ex-intended's dastardly game, she noticed Miss Lindner more. Tonight, she noticed the Lindner coach. A private coach — well sprung, expensively made, designed to stand the test of time and use. The sort of conveyance one could take long distances, if need be.

Well, I have need, and Miss Lindner should have understanding. Daisy remembered how Elizabeth disappeared for almost the entire winter after she dropped Trouston. Of course she'd feel natural empathy with Daisy's need for solitude and escape.

Which was why Daisy watched the other woman like a veritable hawk the entire evening, waiting for just the right moment to snag her elbow and draw her into an abandoned sitting room. It worked beautifully, save the complete dismay painting her new friend's features as they faced each other.

"My apologies." Daisy refused, absolutely refused, to ever say "sorry" again unless forced to do so. "We don't know each other very well, but I've a desperate need to speak with you."

Miss Lindner didn't nod or say anything encouraging but neither did she sidle toward the door. Surely that meant something good?

"I believe we have something in common, you and I." Daisy walked over to a sofa and took a seat, patting the cushion beside her in an invitation Miss Lindner could choose to refuse.

"It is my fervent hope you refer only to our good sense in not marrying Mr. Dillard." She walked to the door, and Daisy's heart sank at the thought she'd lost her chance. Instead, Elizabeth closed the door and joined her on the sofa.

"Mostly." Now that the moment arrived, Daisy found she couldn't mention her disgrace. Their disgrace. It was all just too . . . disgraceful.

"I see." Her companion's eyes went soft but somehow angry. "Though I hope our reasons differ somewhat?"

"I —" She couldn't hold back a telltale sniffle as the enormity of the situation crashed over her once again. "I'm afraid not, Miss Lindner."

The other woman didn't say a word, simply passed a perfectly pressed handkerchief and took one of Daisy's gloved hands in her own. This show of sisterhood, after being without Marge during such a confusing and important time, proved Daisy's undoing. Tears ran down her cheeks and dripped from her nose.

"I need to leave." She barely got the words out between sobs. "My cousin went out west — I miss Marge. I thought, of all people, you'd understand." Daisy dissolved into tears once more.

"You've no idea just how well I understand. I went to Vicksburg to visit my grandmother for a few months after . . ." A fluttery hand gesture finished a sentence neither of them could speak aloud.

"Will you help me, Miss Lindner?"

"It's Elizabeth, and of course. Any way I can."

Swiftly, Daisy outlined her plan — Marge's home out west, Elizabeth's carriage to take her there safely. When she finished, silence stretched between them.

"It belongs to my brother — you'll have to convince him. I'll do my best to help." Her new friend rose to her feet. "Take a moment to compose yourself while I find him," she advised as she slipped through the door.

Daisy wasted no time blowing her nose and drawing a few deep breaths to restore her color. To gain an extra moment between tears and facing Shane Lindner — an imposingly clever man who never failed to make her tongue-tied — she kept her back to the door. She heard it open and closed her eyes for a quick prayer that things would go well.

"What have we here?" Trouston's voice oozed across the room. "A pretty little flower — already plucked but still fresh enough to enjoy."

She sprang from the sofa and faced him. *I won't let it happen again. I won't. I can't let him drag me further away from the person I'm supposed to be — the Daisy people think they see when they look at me.* Remorse somehow lent her strength. "Leave."

"No." He unbuttoned his coat, revealing the waistcoat beneath. The motion made Daisy's stomach churn in remembrance. "You've disappointed me, holding private conversations with my other forgotten fiancée." A cold gleam lit his gaze as it traveled over her. "And I'm of a mind to teach you how to behave."

CHAPTER 23

"I'm not yours to teach." She all but spat the words as he advanced. Torn between fleeing and launching herself at him, nails digging into his face, Daisy stood her ground. *My gloves would make it useless anyway.*

"You're mine, all right." Instead of respecting her newfound courage, he advanced. "Mine to teach. Mine to touch."

"No!" She backed away a second too late as his arms caught and drew her to him in a heavy clasp.

"Yes." Trouston seemed amused by her determination to keep him at bay as she straightened her arms and leaned as far back as possible to avoid him. He snagged both her wrists in one hand and jerked her close. "Mine to take, whenever I choose."

Pulling back one foot, regrettably clad only in a satin evening slipper rather than a pair of sturdy half boots, she delivered a vicious kick to his shin. A cry of pain broke from her lips as her toes took the brunt of the assault meant to cripple *him,* but, incredibly, he was letting her go. . . .

Daisy took advantage of his distraction to scamper toward the door, realizing the moment she got underway that it hadn't been her kick that stopped Trouston. Shane Lindner held him by the scruff of the neck. Odd, she'd never realized that his remarkable height lent him enough strength to lift a grown man off his feet.

But that's exactly what Shane did to Trouston now — if only for a moment. Abruptly, he released her attacker, letting Trouston fall heavily on his feet. Not that he stayed there. Shane's swift right hook sent him sprawling across the carpet. Trouston didn't get back up.

"I always thought he had a weak chin," she marveled, looking at Mr. Lindner with new respect. "Thank you for putting it to good use."

"My pleasure, Miss Chandler." A reluctant smile lifted his lips, though he tried to repress it. His efforts only brought out a well-hidden dimple Daisy never noticed before. "Now, I hear you need some transportation?"

■ ■ ■ ■

Marge stared at the drop front desk in the guest room — a luxury this far west. Gavin ordered, transported, and implanted beautiful things. He surrounded himself with only the best.

I need to remember that. She stayed seated on the bed, fisting her hands in her lap, riveted by that desk. *I don't belong with the fine things he brought to Buttonwood. He made a home to showcase his finest prize: Daisy.*

It would be so easy to pretend it all away and act as though Gavin wanted her. If she chose, Marge could walk down the aisle with her head held high, her future assured, and no one the wiser. One of her favorite verses came to mind. *"When I was a child, I spake as a child, I understood as a child, I thought as a child. . . ."*

She'd grown up long ago, surpassing the point of make-believe and happily-ever-afters. Deep down, she'd known Gavin's letter for what it was — a tantalizing glimpse into a life not meant for her. Only, she'd wanted it so badly, she seized hold and rode out to meet it. Reality won.

Mostly.

Marge couldn't take it any longer. She rose from the bed, crossed the room, and laid one hand atop the desk front. Sliding one finger along the groove, she unlatched the hinged compartment, cradling it so it wouldn't stress the chain meant to hold it up as a writing surface. It opened to reveal the secret within.

Purple daisies, once crushed, wilted within a crystal vase. Deprived of sunlight and fresh air, they faltered far faster than they would if Marge bore the courage to display them on her night table. Instead, she hid them away. *"For where your treasure is, there will your heart be also."*

Perhaps she hadn't outgrown childish games entirely. Marge reached out to finger the soft, fragile petals of one blossom. After Gavin stalked out, she'd seen him hurl the flowers in the dirt, and something inside her howled at the sight. She'd resisted the urge to run out and gather them all up, instead biding her time until Gavin stayed at the mill and Ermintrude rested her eyes for a while.

Then she'd ventured outside, carefully selected just enough of the flowers to fill the crystal vase she'd brought from home, and snuck back inside. Unearthing the vase took longer than she expected, and once she had them properly placed, Marge realized what she'd done — what it would look like to Gavin or Ermintrude if they saw her keepsake. She'd seem a lackwit.

So she kept them closed away in her desk, companions to the words Gavin sent burrowing into her heart after she'd challenged his choice of daisies. *"Purple is your favorite. . . . You said so."*

Yes, she said so. Gavin thought it important enough to remember though. That meant something. It didn't mean a passionate, undying love. It didn't mean he'd been expecting Marge to step off that stage. But it still . . . counted.

"You're a flower every bit as much as your cousin." This is what made her sneak out to save some of those daisies. The sound of his voice, so earnest as he said sweet words. Not flattery or compliments or a calculated bid to earn her favor. No, these were sweet words uttered in exasperation. *True words.* She turned the vase slightly as she deconstructed that lovely sentence for the hundredth time.

The teacher in her couldn't resist diagramming it — pulling out the root sentence. *You're a flower. You are a flower.* Without bothering with grammar, she replayed the meaning of it. Flowers were known for color, scent, texture — sensory appeal. It took time for them to blossom, time for them to be appreciated.

I am a flower. No wonder she couldn't stop smiling whenever she opened her desk. Even better, he'd compared her to her cousin and found her equal. *Every bit.* He hadn't said, "just like." Otherwise, Marge would have discounted the entire comment. She and Daisy weren't alike. Flowers were unique — no two the same — but they could be equally attractive. *If only I knew how to thank him and apologize for how I interpreted things. . . .*

"That's a big sigh."

Marge slammed the desk shut at the sound of Ermintrude's voice. She turned to see, and sure enough, the older woman stood in her doorway. Who knew how long she'd been watching Marge moon over a stray sentence? Her only hope lay in the idea that her body blocked the flowers from view. Surely Ermintrude hadn't seen the vase.

Lord, this is the type of thing I pray about without thinking — asking Your protection and strength. This time, I can't. My treasure and my heart aren't supposed to be of this earth, much less locked away in a drop front desk, hoping for the love of a man who wants someone else. Please help me control myself and follow the way You set out.

"Big sigh then holding your breath?" Ermintrude made her way into the room, apparently finding an invitation unnecessary. "Thinking about how much luggage you brought, wishing you'd shown a little restraint?"

"It won't do me any good cluttering the place and waiting to be repacked. I tried to hope for the best and pack for the worst." Marge eyed the mountain piled against the far wall, sprawling out into the surprisingly large room, and started to wonder where she'd put everything once she took up her official post as teacher.

Settling herself on the bed — and managing to look exceedingly comfortable — Ermintrude fixed her attention on Marge. "It's not doing you any good all boxed up."

"Yes, but it doesn't make any difference." Marge couldn't keep herself from admitting the sad truth. "Nothing I brought will help with the contingency of my groom expecting another woman."

"There's much to be said for versatility. You've been debating for days about the uselessness of hiding from disappointments."

"I'm not hiding from my luggage." *Though there are some things I don't want to unearth.*

241

The very notion of seeing her wedding gown proved enough to make her sit down. Honesty compelled her to add, "Most of it, anyway."

For an uncharacteristic moment, Ermintrude held her peace. Stillness reigned for an endless moment the likes of which teachers dream about often. How many times had she faced a classroom of students, or her overly enthusiastic cousin, and longed for silence only to be given none? Now she had quiet so fresh it crept through the room — a crisp, intoxicating delicacy.

One Marge suddenly lost her taste for. *Why did I never realize silence simply offers an invitation to be filled? If not with sound, with the thoughts one wouldn't care to speak aloud. The sort that plague a person, preying on dreams and surfacing doubts until one realizes just how lonely quiet can be.* She blinked suddenly stinging eyes. *I miss Daisy.*

"You don't like it either." Ermintrude ended the episode. "Let me tell you something, Marge. It gets worse as you grow older. The hopes filling the silence now slowly fade into memories and regrets."

A shiver ran down her spine at the truth she sensed in the warning. *Lord, don't let me become bitter.* Immediately she felt better — good enough to challenge a prickly old woman whom she'd come to think of as a friend. "If you don't like silence, why do you shut yourself up in it? You don't attend town functions, invite people into your home, or accept invitations when they're offered. Why punish yourself?"

"I don't. I don't have to. Life's done enough of that." A pause told Marge Ermintrude realized how snappish she sounded. "No, I keep to myself because the contrast of company makes things worse when the silence returns. This way, things stay on an even keel. But on to the matter at hand." She gestured to Marge's trunks. " 'Waste not, want not.' "

Inspiration struck, and she offered a bargain. "If I accept your version of the homily, will you accept mine?"

"You'll unpack a bit and settle in if I do?" A shrewd light lit the old woman's gaze, her capitulation too easy. At Marge's nod, she didn't hesitate. "Agreed."

Marge wondered for a moment if Ermintrude was so set on her unpacking because she thought it would be another step toward making Marge stay. *She's lonely....* "You're going to start attending functions then."

"How does that have anything to do with my adage? 'Waste not, want not' refers to using what's at hand."

"Town events are close at hand, and I said you'd abide by *my* version." She bent to open the first trunk, drawing out a beautifully worked starburst quilt. "Too late to change your mind now."

"What is your version?" Curiosity overpowered the irritation in her friend's question, and Marge knew she'd won.

She eyed the small trunk in the corner, knowing she wouldn't open that one but still wishing she'd have reason to someday. "Want nothing, waste away."

CHAPTER 24

The day proved particularly difficult. But then, the two days since he'd tried to give Marge those daisies seemed filled with small difficulties. He needed that mill pick — the grind of the flour became progressively rougher, and he had to rerun entire batches. Not only did the process waste time, it took intense concentration to adjust the distance between the stones and judge the length of time needed.

Waiting became tedious as he hovered in the mill, keeping a vigilant ear for any problems once he had each round going smoothly. By the fourth time he emptied the hopper, Gavin's restlessness proved his undoing.

Reading my Bible isn't an option. Even if it were something I'd try to undertake with only half my attention, it would draw me in until I might miss a signal something's gone wrong. Pacing wasn't enough. He'd already smoothed, oiled, straightened, swept, and done every bit of maintenance possible. *I'll try my hand at whittling again.*

It's what his father used to do on days like this, but Gavin usually didn't bother with a pastime he didn't excel in. Anything he attempted to carve wound up slightly awkward or downright unrecognizable — somewhat like his attempts at courting Marge.

Maybe I should carve something for her. He grinned as he walked toward the house for his whittling knife — far more lightweight and easy to wield than the blade he always carried. *Then she'd appreciate the flowers more.* The grin faded.

Things had grown . . . stilted . . . since that morning. The easy conversation between Grandma and Marge dried up when he came to the table. More than once he'd caught her eyes on him, asking something of him, but he didn't know what. Jokes fell flat. She'd started retreating to her room in the evenings rather than reading alongside him in the parlor.

Strange that he hadn't noticed how much he enjoyed her quiet company until she took it away. If he could unearth a way to ask her back without sounding either demanding, or worse, foolish, Gavin would see her in the matching armchair across from him that very evening.

He liked how comfortable she always looked. It made him feel like he put her at ease, and that, in turn, made the place seem more . . . well, homey. There was something homey in the way she curled her feet up beneath her skirts and nestled in to enjoy something edifying or entertaining.

But the very best part, the part he missed the most, was something Marge probably wouldn't believe. She only wore her spectacles while reading. The first time she'd tugged them from a case in her pocket, looping a fine chain about her neck and slipping the delicate golden frames atop her nose, Gavin sat transfixed. Only one night since had he missed that moment — when Grandma asked him to fetch some water. Otherwise, he cast furtive glances over the top of his own book until the time she transformed.

Because that's what happened. Marge unearthed her spectacles, and somehow, they unearthed something hidden about her. They made her face softer, drew attention straight down her pert little nose to the way she absently nibbled her lower lip while she read or parted them in surprise and delight — depending on what she found between the pages.

The best part about the whole thing? Gavin felt fairly certain no other man ever witnessed this nightly revelation. Just him.

Except he hadn't seen it the past two nights either. *I'm losing ground instead of gaining it.* This sort of situation made a man reevaluate, and the more he looked, the less Gavin liked what he saw. A couple short weeks ago, the stage brought him a bride. An inconsequential error — a mere technicality — robbed him of the possibility of a union once she discovered the truth. And in trying to change her mind, he'd forfeited even the simple pleasure of companionship.

The more he thought about it, the angrier it made him. *Aside from labeling that letter ambiguously, I've done everything right. How long is she going to let stung pride get the best of her . . . of both of us, Lord? Or is it just that she doesn't appreciate any of the effort I've made? Did learning I'd proposed to Daisy first harden her heart so much she can't be reached?*

He ignored the sound of feminine voices coming from the guest room. *Her* room. If Marge passed the afternoon talking with Grandma, that meant she wasn't reading, and nothing short of her spectacles could lure him closer than necessary for now.

It took him a few moments of digging

through the chest at the base of his bed, where he kept odds and ends, before he unearthed his whittling knife.

I haven't used it since I moved west. The realization didn't surprise him. What with building a house, reshaping the land, forming a millpond, and building the mill, he'd had precious little time for anything but work. *I sent for her as soon as I got everything ready.*

"Stop shaking your head and say hello to your grandmother." She called orders from where she half sat, half lay on the bed, surrounded by an assortment of girly things. "Marge needed to . . . step out . . . for a moment."

"I see." It felt strange to step into her room, take in telltale signs of unpacking. *She's settling in?*

"She's kept everything boxed up this entire time, so I convinced her to at least sort through."

Neat piles of clothing covered the foot of the bed; a sewing case leaned against Grandma's hip while she perused an album of tintypes. "Quite a collection." Most of all, though, he saw books. Marge's Bible lay on her nightstand, but another Bible, this one looking to be written in French, now lay beside it. Stacks of volumes marched along the floor in orderly lines. The collected works of Shakespeare held vigil next to a complete set of McGuffey's Readers. The travels of Marco Polo vied alongside *Gulliver's Travels,* outgunned by sets attributed to Dante and Milton.

"If you wondered what she packed in all those trunks of hers, now you know. Marge brought a library along with her."

"I believe it — would have believed it without seeing them. It's Marge all over." Words, wisdom, and wonder — that's what books offered. And Marge knew they were rare out west. "Back in Baltimore, we spoke about the lack of education and availability of reading material in the territories." The memory took him off guard.

"Looks like she aims to fix that."

"She's passionate about books." Surely Grandma didn't hear the disgruntled note that entered when he said "books"? *No helping it that I want her to be passionate about more.*

"Paper." Grandma's gaze went sharp as the razor Gavin used, but the hint of a smile deepened the grooves bracketing her mouth. "I need a bit. Get me some from the desk, would you?"

It wasn't a question. Gavin pressed the latch, folding down the drop front to look for some paper. He stopped looking when he caught sight of what else the desk held.

A crystal vase, filled with fresh water, cradled a few slightly wilted purple blossoms. Tahoka daisies, to be exact. Gavin shut the desk, apologized to Grandma for not finding any paper, and made his way back to the mill, mind spinning.

She snuck outside and saved some. It made no sense. It didn't have to. *Marge still feels for me. It's not too late to win her back.*

It seemed so early to retire to her room, yet since the day she'd made a hash of accepting Gavin's gift of the wildflowers, Marge hadn't mustered up the courage to sit across from him in the parlor reading, as they'd settled into.

"Give him time to let that temper of his cool off . . . and then give him an extra day to help him realize what he's missing," Ermintrude had advised after her grandson stalked out that awful morning. She'd also muttered something about a healthy change in perspective for mule-headed women, but that, Marge ignored.

It's been a few days now. Perhaps enough time passed that Gavin's temper cooled and he wouldn't dislike company this evening? The spark of hope died a swift death. *He's scarce looked at me since that day, much less spent a moment alone.*

Refusing to let her shoulders slump, Marge snuffed the lamp in the now-clean kitchen, preparing to follow where Ermintrude had gone upstairs a scant hour before. *Well, here's proof that it's men, not children, who age women before their time. How many seasons have I spent in a room of youngsters without ever turning in early, only to change my habits after mere days living around a man!*

Her head turned toward the parlor as she passed, despite her determination not to peek in. Truth of the matter was Marge couldn't pass up the opportunity to see Gavin relaxed at the end of a long day — even if she simply snuck a glance on her way to self-imposed exile. Evenings showed Gavin in a different light — not just the literal lamp glow either — than his busy days.

He rose with the sun and seemed determined to out-busy it. Sure, the sun shone all day, illuminating the entire world. Gavin put it to shame with his constant motion. After all, everyone knew the sun remained stationary. End of day proved the only time the miller stayed still, dropping into an armchair scarcely large enough to accommodate his width.

Not because Gavin ran too large. Simply because his broad, strong frame dominated furniture. He sat down, settled back, propped his booted feet on an ottoman, and sank into a relaxation so complete it only lacked a sigh of satisfaction. Of course, a sigh might ruin the entire masculine appeal he presented so effortlessly.

He should make things easier on me and start sighing. She felt the wry twist to her lips and knew the idea counted as unreasonable. *I don't care. If Ermintrude is wrong and his temper hasn't cooled . . . and he doesn't miss me, the man needs to demonstrate the courtesy of being less fascinating. That's the absolute least he could do.*

"Marge?" His baritone, rumbling right beside her, made her realize she'd loitered at the base of the stairwell for far too long. "Are you all right?"

An unbecoming flush surely painted her cheeks. "Wool-gathering. If you'll excuse me. . . ." She made for the stairs, mortified to have been caught daydreaming. *Did he see me stare at him?*

His hand caught her elbow, blocking her bid for escape. "Wait."

Even if she'd wanted to leave him standing there, it wouldn't have been possible.

Not when he asked her to stay. Not when he stood so close. Not when warmth spread from his fingertips to rush up her arm, five streaks of heat to rival the strength of her blush. For a heartbeat — no, several. The sound of her own thundered in her ears loudly enough for her to know, after all. For a brief moment she stayed still as a statue, waiting.

"I hoped you would join me this evening." Gavin inclined his head toward the parlor but didn't move his hand.

"Oh?" If the word came out a bit squeaky, Marge could do nothing to help it. *He's asking to spend time with me!* Swiftly on the heels of that thought came one slightly less welcome. *That makes Ermintrude right — I'll never hear the end of it. No matter. It's more than worth the price to have Gavin seek my company!* She beamed like a fool.

"Yes." Now he removed his hand, taking away his warmth.

"I'll just be a moment." She turned to the stairs again, her step light. "Let me fetch my book."

"Of course. Oh, and Marge?" His smile brightened his tone — she could hear it even with her back to him. "Don't forget your glasses."

CHAPTER 25

Had it been over a week since he told Midge he intended to prove a man could adore her? Amos could hardly believe the time went by so fast. He made a point of seeking her out every day and was gratified when she rarely declined a walk or a meal with his family. In fact, the only two days they hadn't spent time together had been the past two Sundays.

She doesn't seem herself on Sundays. The thought plagued him. Amos found it increasingly difficult to keep his mind on the sermon when he noted so many signs of Midge's discomfort without even bothering to look. A simple glance or the number of times her shifting or fidgeting would catch the corner of his eye told a story plain as day. *But what story? And why am I so drawn to it, Lord?*

He'd hurry to catch up with her after church, but she either surrounded herself with friends or hied off like a hunted hare. If she spoke with friends, she smiled too brightly and laughed too hard. If she disappeared, it seemed to serve none of the purpose Amos had come to expect of anything Midge did. So even as he spent time with her and enjoyed more of her wit, humor, and the heart she hid beneath them, Amos discovered more distance lay between him and the girl he'd chosen.

Even now, while he waited for Josiah Reed to finish his short speech marking today's occasion, the puzzle of how to bridge the *Midge gap,* as he'd come to call the problem, tickled his mind. There she stood, beside the Reeds, smiling as her grandfather/uncle turned to face him. It had taken Amos awhile to understand precisely why Josiah Reed could claim either title, but now he knew Josiah was father to Saul and husband to Doreen, Clara's aunt, so he stood as adopted grandfather and great-uncle to Midge. Amos snapped to attention as the mayor of Buttonwood motioned him forward.

"Here's the man who's brought us this far along. The town council felt they'd found a good man for the task of building a fine schoolhouse in the middle of the Oregon Trail, and Mr. Amos Geer didn't disappoint. When the scarcity of wood made it prohibitively expensive, as did the freight cost of brick, it was Amos who suggested using clay from the Red Basin not overly far from here."

"At least," Amos interjected, "not far compared to big cities like Baltimore or Independence."

"So he fetched the clay, made the bricks, and built up the walls a ways to show us how it's done. Now it's our turn for a schoolhouse raising the likes of which the West has never seen!" Cheers filled a brief pause. "We're going to finish these walls and raise the roof, including the bell tower, to-day."

"This morning." Amos didn't mean to interrupt, exactly, but with the large, thick bricks already made and dried, fitting them in place and mortaring them together shouldn't take too long. "Work gets done fast with the whole town to help — yes, the ladies, too. The men should admit we wouldn't be so willing to do this without the promise of the fine dinner we know you're all preparing while we build." Laughter and agreement greeted his acknowledgment, but Amos watched Midge, whose slow smile was all the approval he needed.

He swiftly divided the townsmen into four

teams, one for each wall, as the women dispersed. For each team, he selected a foreman. Adam Grogan, Gavin Miller, and Saul Reed joined him in organizing their crews and getting work underway. Soon they had things up and running in a rhythm Amos hoped would keep on until they finished the walls.

The *glop* of mortar plunked atop set bricks, followed by the *slap* of the next thick brick hefted in place, and then the relentless scrape of trowels removing whatever excess oozed between the layers. Multiply it by the many men working, square it to take into account the four walls, and it formed a symphony of sound the likes of which Beethoven never dreamed.

Amos loved it. The echoes of efficiency provided a sort of workingman's music to the sight of an entire community coming together for the best reason he could imagine — their children. He rolled up his sleeves and got his hands dirty, reveling in the different scents and textures as he always did when working with his hands, particularly whenever he worked in the great outdoors.

The rich, gummy smell of wet clay skimmed over the lighter scent of sun-warmed stone as a soft sandy silt covered his hands and had him breathing in the earth. Amos kept on, working until his crew needed to use one of the pulleys he'd rigged to swing the huge bricks into place on the top of the walls.

With the work slowing, he looked around to see the other teams matching him, or close to it. The sun hadn't reached its height. His optimistic prediction might come true, with their completing the bulk of the work before breaking for dinner.

A glint of red caught his eye, and he turned to see Midge watching him. A smile, a wave, and she turned back to the children who tugged at her skirts in an obvious demand for attention. With the breeze in her hair, a smile on her face, and children gathered around, Midge looked to be in her element. It made Amos think something that had been cropping up more and more as he watched her interact with his brothers and sisters.

Midge will make a good mama. . . .

I'm going to be the world's worst mother some-day. Midge tramped around with an entire herd of scapegraces aping her every move. *Mothers are supposed to be stern, supposed to be genteel, supposed to teach little girls how to be little ladies.*

Midge, for her part, far preferred playing with children to raising them. All the fun, very little of the responsibility — if it weren't for the fact she so badly wanted a little girl to name Nancy and give all the things taken away from her sister, she'd be content as Auntie Midge for the rest of her days.

Auntie. *Not* Teacher. *Teacher* implied responsibility and living up to standards Midge couldn't aspire to. *Even if I could stand and sit still in a classroom all day long — even so fine a one as Amos is having built — I'd make for a poor role model. The children don't seem to mind, but I know better.*

The question is . . . why don't their parents?

A frown creased the space between her eyebrows; she could feel the wrinkle forming. Worse, the kids noticed it.

"Miss Collins," Annie Doan, a bright, outspoken girl of about eight who reminded Midge of her own younger self, spoke up on behalf of everyone. "Did we do something wrong?"

"Of course not." Her smile felt forced, so Midge quickly turned it to one of exaggerated suspicion. She narrowed her eyes in a dramatic scowl and raised on eyebrow. "Did you?"

"I asked if we could play at dodging?"

Billy Geer, Amos's younger brother — and the one he'd pointed out to her as having had diphtheritic croup four years ago at Fort Sumter, and the reason he'd tackled her to keep her out of the sick room — carried a leather ball and eyes full of hope.

With his sandy hair and brown eyes, he was the spitting image of how Amos must've looked at that age. The thought of his almost dying made her heart squeeze up so tight it was hard to get words out, so Midge just nodded. *Thank God Saul came through when he did to save Billy. Otherwise, so much might be different....*

She took a stick and drew a large circle in the dirt, an impromptu playing field for a game of dodge the ball, but stopped once she realized what she'd done. *Thank God?* Shaking her head didn't do much to clear it. *Thank Josiah for sending for Saul. Thank Saul for going and caring enough to be a doctor to help Billy. Thank Amos for pulling me away so I didn't catch the sickness. Thank any and everyone involved, but God had precious little to do with it!*

No. People looked after other people. At least, the ones who cared did. Folks like Saul and Clara were the first she'd met, aside from her own sister. The longer she stayed in Buttonwood, the more people she counted as genuine and caring — what Aunt Doreen would call the "salt of the earth." She didn't even have to explain that one — Midge understood the instant she heard the phrase back when she was thirteen.

Salt of the earth . . . salt was good for two things, flavor and preservation. If someone added something enjoyable to a life and helped preserve or further the good in and around it, the person was like salt. If someone managed that for just about everyone he or she knew, Midge could see a sort of domino effect where the whole world was kept from the decay of people just using each other for momentary wants.

The way people treated Nancy. The way people used to treat her. The way Midge tried never to treat anyone, no matter how despicable. And the way she most deserved to be treated.

Thud. The muffled declaration of a leather ball striking shins through layers of cotton skirts and petticoats came at the same time as a forceful knock to the back of Midge's knees. She faltered, almost corrected herself, but jerked back when little Sadie Warren darted just in front of her. Then it was all over.

Midge went down, hitting the hard prairie

earth with a jarring impact. Her ankle bent at an awkward angle beneath her, a by-product of trying to avoid Sadie. Aware that every child froze the instant she met the ground, Midge pushed herself into a sitting position and tried to reassure them.

The way children handled an upsetting situation said a lot about the type of people they'd grow into, and Midge got a chance to witness firsthand the foundation of Buttonwood's future. Not many could say they saw so far when their rumps hit the ground.

Most of them fretted, asked if she was all right, hovered anxiously. One excitable five-year-old burst into tears and ran for his mama, while a seven-year-old ignored the entire mess and chased down the renegade leather ball. In spite of the usual reactions, a few young ones stood out right away.

Maggie Reed, Midge's three-year-old sister, scampered off in a flash to go fetch her pa the doctor, while her best friend, Tessa Burn, trundled over to offer more immediate comfort. Popping her thumb in her mouth and her favorite doll, Bessie, into Midge's lap, she half sat, half tumbled to cuddle at her side.

Annie Doane announced it was Roger Warren whose throw had gone awry and watched the older boy like a hawk. She gave the impression of a girl ready to haul a criminal to justice the moment he made a false move.

Roger Warren, for his part, mumbled apology after apology, squatting back on his heels and reaching for Midge's hands to help her up. Of course, she couldn't accept his gallant offer with little Tessa tucked at her side, but Midge could tell the ten-year-old had the makings of a fine man. Someday. In fact, Midge wouldn't be surprised if he and Annie were casting more appreciative glances at each other in another five years.

But it was Billy's course of action that most ruffled Midge. At twelve, the boy should know better than to run tattling to his older brother over the slightest mishap. Not that Billy seemed to have learned the value of discretion. Instead, he trotted back toward her with his brother overtaking his pace in long strides.

Midge stifled a groan. *He had to fetch Amos?*

CHAPTER 26

"Mrs. Miller, so good to see you!" "Glad you could join us this morning, Mrs. Miller." "Wonderful to have you up and about, Mrs. Miller, why don't you sit by me?"

Marge watched and listened as the women of the town did precisely as she'd hoped and fussed over Ermintrude. Not only did the divided attention serve her well in helping foist off questions about her interest in teaching when she *must* plan to start her own family soon — the warm welcome went a long way toward putting her friend at ease.

Oh, Ermintrude hadn't said a word about it, but Marge knew she feared she'd avoided the townspeople for too long to be truly accepted so much later. Not that Ermintrude hadn't said a word about anything and everything else having to do with her first forced social interaction in years. But no matter how she grumped, threatened, or harrumphed, the old woman kept her bargain and joined Marge at the site of the schoolhouse raising.

"You put them up to this." The mutters went largely ignored. "Don't think I don't know you told them to make nice to the old curmudgeon who's been making you miserable."

"Don't think I don't know you're intentionally trying to make me show disrespect to one of my elders by giving in to the temptation to tell you to hush." Marge nudged Ermintrude toward a large table. "I did no such thing, and you don't make me miserable except when you're trying to take credit for such an outrageous accomplishment."

The resulting harrumph wasn't up to Ermintrude's usual standard, a sign she enjoyed herself more than she wanted to let on. "Going to deposit me at the biddy table and scuttle off to join your friends now, are you?" Behind the challenge lay a glimpse of the older woman's true worry.

"Not at all." Marge settled herself across from Ermintrude. "Aren't you used to peeling potatoes with me by now? Soon someone else will come to join us. It'll take a lot of mashed potatoes to go around when everyone in town wants a serving!"

"You have no idea." Opal Grogan slid

266

onto the bench beside her. "I'm so glad Adam had them set up these tables beforehand. It will make preparing and serving everything so much simpler. Good morning, Mrs. Miller. It does my heart good to see you. I've been a poor neighbor, I fear, not stopping by more often."

"Not at all." Ermintrude waved her paring knife in as magnanimous a fashion as a knife could possibly be waved. "You've a little one tugging on your skirts and another soon to follow. Before your new-addition-to-be made his presence known, you stopped by a few times. I should've returned the favor but didn't want to impose."

"Impose?" Opal's laughter matched her looks — fiery and full of life. "It'd be a respite to visit for a while."

"I'd thought, with your family and your apiary, you kept as busy as those bees of yours." Ermintrude's peeling picked up the pace, a barometer of her opinion of the conversation.

"Never too busy for a new friend, Mrs. Miller."

"Oh. You have time for new neighbors but can't be bothered to bring Rachel to visit her grandmother?" A sour-faced frump whose name Marge couldn't recall at the moment flounced up to the table and planted her hands on her hips. "I'm sure Mrs. Miller here wouldn't approve your choice."

"Considering you've scarcely bothered to speak two words to me since I came to this town, I doubt you're in any position to speculate on what I do and do not approve of, Lucinda Grogan." Ermintrude's swift reply supplied the name Marge needed.

Ah, yes. This is Opal's mother-in-law. She took the opportunity to look over Lucinda as the woman made a show of settling wearily onto the bench beside Ermintrude. Deep bitterness dragged gray brows to a habitual scowl over a face aged beyond its years, thin features wreathed in the wrinkles of a perpetual frown.

I never would have remembered — much less guessed — this to be Adam's mother. Though, if I think back further and remember that this is a woman who helped keep a feud going, it makes more sense.

It took all Marge's effort not to shoot Opal a commiserating glance. Such things were too often misinterpreted, and Opal, while showing the promise of a good friendship, didn't know her well enough to read her intent. Besides, she might have a soft spot for the unpleasant woman haranguing her and take exception to anything that

268

could be seen as negative.

Although, Marge admitted to herself after catching a glimpse of the grin on Opal's face as Ermintrude took up the cudgels on her behalf, *that doesn't seem likely.*

Ermintrude, who, with at least a dozen years on her new bench mate, put the younger woman to shame as her pile of potatoes grew by leaps and bounds. For that matter, she put them all to shame. Marge figured it was safe to assume her friend was enjoying herself.

"You're mistaken, Mrs. Miller." A disdainful sniff that would have been more in place coming from one of Daisy's snobby town friends punctuated Lucinda's response. "I speak with everyone. If you've chosen not to engage in conversation when the opportunity presents itself, you've no one to blame but yourself." She left unspoken — barely — the obvious truth that Ermintrude had avoided contact with everyone.

"I'm not the one mistaken, Lucinda. You see, I've been watching the way things are done here, getting the lay of the land before joining in, so to speak. You don't talk *with* everyone." Ermintrude paused in her peeling as though savoring the moment. "You talk *about* everyone."

Amos looked over Midge's raggedy retinue then met her exasperated gaze with an amused one of his own. "Children, why don't you run along while I make sure Miss Collins feels all right?" Several were slow to leave, until finally only Tessa and Billy remained.

"I'll go tell Doc you've got it under control." Billy must have been trying to make amends for fetching Amos, because he headed over to the far side of the growing schoolhouse, where several of the men had gone for some water before they started putting up the roof.

"It appears you've been abandoned." Amos hunkered down to be at eye level. "Except for the sleeping beauty there, who almost puts you to shame."

Refusing to rise to the bait, Midge looked down at where Tessa lay curled against her side, thumb still in her mouth. A little one like this could make the hardest heart melt. Sally and Matthew had a lot to be proud of in their firstborn.

"You're right." She craned her neck as though trying to look beyond Amos. "Those Burn men do make some beautiful babies. . . ." She knew every bit as well as he did that Brett Burn, the youngest of the blacksmiths, wanted a wife.

In fact, Brett had started edging closer ever since Pete Speck relinquished his claim on Midge and began courting Amanda Dunstall instead. The gossips said all sorts of things about Pete's defection, but when he and Midge remained close friends, folks started accepting something that looked more like the truth: Midge saw Pete more as a brother than anything else, and she'd finally managed to convince her friend of the fact.

"That's the Fosset side in her." Amos referred to Sally, Matthew Burn's wife and Tessa's mother. He almost managed to sound completely unbothered, but Midge saw the slight lowering of his brows before he caught himself. "Anyone can see that."

"Really? What else can anyone see?" Midge stroked the tips of her fingers through the baby-soft curls covering Tessa's head. To her way of thinking, plenty of things went not only unnoticed but completely unsuspected by the majority of people.

Take her and Pete, for example. Most came to understand the two of them weren't meant to be more than friends, despite the giant-sized crush he'd nursed for a couple years. Yet no one — or hardly anyone, since Midge sometimes wondered whether her friend Opal bore an inkling — so much as guessed Midge sent Pete to Amanda because he was too good for her and deserved better. Midge liked Pete too much to marry him, plain and simple.

Brett, on the other hand, she avoided for less altruistic motives. While all the Burn men worked hard, smiled often, and more than earned their good standing in town, blacksmiths possessed certain traits Midge preferred to grant wide berth. Barrel-chested men with ham-sized hands couldn't be controlled by any measure of quick wit or careful cajoling.

Hadn't she and Nancy learned that years ago, when Rodney's deep chest held an endless well of rage plumbed by huge hands turned to solid fists? No, Midge wouldn't choose a big, beefy husband, no matter how jovial or kind he may seem. Rodney charmed her sister into a life of degradation and filth with such pretense. . . .

The flutter of a breeze on her petticoats made Midge shift, both her feet and her attention. A momentary fear she'd been sitting there with a leg exposed by her little scrape swiftly subsided into astonishment as she watch Amos inch her petticoats and skirt above the line of her lace-up boot.

"What are you doing?" She hissed the question, trying to keep quiet and pull away without waking Tessa or drawing undue attention from any of the rest of the town.

A devilish grin lit his face. "Checking your ankle, something not just anyone — like Brett Burn — can see."

"Neither can you!"

He caught her hand, impeding her progress in tugging the hem of her skirt to cover her ankle. "Billy said he saw you twist it. Let me make sure you're all right."

"It's fine. Really." The concerned determination in his eyes made her hesitate for a split second too long. He had a grip on the layers of cloth again when she tried to shift away, the end result exposing her calf almost to her knee. "Stop it!"

"What's this?" One large hand — large, not heavy or thick knuckled — clamped to hold her skirts at her knee as Amos squinted at the ugly, puckered pink marking her shin. "What did you do?"

"It's nothing." She tried to wriggle away, only to be held fast. Not by force, but by the tender way he used one fingertip to trace around the healing gash. Midge knew it would scar when she had reopened the

273

wound two weeks ago in church, but scars faded. Right now, the mark flushed a deep, angry pink.

"It's not healing well, so I'm assuming you didn't tell Dr. Reed when it happened." He released her knee, his refusal to drop a question Midge couldn't answer making her agitated beyond belief. "That's *not* nothing."

"We just have different definitions of the word." Midge levered herself onto her feet, cradling the heavy weight of the sleeping toddler as she stood. "The fall was nothing, the scrape was nothing, and so is this conversation."

CHAPTER 27

Billy's a good brother. Amos watched his sibling saunter off to leave him alone with Midge. Or, at least, as alone as a man and woman could be with the entire town less than an acre away and a sleeping toddler snuggled against her side. *Lucky toddler.*

Since Midge seemed unharmed, a little teasing was in order. As expected, when he named Tessa her rival, Midge joked back. What Amos didn't expect was the searing shaft of envy that struck him when she seemed to be looking around for Brett Burn. For a wild moment, he considered sweeping her off the ground and hauling her in front of Parson Carter right then.

She wants babies? I'll give her babies. Some of the unreasonable jealousy leaked away at the thought. *Any child of Midge's will be beautiful. Our family will be blessed.*

But he couldn't say something like that aloud. Midge would bolt like a frightened rabbit. Amos knew full well she'd seen this courtship as a farce from the outset. Otherwise, his freckled firebrand wouldn't have capitulated so easily to the idea. If she had an inkling he seriously intended to make her his bride, Midge would no longer play this little game of trying to wait for him to grow tired of her saucy ways.

Instead of voicing any of these thoughts, he ignored her compliment to the Burn men and gave credit for Tessa's cuteness where it belonged, with her mother. As he anticipated, Midge snapped out a response without batting a lash.

"What else can anyone see?" The dry question demanded a comeback, but Midge drew away from him even as Amos sat before her. She traveled somewhere in the landscape of thoughts she didn't care to share, didn't even enjoy having, and Amos couldn't journey with her.

The sparkle in her eyes grew shuttered. The pert tilt to her mouth flattened. Her breaths went shallow then deepened into an occasional sigh sad enough to rend him. There was only one thing to do — jolt her back from whatever memory caught her.

So Amos took advantage of the pretext of her fall to nudge her skirts above her boots. If nothing else, the action would grab her attention and put it back where it belonged — them. Now.

Obviously, Amos acknowledged as the ruffled hem of her petticoat fluttered to reveal slim ankles encased in tightly laced leather, the plan held other rewards. Besides, it worked.

"What are you doing?" If she hadn't been trying to avoid a scene or waking up Tessa, or maybe both — Amos couldn't be certain which reason guided her — Midge probably would've screeched instead of squawked. As things stood, she kept fairly quiet while trying to wriggle away and tug her hem back over the tips of her boots.

As though a glimpse of her boot laces might give him ideas. Amos would've laughed at the thought, if her concerns weren't so well-founded. One peek had him plotting ways to unlace those boots. "Checking your ankle, something not just anyone — like Brett Burn — can see." *A twisted ankle surely needed to be examined more closely. Yep. That boot is coming off.*

"It's fine. Really." Midge's assurance came too late.

Amos made a plan and intended to see it through. Trouble came in when Midge decided to impede his progress by shifting away, inadvertently revealing a length of smooth leg almost up to her knee.

The sight of that fair skin, covered only by the sheer silk of her stocking, just about poleaxed him. He could find no other reason for his ungentlemanly gawking. Amos might have remained speechless for a good while longer if it weren't for the angry pink of a still-healing wound glaring up at him midway between the top of her boot and the bottom of Midge's knee.

She must have seen him notice, because she redoubled her efforts to pull away. He put a hand on her knee, ignoring the intimacy of the action to focus on her injury. "What did you do?"

"It's nothing." For the first time, Midge sounded uncertain. She stopped trying to shift back, and Amos could feel her gaze following where he traced the area around the gash.

His fingertips, made rough from working all day with the bricks, snagged at her stockings, but Amos felt the warmth of her skin and the heat of her embarrassment with far more strength. And interest. *Midge isn't clumsy. Even her fall today came from being hit with the ball.*

"It's not healing well, so I'm assuming you didn't tell Dr. Reed when it happened." He removed his hand before he did something foolish. "That's *not* nothing."

"We just have different definitions of the word." Midge stood up, keeping a firm hold on Tessa so the toddler lay cradled in her arms. "The fall was nothing, the scrape was nothing, and so is this conversation."

She didn't want to discuss whatever caused the cut, or why she hadn't told Dr. Reed about it. *Which means either she's embarrassed, or . . .*

"Who hurt you?" He ground out the words, making it a demand for information more than a simple question. Amos felt his pulse kick into high gear as she paused, seeming to debate whether or not to answer at all.

"I struck my shin on a chest in my room." Midge's explanation held the ring of truth, but her flat tone told Amos more lay behind the story.

"Let me know if you need someone to chop it up." He knew his little joke was the right response when some of the stiffness left her spine.

"No, thanks." She jostled Tessa in her arms, repositioning the little girl so she'd sleep more comfortably. Then she spoiled the mature, maternal image by looking up with a mischievous twinkle. "It's a good reminder that things keep me on my toes when I least expect it."

Amos escorted her back toward where the other women worked and gave her a pointed look. "I know exactly what you mean."

Rage soured the air Gavin breathed as Lucinda Grogan opened her mouth to snipe about Marge's intent to teach and what it meant to their marriage — as though it made any difference to her. He hadn't dealt much with the woman, but he'd heard and noticed enough to take her measure long ago. It was part of the reason why, once the walls were up and most of the men took a short break before beginning work on the roof, he'd headed over to where Marge and Grandma sat with the bitter busybody.

He'd also thought to head off Brett Burn and enjoy Marge's company for a stolen moment or two, but there was no denying Lucinda's tart tongue made for the most pressing reason to stand at her side. Or behind her, as the case may be.

"You're assuming marriage and teaching are mutually exclusive." He didn't even fight to keep his tone even, instead letting the honest irony of his comment fill his words with dry humor. *So does Marge, but we've not discussed it.* Too bad. Now would be as good a time as any for him to point out a compromise that seemed obvious to him.

"They are." Scorn smeared the certainty of Lucinda's statement. "Everyone with a lick of sense knows that."

"We already know your own children don't ascribe to your theories, since two of them wed the children of your sworn enemy, so I suppose we should be thankful you didn't bother with any teaching once you got Mr. Grogan down the aisle." Grandma sharpened her wits on the gossip, and although Gavin knew it wasn't very godly of him, he couldn't help but be glad of it.

If Lucinda didn't watch herself, she'd wind up looking like that pile of potato peels — sliced down and laid bare by Grandma's finest blade — her tongue.

"You know nothing of the situation." How the woman made a sentence sound like a hiss with so few s's was beyond Gavin, but somehow the elder Mrs. Grogan managed quite well. "People shouldn't give an opinion on anything they don't understand."

"Well I, for one, would like to understand more about Mr. Miller's views on married teachers." Opal Grogan stepped in to calm troubled waters, an admirable trait Gavin suspected she used often considering her in-laws.

"Yes, Gavin." Marge tilted her head back

281

at what had to be an uncomfortable angle to see his face. "Explain to the ladies just what, exactly, you mean."

If he detected any challenge in her invitation, her curiosity so vastly overshadowed it. Gavin figured this opportunity could be golden. *After all, one of the things Marge wants is to be appreciated for herself, and teaching is so much a part of who she is. . . .*

"God gave Marge a passion for teaching, and any child who studies under her will be glad of it. I see no reason why our children" — he gave her shoulder a slight squeeze — "should be the only ones blessed by her gifts."

"Thank you." Marge's smile, he'd come to realize, held the key to another one of her intriguing transformations. Not the small, tight smiles she gave when uncomfortable, or the overly wide ones that tried to mask when she didn't want to smile at all, but the wholehearted ones. The ones that spread all the way to her eyes and made the flickering green glow bright against their amber background.

He put his free hand on her other shoulder in a sort of bracing half hug. "You're welcome. I know how important family is to you, Marge. Ours will never lack just because you answer a calling outside our home."

"See that?" Grandma jerked her head toward him. "He gets that from my side of the family. I've made it a point to try to teach the boys to appreciate more about a woman than the children she carries." An uncharacteristically thoughtful pause followed. "You know, Lucinda, it's a lesson you'd do well to apply to your daughter-in-law. Opal seems a rare woman."

"She is." Marge spoke up almost before Lucinda opened her mouth to respond. Almost, but it looked to Gavin as though she ignored the viper's glower. "Opal manages to be a wife, a mother, and a business-woman. Apiaries don't run themselves."

"Oh yes. That's the whole problem, right there." The older Grogan refused to back down, despite the good sense behind Grandma's advice. "Opal keeps my grand-child from me because she has too many demands on her time."

"You're welcome to visit whenever you like." The words bore the flavor of having been oft repeated, as Opal Grogan didn't even look up from the potato she grabbed. "It's your choice."

"Maybe I would, if you weren't such a busy little bee."

Gavin decided he'd had enough of hearing the woman sow strife. "It's good to fill one's time. Keeps folks from more troublesome things." *Like making everyone else miserable.*

"I'm sure I don't know what you mean. I have plenty to keep me occupied."

"What my grandson means, Lucinda," replied Grandma, putting down her knife as she spoke, the pile of peeled potatoes before her larger than any other on the table, "is that it's better to be a busy bee than a busybody."

CHAPTER 28

Our children. Marge kept hearing Gavin say the words, feeling his hand pressing in silent promise against her shoulder, long after he left to rejoin the men. *"Blessed . . ."*

It seemed to her as though her heart could double as a spare bellows for the smithy, the way it expanded many times past its original size, fighting with her every time she tried to close it back down to something manageable. The struggle played out again and again, and each time, Marge lost a little more ground to the swelling happiness when Gavin did something thoughtful or kind or . . . even . . . just spent time with her.

She'd snapped the feelings shut once she learned about his original intent to marry Daisy, determined to contain the damage and never again let false hope buoy her spirits. Because at first, she'd seen no way Gavin could be pleased with her as a substitute bride. Midge's challenge that he prove he genuinely wanted to marry Marge seemed an impossible one.

The entire situation seemed a veritable Pandora's box. So Marge let out the hurt, confusion, and disappointment by refusing to marry a man who didn't choose her. She poured out her heart in prayer, on the pages of her journal, doing her best to rid herself of the anger and upset. The only thing she didn't let out was her hope — the foolish, forlorn hope that somehow Gavin would come to want her. And prove it.

That stayed locked away. Marge knew about the hope, knew it didn't shrivel up or waste away. Felt it grow stronger with each gesture Gavin made. The daisies. His asking her to read with him in the parlor. And now . . . his telling the town gossip how much he respected her judgment and ability. And mentioning, for the first time, the children that would complete their family . . .

It was that confounded hope that swelled her heart until Marge could barely sit still. It seemed she floated through the rest of the day. Had anyone asked, she couldn't have recalled the details of Ermintrude's and Lucinda's constant sniping. Wouldn't be able to describe the food she helped prepare, much less what any of it tasted like. Only two things would mark the day in Marge's memory.

Gavin, and the children.

Not their own. Though the thought made her giddy, it was the children of Buttonwood — her future pupils — who wrested Marge's thoughts away from romance and made the day of the school raising something even more special.

At the beginning of the day, Marge felt the need to stay close to Ermintrude and make sure her friend felt comfortable. Not that she needed to worry, as Gavin's grandmother waded into the social waters of Buttonwood with the bravado anyone who'd met her would come to expect. Marge didn't worry about whether or not Ermintrude would seem at ease . . . but she watched carefully to see whether or not it was all show.

After dinner, when the dishes were cleared and the men were back to raising the schoolhouse roof, Marge decided Ermintrude carved out a splendid niche among the other older women of the town. Save Lucinda Grogan, of course. But in a strange way, Marge would have guessed that having a sparring partner to enliven things is what made Ermintrude feel most at home. After all, there had to be something satisfying in finding an adversary when someone loved to debate as much as Ermintrude.

So with her friend settled, Marge took advantage of the opportunity to join Midge. She'd noticed her friend and coteacher watching over the town's children while the other women got things ready for the massive dinner. Now, she hurried over to the group of youngsters before anyone stopped her for more chitchat.

"Miss Chandler!" Midge greeted her in the same type of loud voice Marge herself used to get the attention of her students during recess. "Glad you could join us."

The controlled flurry of activity around the two women ground to a halt. Older boys looked up from a game of marbles; older girls stilled their jump ropes. Squares of hopscotch scratched into the earth were abandoned; the thin, piping voices of younger children called their friends back from games of hide-and-seek or sardines. In no time at all, Marge found herself surrounded — and stared at — by a group of about twenty youngsters.

"Good afternoon." Marge made a point of smiling at each and every one of them — even the toddlers too young to attend school. Then, especially, the ones who looked old enough they might be needed at home or choose not to attend or do so sporadically.

"Good afternoon, Miss Chandler." The slightly singsong cadence of the classroom greeting started at different times, but all the children ended together. A good sign.

"I look forward to getting to know you." Nervous glances met her pronouncement.

"Why?" A little girl, looking to be about eight years old, cocked her head to the side like a curious little owl.

Marge chuckled. "Because you're each worth knowing."

The other children watched this girl's reaction. She blinked, as though thinking it over, before breaking into a wide grin. "Yeah, we are. Most of us, at least."

"Some of us, you might regret." A towheaded boy who looked to be older than the girl puffed out his chest.

"Speak for yourself, Roger!" Some goodnatured jostling looked like it might devolve into shoving, so Marge cleared her throat. Immediately the children stopped fussing.

Midge raised a brow, a silent acknowledgement she was impressed, and if Marge didn't miss her guess, a warning that the children wouldn't always be so easily reined in. That was par for the course — students always trod lightly in the beginning, growing bolder as time passed.

That's when things got interesting. For now, though, Marge would take advantage of the sweetheart period to establish ground rules of order and get to know the children.

"For teacher." A small girl — most likely the youngest who would go to school — shuffled forward, a slightly wilted ringlet of flowers like the one Midge wore clutched in her hand. The shy offering obviously came not only from the little one but from the group of girls encouraging her to step forth.

"Thank you." Marge stooped, untied her bonnet, and took it off so the little one could rise up on tiptoe and crown her. "It's lovely. What's your name?"

"Rachel." She looked up. "I wanna go to school, but Mama's not sure I'm old enough."

"How old are you?"

"She's five." The curious girl, Annie, spoke up. "And smart, too. I'll make sure she won't be any trouble if you let her come." Her face, Marge realized, was an older version of Rachel's. The two must be sisters.

"Five is a fine age to start learning. Rachel is welcome." A swell of murmurs and giggles made Marge look up from the littlest one's beaming face, to realize almost every child wore a matching grin.

Obviously they approved of her decision. It looked like an extremely well-established group, everyone friendly despite the disparity in ages. Their closeness would be both a blessing and a challenge as she sought to keep discipline, but Midge would be a help there.

It wasn't until after Midge introduced each child then sent them off to play that the two women had a chance to discuss their pupils.

"They're a handful, but good kids." Midge looked fondly over the entire group. "Do you usually have so many?"

"Yes. Baltimore is a large city, so there are plenty of children. They aren't usually so close as these though."

"I see." Her friend seemed to be considering something. "Before we talk about the school, I've been itching to know how things are going with Mr. Miller."

"Oh." Marge felt her smile grow wide enough to make her cheeks ache. "Don't worry — he told Lucinda Grogan today that he doesn't see a reason why I can't be a wife and a teacher, so long as the town approves."

"Good." Relief, almost palpable, made the one word a sentence. "So then, it sounds like you're thinking about being his wife?" She cast a glance back toward the schoolhouse, obviously trying to pick out Gavin from among the men working.

"After today, I've pretty much made my decision."

Midge's gaze whipped back. "Which is?"

She drew in a deep breath. "The next time Gavin asks me to marry him . . . I'm going to say yes!"

Another week passed almost before Gavin could reconcile the passage of time. The town council had scheduled school to begin two days from now, and in the week since the schoolhouse raising itself, he'd gone out of his way to spend more time with Marge before teaching took her away several hours a day.

Well, no . . . he hadn't gone out of his way. More like he'd made sure his way coincided with hers at as many points as possible. Mealtimes simply didn't offer enough time to spend in her company when he'd be missing the opportunity so soon. The time they spent in the parlor reading helped, but Gavin somehow fixed it in his head that if he couldn't convince Marge to become his wife before the start of school, he'd never manage it. And that was a lesson he refused to learn.

Their days fell into a sort of a pattern he wouldn't have expected. He woke up earlier these days — perhaps a side benefit of sleeping on the bottom floor of his mill with the gear housings. The windowless room that used to bother him since he couldn't tell what time it was, and whether or not night ended unless birds heralded the arrival of morning, became a blessing. Without light to tell him when to wake up, he naturally seemed to err on the early side, which gave him more time each morning.

Time he used to go to the house, slip upstairs, and shave every day so he looked his best. Not that Marge ever commented on it, but Gavin knew she noticed by the small, secretive smile he saw tilt her lips once he started coming down freshly smooth. Just one more thing to appreciate about Marge — the way she valued little things.

He even liked shaving more these days, because he could hear Marge and Grandma poking around the kitchen downstairs, smell the enticing aromas of breakfast, and know it all awaited him once he finished. Besides, while Gavin didn't stoop to eavesdropping, the two women sometimes grew animated enough in their conversation for him to overhear parts of it.

Agreeable arguments — that's what Grandma handed Marge every morning. Not because of her agreeable nature, but because of Marge's. That is to say, Marge had an agreeable nature, but she gave as good as she got each and every day, refusing to let Grandma plow her into a corner and get the best of her. Easy to see that they both looked forward to their morning debates.

Not quite so easy to admit Gavin looked forward to them, too. Particularly when he couldn't let on that he listened in to what they said. That would be rude. But he liked what he heard. He liked the way Marge turned things back on Grandma, challenged her to get out and interact more with people in the town. Gavin didn't spare much thought on the matter before he heard Marge point it out, but Grandma kept to herself too much. Besides, when she talked more with other people, she seemed in better spirits.

Best of all, she made better coffee.

At some point, Marge started joining him after breakfast for the morning ritual of opening the sluice gate. She didn't say much, but he could tell by the way she leaned over the railing to watch the water turn the wheel she enjoyed the power and precision of it. Something they had in common.

There was a beauty to the way the rushing water spilled over the wooden slats, pushing them down and bringing the wheel round and round. Everything a set motion, everything a shared purpose as it brought the mill to life. Shared purpose and appreciation is what made things work well together, after all.

It's what would make his and Marge's marriage such a beautiful system.

She sees it, too. I know she does now. That's why she's going to say yes when I propose this afternoon. Again.

Gavin didn't say much over dinner, too busy planning the proposal that would win him Marge's hand once and for all. The smile that took up constant residence on his face fell away for a bit as he pondered. He knew it not because he felt it, but because of the concerned glances Marge kept sending him.

She knows me. She notices my moods. I notice that she notices. Lord, You sent me the right wife. Thank You for not allowing my plans to ruin our lives. And now that I appreciate what You've brought me, I ask Your help in keeping her.

CHAPTER 29

After dinner, Gavin asked Marge to take a turn around the millpond. As he'd pretty much expected, she readily agreed.

Wonder if she knows I'm going to ask her again. I wonder if she plans to say yes. He tucked her hand in the crook of his arm, pleased to note how well her height suited him, how he didn't have to make a conscious effort to slow his steps to accommodate her. *We match — surely she sees that. . . .*

He turned to look at her, drinking in the lines of her profile for the scant second before she turned a piercing gaze upon him.

"What's wrong, Gavin?" Concern shaded her features. Concern and something else — something he couldn't put a name to.

"Nothing's wrong."

"You hardly spoke all through the meal." The other emotion strengthened until he could identify it as anxiety.

She may not want to, but she feels for me. "I keep thinking about the way nothing's wrong — everything feels right, Marge." He heard the sound of a large wagon coming toward the mill but ignored it. The customer could wait while Gavin attended to the important things in his life.

"Oh?" A flash of understanding replaced the anxiety.

"Yes. We get on so well — things have never been better. I know you wanted me to prove my desire to build a life with you, and I think we're already creating one."

"What do you mean?" She stopped walking, but it didn't pull him up short. Like so much with Marge, it seemed natural.

"The time for wondering and waiting is over. Marge," he murmured, clasping one of her hands in both of his as he spoke, hoping that her sudden paleness boded well, "you must know what I want."

"Daisy?" She whispered her cousin's name, a faint question calling into doubt the outcome of his proposal.

"How could you think that?" A swell of anger almost kept him from noticing that she didn't look him in the eyes. Almost. "Look at me, Marge!" He dropped her hand, reaching to brace her shoulders.

"No." She stared past him as though fixated. "It's Daisy." A few swift blinks, and she shrugged his hands away, stepping past him.

It was only when he reached for her elbow to stop her from leaving that Gavin saw what Marge had seen moments before.

The sound he'd heard wasn't a wagon. Their visitor was no customer. Instead, stopped before the mill, sat a grand, glossy black coach the likes of which didn't belong on the prairie. And beside it stood someone who belonged there even less.

"Daisy?"

Dusty. Dry. Desolate. These were the words Daisy would use to describe the great mythical American West. *And really, that's a shame, because so many people are going to be disappointed when they get here.*

She alternated between peering out the coach windows and keeping them closed so as little dirt as possible clogged the stuffy air within. *Worse, all those words start with* D. She frowned. *D was her favorite letter, after all. Why did I never notice how many dreary words begin with it until now?*

Dreary. Oh no. There's another one. Between what Trouston had done, days on end with no one to talk to, and the mounting suspicion that her escape would be rather

298

disappointing, Daisy felt dangerously close to the doldrums. *Now that I've started thinking in D's, I can't seem to stop. How depressing.* But the more she tried to stop, the more she noticed it until it became a sort of awful game.

She had a small notebook in her reticule filled with words starting with *D* now. If nothing else, it helped pass the time when the ruts in the earth grew too bothersome to allow her to doze off. Yet all the way through, she clung to the hope that Buttonwood would prove some sort of shimmering oasis on the Oregon Trail — a haven for weary travelers where she could anticipate lively entertainment and the bracing sympathy of her cousin while she recuperated from Trouston's abuse.

But Buttonwood, when they finally pulled up to the town, was just that. A town. To be sure, it boasted more than any other outpost she'd seen for days, complete with a church, smithy, general store, café, and what looked to be a schoolhouse. All in all, quite adequate if someone wanted to . . . subsist. Or carve a niche in the unforgiving prairie. Daisy wanted neither.

Actually, at the moment she wanted two things: a good chat with Marge and a bath. *Although* — Daisy wrinkled her nose as she stepped from the coach into the dry heat she should expect by now but always hoped against — *perhaps the bath should come first.*

Nevertheless, she pasted on a bright smile for the driver, as she always did, and looked around. A three-story building — the mill — dominated this area. She'd seen a nice little house when they drove up, too, so perhaps Mr. Miller created a corner of civilization here. But the best thing in sight was the figure staring at her from the far side of the millpond.

"Marge!" Daisy didn't waste another moment. She grabbed handfuls of her sea green traveling costume to lift the hem out of danger and started to run. "Marge!"

Odd that Marge wasn't moving. *Must be shock. She and Gavin are so surprised to see me!* It didn't matter. Once she'd gone about halfway, her cousin came to her senses and started rushing to meet her. Gavin stayed where he was, but Daisy liked that. Her sister's husband didn't really belong in the moment of their reunion, after all. *Good for him for realizing that!*

Then the time for thinking mercifully ended, and she met Marge's embrace. Folded into the familiar comfort of her cousin's hug, Daisy took the first deep breath she'd managed in weeks. It smelled faintly of lemons. *I forgot that Marge always smells like this. Fresh and new — just what I need.*

She clung to that hug for longer than perhaps she should have, but Daisy needed a moment to collect herself. It simply wouldn't do to face Gavin with red-rimmed eyes. Already she'd arrived unannounced, and while Daisy knew Marge would welcome her with open arms, uninvited houseguests weren't the most beloved individuals in the world. Weepy ones sank to the bottom of the list, so she took a few more of those wonderful deep breaths before letting go of Marge.

Strange. Gavin only now began to approach them. No smile warmed his face. Unease twinged between Daisy's shoulders. Or perhaps that was one of the side effects of traveling so long? In either case, the sensation didn't strike her as pleasant.

Worse, Marge didn't look overjoyed either. Oh, her cousin smiled, obviously pleased to see her; but something shadowed the hazel of her eyes. Since Marge didn't make a habit of pouring out her heart and seeking comfort for whatever troubled her, Daisy knew she'd have to pry it loose.

But then, it might be good to focus on someone else's problems for a while. Heavens knew she'd gotten far too much time to ponder her own, trapped in that coach. *Time to move on.*

"Marge?" She reached out and grabbed one of her cousin's hands. "What's wrong?"

What's wrong? Marge blinked, trying to process her cousin's sudden appearance, still attempting to understand what it all meant. *You're here . . . for starters.*

But she couldn't say that and hurt Daisy's feelings. It sounded all wrong, because the truth of the matter was Marge wanted to see her cousin. *Sort of.* Admittedly, now didn't rank as the best timing. *Or does it?*

She resisted the urge to glance back toward Gavin, whom she knew hadn't yet joined them. Somehow she always knew where he stood — how far away, what direction, and so on — without needing to actually see him to verify it. If he stood directly behind her, waiting for a turn to greet Daisy, Marge would feel a pleasant prickling along the back of her neck.

Instead, an ominous churning in the vicinity of her stomach told her Gavin still hadn't recovered from the surprise of her cousin's arrival. *Is he happy to see her? Glad she showed up before he proposed again?* Because if Marge didn't miss her guess — and, after all, she rarely allowed herself to be mistaken — that's what he'd been building toward when she caught sight of Daisy.

Lord, does he still want her? Is he looking at the pair of us, even now, remembering why he chose Daisy in the first place? Seeing her delicate beauty and realizing anew just how far short I fall of her standard? I'd hoped . . . Oh, Father, why did You bring her now? Why not in a few days? After —

Suddenly other troublesome aspects of Daisy's appearance hit her. Not just the repercussions for her and Gavin, but the timing. What it meant. Marge craned her neck, realizing Aunt Verlata should have joined them by now. But no one else emerged from the coach. No one.

"I should ask you that same question, Daisy." She searched that beautiful face, noticing much later than she should have the tension drawing Daisy's forehead too tight, the slight puffiness around her eyes, the darker imprint along her lower lip that tattled of her nervous nibbling. . . . "What's wrong?"

A pronounced sniff preceded the answer. "I *missed* you, Marge." But Daisy's green eyes looked downward as they always did when she tried to hide something.

"I've missed you, too." Marge's re-

303

assurance won a far-too-brief smile. "But where is Aunt Verlata? Where is your fiancé?" *Why are you here, when you should be in Baltimore preparing to become Mrs. Trouston Dillard III?* Questions crowded her mind — all of them suggesting a scenario Marge didn't want to contemplate. "You're to be married this weekend! How are you here?"

Only two possibilities presented themselves. Either Daisy hied off, abandoning her engagement without a word to Aunt Verlata or Mr. Dillard, deciding to avoid the unpleasantness of breaking it off, or Daisy had already married him and found she disliked the company of her husband.

Lord, help me, I hope it's the second. If Daisy's in a sulk over married life not being as grand as she'd hoped, I can handle that. Soothe her ruffled feathers and send her back. But if she's run off, I can't salvage her reputation or engagement.

Which would mean Daisy was single. In Buttonwood. Right under Gavin's nose.

CHAPTER 30

There she stood, looking like she'd stepped from the pages of a *Godey's Lady's Book* his sister used to be so fond of. Daisy Chandler stepped from that glossy black private coach looking fancy enough to call on the queen.

Well, perhaps not, but that green fabric — and it sure looked as though they'd used an awful lot of it to make one dress for such a small woman — had to be expensive. Lace decorated the sleeves and collar, matching ribbons fluttering along the brim of her hat. Except some of those ribbons kept snagging on something that looked like, of all things, a bird's nest perched among them.

Other than that, though, Daisy Chandler looked perfect, from her perfect black ringlets down to the tips of her black boots that kept their shine despite the dust her coach kicked up. Perfect, and perfectly out of place.

Gavin kept his distance as the two cousins

embraced, trying to marshal his thoughts. Not so much thoughts but questions in a quantity to clog the gears of his mind. *What brings her here? What am I supposed to do with two of them? Where is her aunt? Her fiancé? Isn't she supposed to be married this week?*

Suspicions rode hard on the heels of those questions. *Did Marge write to her and tell Daisy of the mix-up?* Despite the heat of summer, cold swept down his spine. *Is she here to take her rightful place as my bride-to-be, when I've been courting Marge this whole time?*

But no. Even if he didn't remember Marge's sudden pallor when she spotted her cousin, one glance at the confusion and concern on her face now told him she didn't expect Daisy any more than he had. It didn't solve everything, but the realization made it possible to walk over and behave with some semblance of normalcy.

He approached slowly, giving the women a moment to themselves — and himself an extra measure of time to decide how to handle this new development. Gavin knew full well he couldn't go stalking up and demand to know why Daisy had come.

Thankfully Marge asked for him. Oh, she did it as a concerned cousin and in a way that couldn't possibly offer any insult — in short, far better than he would have managed — but she still got the question out at just the same time he joined them.

"I *missed* you, Marge." A forlorn answer, in keeping with Daisy's downcast gaze, spawned a new set of suspicions.

That can't be all there is to it. Not when she arrives alone scant days before her wedding. Gavin tugged the brim of his hat both as a gentlemanly acknowledgement of her arrival and to hide the way his eyes narrowed.

He needn't have bothered. Daisy didn't so much as glance at him. She seemed too busy processing the volley of questions Marge lobbed at her. Gavin grinned for the first time since their unexpected visitor showed up. Leave it to his Marge to ask everything on his mind. All at once.

"Mama and Mr. Dillard remain in Baltimore, of course." She still didn't meet Marge's gaze, instead turning her smile on him. Dazzling and full of charm, Daisy's smile could blind just about any man.

Gavin knew — he'd been one of them. *How did I not notice how empty it is? How practiced?* Because the sad truth staring him in the face was that Daisy's smile was just for show. It didn't reach her eyes or light up her face the way Marge's did.

His lack of response — teamed with Marge's waiting silence — must've made Daisy uncomfortable. All at once, a flood of words poured from her mouth. A garbled explanation of words stumbling over each other, blocking one another, stopping anything from making sense as she kept piling on more explanations.

At some point, Gavin tuned it out in favor of waiting for her to finish. Watching the two women, he couldn't help making comparisons. Not because it was fair to do so, or even right to, but because he couldn't help himself.

There stood Daisy, resplendent and picture perfect, ringlets bouncing, hands waving, eyes widening and mouth going a mile a minute. She looked gorgeous, as always, but her blabbering made her far less attractive than Gavin remembered. He also noticed that in what he could catch from what she said, she didn't ask anything about how Marge fared.

Everything about Marge seemed simple by contrast. From the slim lines of her deep blue skirt and crisp white blouse, the mother-of-pearl buttons its only decoration, to the way she held still, tilting her head to take in her cousin's words, Marge exuded calm and caring. No ringlets bobbed around her face. She secured her chestnut waves in a practical bun at the nape of her neck. Dust speckled the tips of her brown boots, silent evidence of the walk they'd been enjoying before Daisy descended upon them.

Gavin liked that dust. Liked walking with her. Would have liked to finish that conversation. Instead, here he stood, waiting for an unwelcome visitor to finish speaking her piece so he could have Marge translate what it all meant. He waited a long time before Daisy wound down and Marge looked up at him.

"What?" He didn't need to be more specific — Gavin knew Marge would understand exactly what he asked.

"Daisy decided she and Mr. Dillard wouldn't suit and broke off the engagement, and he's made a spectacle of the entire thing to punish her." She glanced at her cousin, who nodded in a way Gavin would have thought overly eager for such a glum topic, but he didn't pretend to understand women.

"So she decided she needed a change of scenery and came to visit — without Aunt Verlata's agreement or knowledge." Marge's voice took on the sharp edge of remonstrance — as well it should. "You know she'll be worried silly."

"I left a letter." Daisy wrung her hands.

"Like I said I did. And at the last op-portunity I sent a telegram letting her know nothing befell me. Mama won't worry over-much."

"Yes, she will." Gavin didn't know Verlata Chandler too well, but she doted on her daughter — which might be partly out of necessity as well as devotion.

"Not once she knows I'm safely here with you and Marge." Nothing there to misun-derstand. "Mama knows she can trust Marge, and there's nothing to damage my reputation while I stay with my cousin and her husband."

Gavin shot Marge a glance she didn't meet. Obviously Daisy didn't have the slightest idea of the true state of things.

Husband? He let out a grin. *Marge can't wiggle out of this one. Once Daisy knows the state of things, she'll help me get her cousin to the altar. . . .*

"But, Daisy . . . I'm not her husband."

"I'm not her husband." Gavin's words struck her with the force of a physical blow, but somehow Marge remained standing. His grin as he informed Daisy he was still a bachelor sent secondary ripples of pain skit-tering across her bruised heart.

He discovers Daisy's available, and his first

step is to reassure her that he is, too. Marge closed her eyes, though no tears threatened. Strange how the ache seemed too deep to provoke tears. *She got here just in time. Even one day later and I would have accepted his proposal. . . .*

Now the pain rose to claw at the back of her throat, stinging behind her nose. *Because Gavin meant to ask me today. Just now. And I would have said yes.* Shame over her foolishness burned back some of the sorrow. *I believed we'd reached a point where we'd form a solid marriage. Convinced myself I could make him happy . . .*

But one look at the grin stretching across his face as he told Daisy he hadn't married her put an end to that notion. It couldn't be more obvious what truly made him happy.

"Marge?" Her cousin sounded somewhat shrill, the way she always did when forced to repeat herself. "I asked if this is true. You two haven't married yet?"

"It's true." *Not yet. Not ever.*

Daisy looked from one of them to the other, confusion showing in her pretty pout. "But . . . why?"

Because I'm not the woman he wants to marry. Marge wanted to shout the words. Wanted to burn them and bury the ashes of their truth. *You are.* As things stood, the confession stuck in her throat — a raw lump she couldn't dislodge. She might well have stayed that way, frozen in a morass of self-pity, but for her cousin's reaction.

"You!" Daisy rounded on Gavin, indignation drawing her up to her full — if not imposing — height as she whipped off her gloves and advanced. "What — did — you — do . . ." A stinging patter of blows rained upon a bemused Gavin as Daisy flailed her gloves at his shoulders and hat, her voice rising to a screech as she continued. "To — my — cousin?"

"Daisy!" Marge ripped the gloves from her hands. "Stop that this instant!"

"Give them back, Marge." Her brows almost touching in the middle, chin set in an expression of absolute rage, Daisy extended one hand. "I'll take care of this."

She kept a firm grip on the gloves with one hand and snagged Daisy's elbow with her other to make sure her cousin didn't launch another attack. "Take care of what?"

"She's berating me for not having married you yet." Gavin, for his part, hadn't lost his grin. Obviously the wretched man found the entire scene hilarious — the woman he'd actually proposed to giving him what for over not marrying someone else.

312

"If you want him, he'll marry you." Daisy jerked her elbow from Marge's hand but didn't move otherwise. Her voice went so low Marge almost couldn't hear her. "If he's done anything to change your mind, you don't have to."

"What?" Gavin asked the question echoing in Marge's mind.

"I said," Daisy repeated in an exaggerated voice, "if she wants you, you'll marry her. If she doesn't, we'll go home."

"Daisy, you don't understand." Marge realized she had to tell her cousin the truth. Immediately.

"Yes, I do." Her scowl remained. "It's plain to see you're not happy, Marge. We're leaving."

"No." Gavin moved to stand directly in front of Daisy when she would have swept past him, a determination such as Marge had never seen hardening the lines of his jaw. "You're not going anywhere."

Chapter 31

"You can come with me or you can stay here, but I've a mind to visit Marge." Midge recovered her wits the moment the black coach drove out of sight.

It'd stopped at the smithy for just a moment — not even long enough for the dust to settle — and then taken off in the direction of the mill. Since nothing else lay that way, and it branched off the Oregon Trail, nothing could be more obvious but that the driver had asked directions and intended to take his passenger to the mill. To Marge, if Midge didn't miss her guess.

And, of course, she aimed to find out that she hadn't.

"Visit Marge or follow that coach?" Amos knew what she intended and let her know it.

"Both. Will you escort me?" He had her hand nestled in the crook of his arm, where, Midge admitted to herself, it felt quite comfortable. So long as it stayed there though, they remained attached — a problem, since Amos showed no signs of moving in the direction the coach had taken.

"What if I don't want to encourage you to be nosy?"

"I'd be forced to remind you that hypocrisy makes men far less attractive." She gave him an arch glance. "And considering the way you kept asking questions about me when I showed no interest in answering, you've a good dose of nosy in your own makeup."

"I don't indulge in nosiness." His brows rose so high his hat brim went up. "When I have a vested interest in matters, I may, however, investigate."

"Very well." Truly the man deserved no end of teasing for his wordplay, but time wasted while they wrangled. "I've a vested interest in Marge's well-being and would like to investigate. Either turn me loose or accompany me, but make your choice, Amos Geer."

"What makes you think whoever rides in that coach might present a threat to Miss Chandler's well-being?" He began walking. Slowly. Far, far too slowly for Midge's liking.

"An instinct, you could say." *That, and the*

315

fact I know far more about Marge than you do but can't tell you any of it. Because if I don't miss my guess, Marge's relatives have come to visit . . . and might ruin everything!

"Not reason enough." If possible, he slowed his pace.

"I'm privy to more than you are when it comes to my friend," Midge reminded, plowing forward as though sheer determination would force him to move faster. "And if her visitor is the woman I suspect, things might become very difficult for her and Mr. Miller in short order."

"That's their business." He stopped altogether, his hand clamping down upon hers to ensure she stopped alongside him.

Midge glowered and tried to pry herself free. "She might need me. I won't leave her to deal with a shock like this all on her own."

"She's not alone. If, as you suspect, it's her family in the coach, she has them and Gavin." Amos showed no signs of budging. "Besides which, it's not your place to pop up every time trouble comes calling. Even your closest friends have to learn to stand on their own feet."

"People shouldn't have to stand on their own."

"We never do. The most important support and best friend Miss Chandler can call on is always available."

She gave a mighty tug but didn't gain so much as an inch. "Not with you keeping me in town!"

"Silly." His fond smile might have charmed her at any other time. "I meant the Lord. He's with them at the mill, His hand is upon them, and it's not your place to intrude on whatever family matters unfold there this afternoon."

"You're serious." Midge held stock still. "That's your answer when a friend faces trouble — prayer?"

"Absolutely. Better yet, I add my prayers to theirs."

Prayer. Midge swallowed a sneer. It always came back to prayer with the good folk of Buttonwood — talking with Someone who either couldn't hear you or only listened enough to get the wrong idea when He bothered to help at all. Why hide behind something as insubstantial as prayer when a body could do something in the here and now?

"Be practical, Amos."

"I am." Something in her tone must have grabbed his attention, because his smile vanished. "You don't see prayer as being practical in nature, Midglet?"

"Midglet? What is this?" The man chose a

strange time to create an endearment.

"Little Midge . . . Midglet."

"It sounds like *piglet.*" She couldn't let him know she liked the name — not that easily. Not when they were about to argue. Not when she probably wouldn't hear him say it again.

"I like baby pigs, and I like you even better. Now answer the question." The teasing faded away, leaving him serious. "You don't see the use of prayer?"

"No." And no amount of cute nicknames could change her mind or make her cushion the truth of how she saw things. Even if it did make her wish he'd either started calling her Midglet earlier or never started. For him to show such affection now, when he was about to decide not to spend time with her anymore, seemed an awful sort of joke. "Prayer isn't practical at all."

"You think God asks us to do something without purpose?" If his brows raised his hat brim before, now it rested so low on his forehead it almost hid the intensity of his gaze.

"I don't pretend to know God's purpose, Amos."

"What do you know?" No teasing lightened the words, but neither did belligerence underscore them. Amos sounded thoughtful, hesitant, as though treading lightly.

That I don't want to talk about God. Midge sighed. "I know that I want to go visit Marge, and you're stopping me."

"You can't keep her here." If the man didn't move, Daisy would shove him out of her way. She'd made the decision after her last encounter with Trouston that no man would bully her again — and that went double for Marge.

The very thought that he'd lured her cousin here with the promise of marriage only to keep her trapped in the middle of nowhere with no wedding and no hope for escape enraged Daisy beyond all measure. She hadn't intended this visit to Buttonwood be a rescue mission, but obviously that was precisely what was called for.

Pity Gavin Miller has such a strong-looking jaw instead of a weak chin like Trouston. I might be tempted to try that maneuver of Mr. Lindner's. . . .

"He's not holding me in Buttonwood against my will, Daisy." Marge's dry tone went a long way toward convincing her. "There are stages coming through here regularly — I could have chosen to return at any time."

"Looks like Mr. Miller disagrees with that

319

assessment." Daisy shouldn't have had to point out the forbidding expression overtaking the man's face at Marge's mere mention of leaving, but something told her it was important.

"I do." He crossed his arms. "I brought Marge out here to be my bride. She can't just run off at the first sign things won't be a fairy tale."

"Surely you aren't referring to me?" Daisy matched him glower for glower. "I didn't run away from my fiancé, Mr. Miller."

"Sounds like it."

"Gavin" — Marge moved forward — "we don't know what happened with Daisy and Trouston, but I would think you'd be glad to see her." A strange look Daisy couldn't quite interpret flashed across Marge's face. "I, for one, never cared for the man. And I told her so."

"I should have listened." One of those pesky waves of regret threatened to swamp her. "But I didn't run off, Mr. Miller. Trouston Dillard drove me away. There's a difference."

"Makes a man wonder if Mr. Dillard sees things in the same light." Disapproval radiated from Gavin so strongly, Daisy almost wondered whether he suspected the truth of the matter.

She sniffed. "Of course he doesn't, though I wouldn't believe a word he says if you ever have the misfortune of speaking with him."

"It does seem men are not inclined to admit when they've made a mistake." That time, the look Marge threw Gavin spoke volumes. Perhaps Marge didn't want to flee, but her fiancé still had a lot to answer for.

And Daisy aimed to make sure he did.

"I've owned up to my mistakes."

"Privately, perhaps." Something glinted in Marge's eyes, but Daisy couldn't tell for sure whether it was moisture or determination. "Publicly makes for another matter, doesn't it, Gavin?"

Daisy sucked in a breath. *Some mistakes should never be made public. Not when there's nothing to be done about them . . .*

"Some truths serve better as secrets. It protects people." His explanation almost echoed Daisy's own thoughts.

"From embarrassment?" Marge gave no quarter. "Things will be worse now for having waited to tell everyone about the mix-up. They'll wonder why we didn't say something from the start. Why —" It seemed as though her cousin caught herself just before she spilled the most interesting bits.

She always does that.

"They won't wonder about a thing.

There's no need."

Marge's head snapped back. "I know they won't wonder why once they see Daisy. It's obvious why a man would want to be her fiancé. They'll wonder about the reasons things didn't work out."

"Do folks here know about Trouston?" Her heart fell. *So many miles away, and I still can't escape the past? Are gossips truly that effective even out in the wilds where they have no telegraphs, railroads, or newspapers?*

"That's not what I meant —"

"I know," Marge outright interrupted Gavin — his mouth was still open and everything — "but Daisy doesn't know what you're talking about. She thinks we're discussing gossip about her leaving her fiancé in Baltimore — not the situation right here in Buttonwood."

"What situation?" Daisy got the distinct feeling she'd missed something. Something important.

"Marge," his voice came, holding a warning Daisy, for one, would have been too cowardly not to heed, "don't."

Marge always had been the brave one. Pain and pride warred in her cousin's eyes. "The reason Gavin and I aren't wed, Daisy, is that I'm not the Marguerite he wanted."

"You mean?" She gasped and stared from

Gavin to Marge and back again. "The letter . . ." Daisy wouldn't have believed it to
be possible, but suddenly she felt even
worse than she had before.

Marge blinked, and Daisy knew with
bone-deep certainty the glint had been tears
all along. "Gavin doesn't want me."

"No." His growl went ignored by Marge,
but Daisy heard the vehemence in it.

"Yes. He proposed to *you*."

CHAPTER 32

Amos Geer didn't consider himself a coward. Far from it. When trouble reared its head, he faced it. When his family needed something, he set out to get it. When tragedy struck, he called on the Lord and plowed ahead until he overcame the challenge or learned enough from it to make it worth the trial.

But for the first time since Pa's death, Amos found himself tempted to avoid something, ignore the warnings clanging in his mind. Wish it away, or at the very least, borrow an ostrich's trick of burying his head in the sand until trouble passed on.

I could do it, Jesus. I could set my feet to walking, take Midge to the mill, and leave the questions knocking on the back of my brain right here on the road. All it would take is not asking anything more. Not taking the chance that I'll hear what seems most likely, given everything Midge tells me so far.

Only problem was he couldn't. Lead might as well coat his feet for all they moved. It certainly felt as though something that thick and heavy clogged his chest, strangling the contentment he'd enjoyed the past week as his courtship progressed.

You don't give us a heart of fear, Lord. But then again, You haven't given me the wife I desire either.

He looked at her, reading the obstinance and impatience dotting her thoughts as clearly as those pert little freckles sprinkled her nose and cheeks. *I assumed she belonged to You.*

Please, please don't let me be wrong this time, Lord.

"Well?" She huffed the word out. Midge obviously didn't want to speak about the important things any more than he did. Most likely, they both knew where such a conversation would lead.

Can it be that my prickly little Midglet doesn't want to divide us any more than I do?

Some of the weight eased from his chest, though not much. "Let Marge handle her visitor as she sees fit. This is more important." He walked her over toward a bench outside the church.

"What is?" The closer they came to the church, the heavier her steps became.

"Amos?" Fear didn't color her voice, but hesitance shaded each syllable, telling him as clearly as if she'd shouted it that she didn't want this conversation.

He sat her down on the bench, noticing she sank onto it as though relieved. *Relieved I didn't take her inside the church?* His suspicions solidified more with each passing moment, coagulating into a clot of foreboding.

The way she fidgeted through every sermon — even more restless than usual. Her constant moodiness on Sundays. The way he'd never heard her refer to God, never seen her volunteer to pray, never spotted her with Bible in hand. Everything pointed to the one thing he'd never thought to see, never thought to look for in a woman raised by such an obviously religious family. *But the Reeds didn't raise Midge, they adopted her.*

"You're right." Amos didn't sit beside her, instead standing in front. He had two reasons for the posture — first, it kept her attention on him, making it overly difficult for her to hop up and rush away, and second, he knew good and well he couldn't sit calmly with his thoughts in such turmoil.

"Of course." She raised a brow as though prompting him to continue. When he didn't, she sighed. "About what this time?"

"I was nosy when it came to learning everything I could about you. Whatever watching couldn't tell me, I tried to pry out of you. If that didn't work, asking others usually did."

"No need to admit it. I already knew."

"The thing of it is," Amos continued, pacing a few steps away and back as he tried to best phrase what wore at his mind, "I never thought to investigate the most important aspect of your character. When it came down to the crucial matters, I made assumptions. Assumptions I'm starting to think were wrong."

"Dangerous things — assumptions." She reached up and fiddled with the battered locket she always wore. "I suppose now that you've spent time with me, you've found flaws in my character that lead you to believe I would make you a poor wife?"

"Dangerous things — assumptions." He managed a small smile. "I've not unearthed any flaws to make me stop courting you, Midglet. But questions have risen to the surface, and I can't ignore them or pretend the answers won't matter."

"If you've not found the flaws, you've not looked hard enough." The slight movement of her jaw told him she ground her teeth in between sentences. "It's only a matter of time, so perhaps the wisest course of action would be to part ways now?"

"Fatalism is every bit as unattractive as hypocrisy."

"Seems to me fate's never been pretty." She stood, her nose almost touching his chin when he didn't step back. "So there's no reason for you to be surprised."

He put a hand on her shoulder and pressed her back onto the bench. "Why don't you let me be the judge of that?"

"Me?" Daisy's squeak made Marge wince.

Well, if she felt like being completely fair, it wasn't so much the squeak as the reason for it. But Marge didn't feel like being fair. *Honestly, what's the point of it anymore? If I spend my time trying to give everyone else a fair shake, I'm the only one who winds up exhausted and with nothing to show for it. In the end, being fair doesn't end up fair at all!*

"Yes, you." Since Gavin seemed to have decided not to say a word, Marge confirmed the awful truth.

Awful to her, at least. Not so awful for Daisy, whose charmed life showed no signs of slowing down. Lose a fiancé, come to visit her cousin, find one she didn't even know she had. . . .

I wonder what it must be like to have so many options. A rueful little bubble of laughter swelled up, but Marge didn't let it out. If she let out any emotion, everything might come pouring forth in one massive flood.

"But I had already accepted Trouston's proposal!" Daisy protested as though tacking on some facts could possibly change others. "You couldn't mean to propose to an engaged woman."

"I didn't know you'd accepted another proposal." Gavin's annoyance came through loud and clear. In fact, even though he didn't roll his eyes, Marge could see his resisting the impulse.

She almost didn't blame him. At least, she wouldn't blame him if the entire wretched mess wasn't *all his fault!* Imagine proposing to a woman using a name she shared with another single woman in the same household and expecting the occupants to read his mind as to which woman he wanted.

Except I did know which woman he wanted. From the very start. That pesky propensity toward fairness wouldn't leave well enough alone. *As a matter of fact, Daisy thought the same thing. Why else would she tear apart her desk to unearth the list of wedding invites and make sure Gavin hadn't been writing to her? We both knew which cousin would be his first choice. . . .*

She closed her eyes, hoping to blot out the truth. Or, if not the truth, at least the appalled look on Daisy's face.

"Oh, Marge. I'm terribly sorry." Her cousin's voice sounded . . . defeated. "I'd so hoped one of us would find happiness with our fiancés. Instead, neither of us will be wed."

"Let's not be overly hasty." Gavin cleared his throat. "While you have my . . . condolences . . . that things didn't work out with Mr. Dillard, that by no means invalidates my engagement."

"But . . . we aren't engaged." Daisy's blink might as well have been a hammer's blow to Marge's heart. "I never accepted you, Mr. Miller. Marge did. Mistakenly, but . . ."

"Mr. Miller's proposal wasn't mine to accept." *Really, this conversation is worse than a Cheltenham tragedy — or a farce.*

"Marge, we've discussed this." Gavin sounded as though he scarcely held on to whatever thin layer remained of his patience. "I used your name, you accepted, I accepted your acceptance — no matter the technicalities of intent, you remain my fiancée."

"We have discussed this." She snapped out the words, refusing to pretend a calm she

330

didn't even remotely feel. "Intent comprises far more than a technicality when it comes to a proposal. Daisy was your intended fiancée."

"This is why you haven't married him?"

"Yes." For once, she and Gavin had the same answer — at the same time.

"Yet you still offered to wed her, once it became clear what happened?" Daisy's mouth hung open in what, even to Daisy, classified as an unappealing manner. She probably realized it, because she closed her jaw after just a moment. "Why?"

That did it. *Even my cousin can't fathom why Gavin would make such a sacrificing gesture?* "Thank you." She kept the irony from her response and straightened her shoulders, ignoring Daisy to look Gavin in the eye. "I've been wondering the same thing for weeks and am no closer to understanding it."

His roar was immediate — and deafening. "Have you both gone daft? Do all women lack sense, or is it limited to those bearing the name Marguerite?"

"Well, we Ermintrudes happen to be renowned for our good sense." She half stalked, half hobbled into their midst, making Marge wonder how she hadn't noticed the old woman's approach. "But on behalf

331

of womankind, I'd say it's men who bellow insults at the two women to whom they've offered proposals who may just be lacking their wits."

A spurt of laughter escaped Daisy, though she quickly stifled it. "I agree, and though it didn't seem to be the case, I meant to ask Marge why she refused to wed you. Now, of course, I needn't ask. You're not nearly so agreeable as I remember!"

"I presume that you, of course, are Daisy." Ermintrude glanced from the newcomer to Marge as though looking for similarities. She'd find precious few, Marge knew.

"None other. I'm pleased to make your acquaintance, Mrs. Miller." Daisy bobbed an informal curtsy. On the prairie. For the grandmother of the man who'd mistakenly proposed to her cousin. The same grandmother who now eyed her as though she were a prime candidate for Bedlam.

"Afraid I can't claim the same, missy. Your arrival throws a spoke in the works." As usual, Ermintrude didn't stop to sweeten her thoughts with a coating of diplomacy. "My grandson made great strides with that one" — she poked her cane toward Marge — "until you showed up. Now that's all gone out the window."

Somehow Marge managed to keep her

expression impassive, while on the inside she vehemently agreed with the old woman who'd come to be her friend. *Absolutely. Now that Daisy's here, things can be rectified. Gavin will court the woman he always wanted, and I'll gracefully bow out and focus on teaching.*

Never mind the streak of pain that came every time she imagined Gavin speaking the wedding vows to her cousin or the dull, throbbing ache that seemed to have taken up permanent residence in her chest. That would ease in time, as did the pain of every sort of loss. Yet there seemed to Marge an odd creaking from the vicinity of her heart as all three of them made their way toward the house.

It wasn't until after they'd given the coach driver something to eat and sent him on his way that Marge managed to identify what it was.

Pandora's box . . . with Daisy here, even hope has left me behind.

CHAPTER 33

"Why should I let you decide?" Midge sat down despite the defiance of her words. *Why wait for the inevitable?*

"Because we don't always make the same decisions, you and I." This time, he sat beside her, his knees angled toward hers in a silent display that he didn't intend to leave just yet. "You might like mine better."

"I'm used to depending on myself." *Which means I shouldn't like the fact you're still here. It shouldn't matter.*

"Most people admire self-reliance."

"Not you?" She raised a brow. "Strange, since you seem remarkably self-reliant and capable in most things you do."

"Ah, but that's not true." He leaned back, but somehow his shoulders filled even more space.

"I've watched for long enough to know."

"Depending on yourself again? What you see and what you hear shapes everything you believe?" Amos held himself too still to be as comfortable as his stance indicated.

"What I see, hear, touch . . . everything I experience. The things that happen around me, things people do to show who they are. I watch and listen and learn." The more tension he exhibited, the more comfortable Midge felt. "And you do the same thing. It's part of why I avoided you for so long."

"Afraid of what I'd see when I looked at you?" He pinned her with the question — asked in his words and his eyes.

"Not afraid." *Uneasy, yes. Uncomfortable, yes. But afraid?* Midge Collins was no coward. "Just . . . aware."

Amos kept silent precisely long enough to make her wonder if she'd won that easily, only to come back with the last thing she'd expected. "Aware of me, but not aware enough to know what I truly rely on?"

It fell into place so swiftly Midge felt as though she should hear a *thud.* "God. You're going to say that you rely on God more than you rely on yourself. Am I right? Is that it?"

Of course it is. That's what all Christians say, even while they do all the day-to-day work of taking care of themselves and their loved ones. God doesn't do it, and they don't expect Him to. People see to the details of life. I do. Saul does. Amos does. The only dif-

335

ference lies in who gets the credit. I don't give mine away.

"Yes."

This time, Midge let the silence spin out between them, deepening, widening until it became a heavy, noiseless gulf. An uncomfortable ocean she didn't have the means to cross, because she didn't share his belief in the benevolence of a God who let people suffer every day. Even good people who deserved better. Maybe even especially the good people who deserved better.

"What are you thinking?" Amos broke through the barrier she could not, for all the good it would do.

"You don't want to know." Midge gave him the truth and waited for him to refute it, insisting that he wanted to hear whatever she preferred not to reveal.

"There's some truth to that. No one wants to know things that make someone special seem farther away." Somehow his acknowledgement of what was happening helped bridge the gap.

Midge looked at him for a long moment. "Then don't ask."

"I already did."

"You already know the answer."

"It's not the same as hearing it from you, Midge." He seemed determined to make this as difficult as possible.

"Fine." The fact she sounded like a petulant twelve-year-old gave her pause, so she modified her tone. "Fact of the matter is I don't believe in prayer because it's never worked for me, and I've seen it fail the people I care about. Logical people form theories based on observation."

"Now you sound like the daughter of a doctor." His wry grin salved some of the sting from his words.

Though, in truth, the sting came not from his opinion that she sounded like Saul's daughter but from the irrefutable fact she wasn't. "I'll take that to mean it sounds like good sense."

"To an extent, but it leaves too much unaccounted for when you rely on your own sense. Or senses, as the case may be." He stretched his legs out as though settling in for a long conversation — which, come to think of it, he most likely was.

"Personally, I prefer to leave things unaccounted for, with room for potential error, rather than assign credit where none is proven due."

"You speak of faith as though it's a fallacy."

"Do I?" She leaned back against the bench, resigned to following the conversation all the way through to its natural end. To their natural end. "Although I never thought of it that way, it's a good way of putting it."

"No, it's not." He straightened up, planting his boots in the dirt. "You're discounting the way faith has different roles to play, Midge. Faith doesn't merely exist to serve."

"Did I say such a thing? Faith offers comfort to those who can't or won't understand the true nature of the world around them, Amos. False comfort. I want no part of it." There. She said it. Any moment now he'd stand up and walk away, just like she'd always known he would.

Sure, it had taken him longer than she expected to realize the truth about her, but he'd figured it out. Eventually. More importantly, his newfound realizations would prove her right . . . again. Amos would lose interest in her and prayer didn't work — two different things he wouldn't have agreed with, but Midge knew better.

"So it's not just prayer you don't believe in. It's God, too?" If words could drown in sorrow, his would.

"Don't be ridiculous, Amos. Of course I believe in God. Any reasoning person with the eyes to see the world has to know it didn't just sprout up willy-nilly or by chance. Complex systems don't simply appear, and there's far too much order to the natural world for it to be accidental. God exists."

Confusion beetled his brows. "Then why don't you believe in prayer, Midge?"

"I didn't say I don't believe in God, Amos. He simply hasn't done anything to justify having faith in His goodness." She stood up and started to make her way back to the house. *I'll visit Marge tomorrow. He may have a point about her having to handle things on her own.*

"In a nutshell, you've decided God exists but that He's not worth having faith in?" Amos's voice called after her, letting her know it had begun. He wasn't following anymore.

Midge wondered why she felt none of the grim satisfaction she'd been expecting. "Exactly."

"What are you doing?" Gavin waited until Daisy excused herself for a "private moment" before pulling Marge aside. As things stood, the only way he caught hold of her alone was lying in wait in the hall for her to wander back from showing her cousin to the necessary.

"I assumed Daisy and I would share the

guest room." She stared at him with a blankness he found unnerving. "It simply wouldn't be proper for one of us to sleep in the master bedroom — even while you continue to bunk in the mill."

"That's not what I meant." Although for a fleeting moment the thought crossed his mind that with Daisy there as an additional chaperone, it might be possible for him to move back into the house without provoking undue gossip. "What were you thinking, telling your cousin I meant the letter for her originally?"

"I thought it best to tell the truth. After all," she declared, closing her eyes and pausing before continuing, "you're the one who told her we aren't married. Surely you knew she'd ask why?"

"Yes, but we could have told her the same thing we told the rest of the town — that we waited until you felt comfortable and certain you wanted to make a life here in Buttonwood." That sounded weak when spoken aloud, but Gavin couldn't very well take it back now. "Or that until you had the school up and running, that took the bulk of your focus."

"She's my cousin, I'm tired of half-truths, and this concerns her directly."

Her remonstrance hit the mark, making

him uncomfortable with the way they'd been deceiving everyone in town. "Half-truths are better than whole lies, particularly when one works toward making them more and more real."

"I'm finished fooling myself, Gavin. Whole truths are best." Marge made as though to move past him and return to the parlor.

"Wait. If you wanted to tell Daisy the whole truth, why did you leave out the most important part?" Her expression told him plain as daylight she didn't know what he meant. "You left out the fact that I'd proposed to you since we discovered the switch. You told Daisy all about the way I'd originally written to her but didn't say how I've courted you ever since."

"She knows you offered to go through with the arrangement. Don't worry. Daisy doesn't think poorly of you for not marrying me. She knows you tried to stand by your word, even when you hadn't given it." The confusion cleared from her features, replaced by that dull, vague look he found so disturbing.

"That's not the same thing, and you know it."

"What do you want from me, Gavin?" For a split second, the blank mask fell away, revealing the conflict raging beneath. Fierce, proud, despairing — she embodied all these things and more as she rounded on him, enough to drive away a man's breath.

His lack of response settled her back to impassivity, making Gavin wish he'd thought more quickly.

"Daisy knows you initially proposed to her. She knows that once you discovered the mistake you stood prepared to do the honorable thing and marry me to uphold your word." It sounded almost as though she ticked things off some sort of mental list. Knowing Marge, she most likely was. "She sees the house and mill, knows you from back in Baltimore, and understands that I wouldn't let you marry me out of a sense of duty. That doesn't reflect poorly on you."

"None of that matters." He reached for her hand, but she shoved it into one of those ever-present pockets hiding within the folds of her skirts. "What matters is that she doesn't know how I've pursued *you*, Marge."

"That doesn't signify." She shook her head, her smooth bun scarcely moving at all with the motion. "She needn't hear my tales of your thoughtfulness, Gavin."

"So long as you remember them, I'm satisfied."

"You owe me nothing." She straightened her shoulders as though brushing away all his efforts, an impression verified by her next words. "You're free to woo Daisy, as you always wanted."

CHAPTER 34

Marge almost made it past him when his hand closed around her forearm. *Why won't he let me go? I've not harmed his chances with Daisy. Does he want my promise to put in a good word, help his cause?*

The ache in her chest echoed at her temples as the thought hammered home. *Daisy changes everything, except the parts I most wish she could.* Her cousin's vivacious beauty snatched attention, admiration, and the marital aspirations of the one man Marge wanted. It seemed a cruel hoax that, in spite of everything taken away, Marge was left with the regrets and disappointments of all that came before.

"How can you think I'd transfer my attentions to your cousin so swiftly?" Gavin's grip tightened a fraction before easing, as though he fought the urge to shake her.

Marge put her hand over his and pulled his fingers away. For once, the contact didn't send spirals of warmth cascading through her. If anything, she felt colder once he let go.

"Why wait, Gavin? You planned to be married to her weeks ago. Don't postpone things for the sake of pride."

"Pride?" A muscle jumped in his jaw. "You think I choose not to pursue your cousin out of misplaced pride? You sell us both short, Marge, if you can think of no other reason."

"Some of the members in town will think you fickle." The admission brought a kick of vindication she carefully didn't show. "Until we explain what happened. Then no one will see you poorly. I'll make sure they have no questions about your integrity, Gavin. I promise you that."

"What of your integrity, Marge? As far as everyone is concerned, *you* are my fiancée."

"Oh." *He's worried about my reputation.* She dragged in a deep breath. "There are some who will be unhappy, maybe even hurt I didn't confide in them, but Clara and Opal will forgive me in light of the circumstances."

"That's not what I meant." Anger marched along the set of his jaw as he stared at her.

Lord, how is it that I'm reassuring the man I

thought You'd sent me to marry that it's perfectly all right for him to abandon me? No, I know why. I know it's the right thing. But my heart doesn't understand why You've let me go through all this, if the outcome is so harsh.

"Midge already knows the truth, as does Ermintrude. The town council has been aware from the beginning that we might not become man and wife. In fact, this makes me a better choice for schoolmarm in a lot of eyes." If Marge could have dredged up a smile, she would have, but it proved an impossibility.

He stepped forward, his boots brushing her skirts, his head tilted so she couldn't avoid his eyes or words. "Forget the rest of the town, Marge. They don't matter. What about you?"

Her heart clenched and collapsed at the intensity she read in his face, at how fiercely he asked after her well-being. *Why, oh why couldn't he want me? Why is he only worried or showing any sort of tender feeling now, when it comes down to his ability to leave me behind?*

"I don't blame you, Gavin." She took a step to the side, pressing against the wall to sidle past him to the safety of the parlor . . . of Ermintrude's company.

"You shouldn't. I tried my best to make it

346

work. You're the one sending me to your cousin." The more softly he spoke, the deeper his voice became and the darker his mood sounded. "If you've anyone to blame, Marge, it's yourself."

She froze. "What?"

"I didn't say anything, Marge." Daisy breezed through the door. "Though I am a bit tired after all that traveling. Would it be too terribly selfish to ask to be shown to our room for a little rest before supper?"

"Not at all," Gavin answered for her, turning on his heel and stalking into the parlor. "Marge will be happy to show you. I'll let Grandma know before I get back to work."

Marge watched him go, fighting the urge to stop him and demand what he'd meant by blaming her for anything when there was no possible way for her to be more understanding. *What good can come of it?* She tamped down the newfound spring of resentment and led Daisy up the stairs to the room she'd come to view as her haven.

Another thing I can't think of as mine anymore. Shame flooded her. *It's little wonder hope left me — I don't deserve it. Gavin needs a better wife than I can be if I've become such a bitter wretch I begrudge my cousin anything. Daisy is the sister of my heart!*

But no sooner did she open the door to the room than a traitorous voice added the sort of thought she most needed to avoid. *And going to be the wife of the man who holds that heart. Little wonder you're not as pleased to see her as usual.*

"How charming!" Daisy stood in the center of the room and did a little twirl. "Small, though I'm sure we'll manage."

"It's a good-sized room when not filled with luggage." Marge didn't just mean her own; for a girl who'd snuck out right beneath Aunt Verlata's nose, Daisy managed to pack an astonishing amount. "Between the two of us, we must have brought half of Baltimore to Buttonwood."

"Good." Daisy bounced onto the bed. "From what I've seen, the place could use a few more touches of civilization!"

"If by civilization you mean crowded streets, air filled with soot, and the smells of far too many people packed on top of each other, I far prefer the wild West." Marge sank onto the chair positioned before the drop front desk that hid a few now-drying purple daisies.

"Don't be so negative. I'm talking about paved streets, shops and businesses, parks, and the like."

"The general store here is enormous, and

whatever they don't carry one can order via catalog. With the mill, the smithy, a church, the new schoolhouse, and even a café, Buttonwood has everything we could need. Besides" — Marge gestured toward the expanse of land and sky shown through the window — "the prairie puts any park to shame."

"No dressmakers or cobblers or haberdasheries or confectioners or lending libraries . . ." Daisy frowned. "I'm glad you're content with so little, Marge, but you'll not convince me a place like this is any match for the comforts of home."

"But . . . you just learned that Gavin proposed to you." A faint flutter signaled the return of a hope Marge began to feel she was better off without. "How can you decide against staying when you've only been here an hour?"

"Don't be silly, Marge."

"When have you known me to be silly?"

That brought her up short. Daisy thought for a moment, and probably would have thought long and hard, but it seemed too important to waste the time on something as trite as thinking. "Never. So don't start now. Gavin might have written that letter to me weeks ago, but we both know I'm

not the Marguerite he wants to marry anymore."

Marge blinked but didn't say anything,
which could be a good sign or a terrible
one. To tell the truth, Daisy never saw
Marge speechless, so she couldn't say for
certain which way it went. She decided to
be optimistic.

"We just have to make sure he realizes it."

"Daisy, Gavin wanted *you*. He got the
surprise of a lifetime when I stepped off that
stage, and while he's acted nothing but a
gentleman and offered to do his duty" —
her cousin grimaced, and Daisy couldn't
blame her — "by marrying me, I turned him
down. That means he's more than free to
pursue you. Since you're no longer engaged,
it's the perfect situation."

"You can't be serious." *She isn't serious.
That's all there is to it. Marge isn't offering me
the man she wants to marry — the one she
got so excited about building a life with she
wrote endless lists of what to bring to the
wilderness. The only thing that ever inspired
her to care about what dress she wore. She
isn't trying to convince me to take her place?*

Belatedly, Daisy realized Marge had been
talking the whole time she'd been lost in
thought. *Oops. No matter. Whatever she said
doesn't change the fact that, deep down,*

Marge wants to be Mrs. Miller. And I don't. Guilt and shame tugged at her stomach. *Even if I did, I couldn't . . . now that I've been ruined.*

"I cannot believe you're trying to convince me to spring from one failed engagement into the midst of another failed engagement, Marge." When all else failed, Daisy learned long ago that tears worked. That proved fortunate, since they sprang up so very easily these days. "You and Gavin didn't work out, so you're trying to foist him off on me, when I'm still recovering from what happened with Trouston?"

"Oh, Daisy." Marge got up from the spindly desk chair and walked over to sit beside her on the bed. "How thoughtless of me. I'm sorry. Tell me all about it."

In an instant, Daisy realized her mistake in bringing up the fiasco that had been her abandoned engagement. She'd known Marge would ask about her reasons for breaking things off with Trouston, but she hadn't planned on bringing it up directly. Avoidance would have been best for as long as possible. Especially since she hadn't yet decided how much to tell Marge.

"It's just all so upsetting." She indulged in a satisfyingly loud sniff. All right — a great galumphing snort of a sniff. The likes of which would horrify her mother, who wasn't here to remind her to be ladylike at all times. *Perhaps there are benefits to the West, after all.* The thought cheered her, but she refused to smile. If she did, Marge would expect her to be more forthcoming

"You used to be so devoted to him. Is there . . . is there any chance you're put out with him now but you'll forgive him later?" Marge spoke slowly, softly, as though testing the waters.

"No!" Daisy's response came out sharp enough to make her cousin jump. "Absolutely not. I'll never go back to him, no matter what he says or does or promises."

Marge slid an arm around her waist and rubbed her back. "I've never seen you so . . . put out. What did he do?"

Her cousin's kindness proved Daisy's undoing. Everyone else had demanded to know, or asked in such a way as though making her out to be some sort of flighty chit out for attention. Not Marge — Marge understood just like she always had.

"You wouldn't believe it." The tears burst forth — not gently sliding down her cheeks anymore but pouring out in great gushes that had her going through both their handkerchiefs in minutes. "He pretends to be such a gentleman, so upstanding, so

352

considerate and attentive, as though he'd make a perfect husband. But it's all an act, Marge! If you knew what he's really like, how terrible a monster lurks beneath what he shows everyone else, you'd be positively horrified by how close I came to marrying the man. I know I am." *And you'd be even more horrified to know that it's my fault for letting him ruin me.*

"He's a fraud then?" Marge's tone indicated that she'd suspected as much.

No . . . I'm the fraud. But so was Trouston. In fact, hadn't Marge warned Daisy Trouston seemed too good to be true?

"I believe it. He seemed something of a ladies' man, but it looked like you had him in your pocket."

"You're right." Daisy seized on the opportunity to explain the problem without revealing her own lapse. "He's the most horrid womanizer, Marge. I can't live with that."

"You don't have to. We should have known, Daisy. Trouston was too smooth and polished to be anything but a slippery eel."

"A trout." Daisy wallowed in the most gratifying blubber of her life. "Did you ever notice it's what his name sounds like? And sort of how he looks, if you truly think about it." She gave a vindictive *honk* into her third handkerchief.

Her cousin didn't hesitate for an instant. "With his pale skin, thin whiskers, and the way his eyes bulge out when someone surprises him? Yes, I noticed, but you were so taken with him it seemed petty to point it out at the time."

"Don't forget his weak chin." She fought a smile at the memory of Trouston crumpling to the ground beneath Mr. Lindner's fist. "Surely that contributes to the entire impression of fishiness."

"Without a doubt." Marge handed her a fourth linen square, although Daisy didn't think she'd be needing it.

"I feel much more myself now." She let out a small smile. "Coming to Buttonwood was the right choice."

CHAPTER 35

"So you figured it out." Dr. Saul Reed ushered Amos into his exam room and diagnosed the trouble in one glance. "I wondered how long it would take. You strike me as highly observant."

"She's not a believer." He walked in but didn't take the seat the older man indicated. "That's not the sort of thing I expected to discover, Dr. Reed. It is the sort of thing I would expect a man to reveal to another man who asks permission to court his daughter."

"As you pointed out at the time, when I remarked that it seemed like a conversation you should have broached with me in private, you weren't seeking her hand." Reed raised a brow. "You sought permission to spend time with her and grow to know her well enough to determine whether or not you'd be a good match. Rest assured, had things progressed beyond this point, I would have made certain you knew of her beliefs."

"Or lack thereof." Now, Amos sat. "I doubt most of the town knows that she attends church more for your benefit than her own?"

"Very few are aware of where Midge stands spiritually. Her heart and the way she treats others speak for themselves in most instances, and folks take her at face value."

"You mean they assume, as I did, that she believes in the Lord based on the way she lives."

"Midge puts many Christians to shame when it comes to carrying through biblical precepts in daily life, though she doesn't realize it." Reed took a seat across from him. "She is, however, all too aware of the hypocrisy of many Christians."

"I see." *Then the problem has more than one facet. The human witness and the divine evidence both present challenges to her.*

"Do you? I'm not sure how much of her past she's discussed with you, Mr. Geer, but the Lord is working mightily in Midge's heart." Dr. Reed leaned back. "And He has been for the four years since He entrusted her to my care."

"We've not discussed her past. Any hint

that the conversation headed that direction, she shut it down or changed the topic." Amos bent forward to rest his forearms on his knees. "Nor did I suspect her lack of faith. Although once she mentioned her views on prayer, it seemed so obvious I couldn't believe I'd missed it."

"We frequently miss what we don't look for. Midge counts on that to maintain her place in this town and protect my standing. It's what I believe Doreen referred to when she mentioned it being a good thing Midge attempted to avoid you. You see more than most."

"Not enough."

"Not yet. But you care enough to keep asking. That's good." Dr. Reed rose to his feet. "I begin to think you might be the match we've prayed for."

"I won't be unequally yoked, Dr. Reed." Following the older man's cue, Amos stood. In truth, Dr. Reed didn't even have a decade on him, but his profession and his family lent him an undeniable maturity. "Midge's disbelief is an unanticipated obstacle."

"Obstacles are created to be overcome." The doctor opened the door. "The only question is whether or not you feel the reward is worth the undertaking."

Amos didn't hesitate. "Undoubtedly. I take it." He eyed the door as he asked, "This means you don't intend to enlighten me about Midge's past?"

Dr. Reed shook his head. "It's not my story to tell, and I won't do you or Midge the disservice of interfering in that way. Best you find her and convince her to confide in you."

"I will." Amos walked through the door and took his hat from where it hung on a peg in the hall. "You can be sure of that."

"You want to come with me to visit Marge?" Midge gave Amos a dubious look the next morning. "Why?"

"To be honest, I'm more interested in having this sack of grain ground up." Amos gestured to the bag on his shoulder. "I'll leave the socializing to you."

She ignored the appealing grin. "Why are you here, Amos?" They both knew he couldn't be unequally yoked — that is, married to a woman who didn't share his belief in God. "I thought we decided I was a waste of your time."

That doesn't sting. I won't let it sting. If I'm not enough for a man on my own, then it's his loss. The bravado sounded hollow even in her head. *All right, it does sting. But I knew from the start I wasn't good enough for a man like Amos Geer, so I've no one to blame but myself.*

"Midglet" — his use of the endearment tore through her — "you're never a waste of time."

"Don't call me that." She started off toward the direction of the mill. "And if you haven't realized I'm a waste of your time, it's only because you don't know me well enough."

He fell into step alongside her. "I'll agree that I don't know you well enough, but I'm trying to fix that."

"You've seen all the good, and it goes downhill from there. It's best to cut your losses, Amos."

"The only way I can lose out is if I let you go without learning everything about you." His words drove sharp spikes of dread and longing through her core.

A broken laugh seeped through her defenses. "Everything?"

"Everything." No doubt clouded his answer. Just certainty, as pure and whole as the man himself — the opposite of anything Midge could offer.

"How about I sum it up for you?" She veered to the right, where she knew she'd find a grove of wild black walnut trees in a few moments. "Follow me and I'll show you exactly what you need to know about Midge Collins. *Everything* you need to know."

He didn't say a word, simply increased his pace to match hers as she hurried to get this over with. What went through his mind she couldn't begin to guess, but before long he'd understand that he should keep far, far away from her.

"Here." She slowed as they reached the trees. These were the oldest, largest plants in the area — just about the only trees aside from a few scrub oaks and cottonwoods. The only reason they'd been left standing rather than harvested by some pioneer for lumber was the walnuts they provided each fall.

"What?" Amos set down his sack of grain, peering around as though waiting for something to become clear. "All I see are walnut trees without any walnuts."

Midge pointed to a stump on the far left, where wind and locusts did their damage until Uncle Josiah chopped it down and carted it away. There'd been no other method of saving the other trees. "That one. You like to observe and investigate. Look closely and tell me what you see, Amos. Everything."

He made his way to the sawn-down tree,

crouching before the barren stump and passing his hand across the weather-worn surface. "It's a stump. Walnut tree, same as the others, but one of the oldest — or would have been if it hadn't been cut down. Looks like the roots go deep, and whoever bothered to haul it away saw no need to remove the rest. It's sat here like this for a couple years, at least. The dark marks show folks have put walnuts here during fall harvest."

"True. All true. But that's not the most important part." Midge moved to stand beside him. She reached out, took his hand, and laid it on the dead bark roughing off in brittle flakes along the outside. "Locusts infested it, so they had to cut it down to spare the others."

"This has nothing to do with you, Midge." He started to straighten, but she put a hand on his shoulder.

"I'm explaining." She guided his hand from the bark to the flat surface. "See how worn away, decayed, corrupted the outside is, but the farther inward you go, the more intact it becomes?" She slid their hands toward the center. "The evil attacked and destroyed the outside, making it ugly, but when they cut down the tree, they showed what was good and right went all the way through to the core."

"Now I see." He turned his hand in one swift motion, threading his fingers through hers. "You both have good hearts. Midge, I didn't need to look at a tree stump to know that."

"No!" She yanked her hand from his, but he didn't turn loose. All she managed was to throw herself off balance, so she sat heavily on the stump she'd brought him to. "You didn't let me finish, Amos." She swallowed back the anger and pride and sadness over how obtuse he insisted on staying — that he forced her to spell it out.

"Finish then." He stayed crouched before her, his thumb rubbing circles at the pulse point on her wrist, making her want to lean forward and get away all at once.

"I'm nothing like this tree. I'm its exact opposite." A ball of heat settled at the bridge of her nose, pressing against the backs of her eyes. "People can't tell when they look at me. I seem all right on the outside, but on the inside, I'm not like the others. They can't remove me or reveal me for what I really am, because it would destroy the Reeds. So instead of taking out the part of the group that's rotten, I stay."

"Midglet, that's a lie." Anger tightened his grip on her hand and deepened his voice. "A foul lie you're far too intelligent to believe, much less expect me to."

"It's the truth." To her horror, the hot ball broke into drops of salty tears she couldn't blink back. "I'm rotten on the inside, ruined by the bad things of the world early on. The pretty parts and smiles are just for show, Amos. Most people just don't bother to look closely enough to notice the truth."

"No one's looked as closely as I have, and I'm telling you you're wrong." He braced his free hand on her other side, closing her in. "The way you see yourself is wrong. No one who's been corrupted and lives with a decayed soul is able to love others the way you do, Midge . . . is able to swallow back her feelings every Sunday and sit in church for the good of her family. Everything you do shows that you care about other people more than you care for yourself, and that makes your core beautiful."

"Sin leaves stains same as the hulls of black walnuts." She lifted her knees into the space between them, braced her heels against the surface of the stump, and pushed back out of his reach, standing up and hopping down as swiftly as possible. "And I already know the way you Christians think, Amos." She kept walking toward the mill, knowing he'd need to go back for his sack of grain before catching up to her.

"You don't know everything, Midglet." He spoke quietly enough for her to pretend not to hear, but his persistence in using that nickname balled her hands into fists.

"You only think a heart is beautiful if it belongs to God . . . and mine doesn't."

CHAPTER 36

"Is that cousin of yours still in bed?" Ermintrude looked up from her embroidery when Marge came downstairs with her set of McGuffey's Readers after putting away the breakfast dishes.

"It's been a long journey for her, and she's not used to dealing with anything so taxing." Marge fought off the feeling she was making excuses and sat down in her favorite armchair.

"Of course sitting in a luxuriously cushioned private coach for days on end must be absolutely exhausting."

"She's also nursing a broken heart." *And keeping secrets, which Daisy's never been able to do well.* Marge kept the second part to herself.

Until she knew the full and precise reason why Daisy broke off her engagement to Trouston Dillard III, she refused to speculate or pressure her cousin to accept Gavin's suit. A gnawing worry pressed against the back of her throat every time she remembered the look of panic on Daisy's face when she'd asked what went wrong.

"A broken heart, unlike a broken limb, does not leave a body bedridden." Ermintrude's snort almost sparked a smile in response, but Marge was in no mood for merriment.

"Daisy's accustomed to town hours, where she stays up late into the night and doesn't rise until long after the sun."

"Foolishness and unnatural. I notice you come from Baltimore — on a hired stage — and didn't indulge in such behavior." Approval rang in her friend's voice. "I say the right bride arrived in Buttonwood the first time. Furthermore," she went on, raising her voice when it became apparent Marge intended to interrupt, "I believe my grandson shares my opinion."

Marge decided to ignore the last part altogether. "Since I've always taught school, even in Baltimore, country hours aren't a switch for me. It's not fair to judge Daisy by my schedule."

"Going to avoid the important statement, are you?"

"I'm going to find the story I mentioned to Midge the other day. After church tomorrow is the field day celebration to mark the start of school on Monday. She should be here any time to go over our lessons." With that, Marge buried her nose in a book. The familiar page before her went unread as her mind churned with a thousand things.

"Difficult to read without turning pages."

"Planning lessons requires thoughtful consideration." Her retort to Ermintrude's prodding lacked conviction — mostly because she hadn't been reading or planning lessons at all.

Truly, she'd brought down the books so she'd have them on hand when Midge arrived and only opened them to avoid an uncomfortable conversation with Ermintrude. Obviously she needed a more clever ruse if she wanted to fool the old woman.

"If you can concentrate on grammar when you think you've lost my grandson, then you never deserved him."

"You know me too well for such a short period of time." Snapping the book shut, Marge set it aside and rose to go stand beside the window. "On the bright side, that means you must know I don't wish to discuss the possibility of Gavin courting my cousin, much less marrying her. At any rate, it seems such things will be placed on hold until such a time as Daisy's heart recovers from the disillusionment she suffered at the hands of her last fiancé."

"Why put them on hold? Let your cousin sleep the days away, recovering, while you marry my grandson." Her rocking chair creaked at a faster pace as the old woman laid out her plans. "Then we'll all be happy, and Sleeping Beauty needn't be disturbed. No delays required."

Thankfully Midge came into sight at that moment, allowing Marge to excuse herself without having to tell Ermintrude precisely how ridiculous she sounded. After all, she'd been raised to respect her elders — even when those elders didn't show much respect in return.

"Midge!" Marge rushed out the door and met her friend several yards from the house, thrilled to make her escape. Thrilled, at least, until she caught sight of Midge's face up close. "Why have you been crying?"

"Amos." She reached up and swiped angrily at her eyes, making the red even more pronounced. "That man simply doesn't know when to accept defeat and call it a day."

"I know a few people like that." Marge led Midge toward the barn, not wanting to return to the house or, worse, venture near the mill . . . where Gavin spent his time. /

wish Gavin wanted me that way — that he chose me, settled on me, and refused to give up until he won me as his bride. But look where my hopes have gotten me so far. I'm better off without them.

"Hurry." Midge cast a disgruntled glance into the distance behind them, where a figure approached at a rapid pace. "He's catching up and I'm in no mood to speak with him now."

"Here." Marge ducked behind the mill and made a straight path to the small barn, where Gavin kept two oxen to pull his wagon and one milk cow for Ermintrude's sake. She remembered thinking how sweet it was for him to have purchased that cow and taken the time every day to milk it simply because his grandmother favored fresh milk and wanted a regular supply. But those were happier times, when she'd first arrived. When she'd still thought things might work out. She blinked and pointed to the ladder leaning against the hayloft. "We can talk up there for a while, and no one will think to come looking for us."

"Good." Midge scampered up ahead of her, settling into the sweetly scented, slightly prickly hay. "Now, I hate to be nosy. . . ." she started, making Marge laugh for the first time since Daisy arrived the day before.

"No one hates being nosy. People just hate being thought of as nosy." She shook her head. "Since I want to know what Amos did to upset you, I'm just as guilty as you are. Go ahead."

"The beautiful black coach that came through town yesterday headed this direction — everyone will be asking you about it tomorrow at church." Most people's eyes grew red after they were exposed to bunches of loose hay, but on Midge it seemed to have the opposite effect. The signs of her tears all but vanished as she waited for Marge to explain.

"Daisy."

"I thought so." The two of them sat in silence for a moment. Midge understood the magnitude of what Daisy's arrival meant for Marge and her budding relationship with Gavin without Marge needing to expound upon it or bemoan the change. "You would've said if she'd arrived with her fiancé . . . or her husband. I forget when her wedding date was supposed to be."

"Today." Marge closed her eyes and didn't add to the damning nature of that one word.

"Ah." If a mind were a maze and thoughts traveled through, the map of their course was printed in the lines on Midge's forehead. Her brow furrowed, lifted, crinkled, smoothed, and creased as she attempted to solve an impossible quandary. Finally her friend shrugged and said the last thing Marge could have expected.

"Amos knows now that I'm not a Christian, and he doesn't want to marry me anymore."

"Where is she?" Amos Geer stalked into the mill with a bag of grain on his shoulder and a scowl on his face.

"Which one?" Gavin muttered the response before considering that Amos had no way of knowing about Daisy's arrival.

"Midge, of course." He dumped the sack onto the floor, where it slumped as though dejected to be left there. If a man could resemble a sack of flour, Amos fit the bill as he slouched against one of the mill's wooden support beams. "She won't listen to reason."

"She's a woman." Gavin tied off the bag of flour he'd just filled, adjusted the opening to the fresh one, and tested the grind between thumb and forefinger. *Perfect.* "They don't seem to be in the habit of listening to reason. At least, not around here. Sounds like things aren't much different for you."

"Midge decided I don't want to marry her."

"Marge decided the same thing." Gavin straightened and returned Amos's confidence with one of his own. It felt right, considering they found themselves in the same boat. "Wonder if it's a stubborn schoolmarm characteristic?" They shared a rueful laugh at his joke, despite the fact it wasn't funny at all.

"I could use some wise counsel, and you're about the closest I've come to a friend I can trust since I came to Buttonwood." Geer's admission didn't surprise him.

"Makes sense. Pretty much the same thing here." Since Amos had been the one to help with the mill, Gavin spent enough time with him to trust the other man had a good head on his shoulders. "Both been too busy with work to do much gabbing like women make time for. Marge's only been here a few weeks, and she's already got a gaggle of friends."

"Women manage that. Women and children." They stood in silence for a moment, wondering at the parallel but refusing to say another word about it.

"So what seems to be the trouble with your Miss Collins?" Gavin recalled the night of the dinner party at the Reed place, when everyone welcomed Marge to town, and how he'd disliked the way Geer's eye fell on Marge. Later he'd come to realize the other man's interest lay in Marge's friend — something he was only too happy to support.

"Understanding it goes no further than this conversation." The other man waited for his nod before continuing, "Midge isn't born again. She knows I won't be unequally yoked, and she's decided this means I can't see anything of interest in her."

"She's not a believer?" Gavin heard the astonishment in his own question but didn't try to soften it. "I never would have guessed. Miss Collins attends church regularly. . . ."

"Church attendance and belief are not one and the same."

"True. But usually you see things the other way around." Gavin wiped the flour from his hands on a spare rag. "There are plenty of people who attend church and claim salvation but don't live it out. Miss Collins lives as though she believes, but if what you're saying is accurate, isn't saved. That's surprising."

"I know. At the same time, it shows that her heart's in the right place." Frustration coated the other man's words. "I'm not wrong in the choice of the woman. It's the timing I have to wait on."

"When the heart's good, the soul follows. I'll keep it in prayer, my friend." Gavin bent down and grabbed the fifty-pound sack of grain.

"Thanks." Geer followed him up the stairs to the storage room, where they poured the contents into the bin leading to the hopper.

"This won't take long once I finish Speck's last batch down there."

"Good."

They tromped back down to the main floor. Amos took up his post by the support beam, and Gavin checked the progress of the flour.

Sure enough, the batch had just about finished running — the mill capacity ran at three hundred pounds per hour, after all. Gavin pulled the lever to release Geer's grain into the hopper. He needn't adjust the distance between the stones, and the type of grain hadn't changed. Fine white flour coated his hands and shirt, settling in his hair as it always did when he bent near the output, but he didn't mind.

Breathing in air mixed with flour made it seem as though all was right with the world, even when it wasn't.

Just as the thought crossed his mind, an ominous scrape sounded, simultaneous with the searing flash of burned powder as a spark ignited, setting the mill aflame.

CHAPTER 37

To say the earth shook with her pronouncement might be somewhat of an overstate-
ment, but not nearly so much as Midge
would have liked. No sooner did she get to
the bottom of what ate at her than a hor-
rendous, grating scrape, followed by a sort
of booming explosion, shattered the stillness of the prairie.

If it hadn't been for the fact Marge sat in
her way and beat her to it, Midge would've
been down the ladder and out the barn door
before the sound stopped echoing in her
eardrums. As it stood, the two of them raced
outside, with Midge pulling up alongside
Marge in a desperate rush for the mill.

"Gavin!" Her friend's gasping scream
sounded the note of desperation thumping
in Midge's own heart — though the name
differed. She reached the door the same moment as Midge, her hand closing around
the handle with the thoughtless determina-

tion to yank it open.

"No!" Midge threw herself between her friend and the door. "Like this!" She pushed them both to the side, behind the wooden barrier as she opened the portal — the only way to offer some scant protection against the possibility that fresh air would make a raging fire belch out the door in new fury. She hadn't spent so much time reading about fire safety only to let Marge succumb to unnecessary injury now.

No flames burst out, reassuring Midge that the tan stone of the mill had done its work in minimizing the impact of the blaze. She looked around the door, felt the heat, and smelled burned flour and something worse, something stronger than the singed stone around them as Marge pushed past her.

"Amos!" Smoke blanketed the room, blinding her for a moment. Flames licked greedily up wooden supports to the beams bearing the floor of the next level above. *If this continues, the upper story will collapse upon us all.* "Amos!" She screamed his name, hearing Marge call for Gavin — hearing Gavin respond.

Cold clutched her in a tight fist when Amos didn't call back or come to her. *No. God, no. Don't let him be hurt.* She didn't care if she was praying. Didn't care if her asking for Amos to be spared meant God might decide to let a burning beam fall atop her. *It doesn't matter, so long as he and everyone else are all right. Do You hear me?*

"Over here!" She followed Gavin's voice — the wrong one, but the only lead she had — eyes tearing from the smoke and her fear. Midge felt more than saw Marge move to the right, and she followed, avoiding the large dark shape that must be the millstones in the center of the building.

"We need to get him out of here." Gavin could only be talking about Amos. He came into view, crouching low over a prone figure.

"Amos?" Midge fell to her knees, scooping her hands beneath his underarms as Gavin picked up his ankles. "Wake up, Amos!" Even as she spoke, she knew it would be best for him to lie still while they moved him. But so long as he remained still, dread clawed at her that the life had already left him.

A low moan, raw and filled with pain, brought a new flood of tears. "He's alive!" Together the three of them lifted him, carrying him around the millstones and out the door.

Eyes streaming, Midge didn't see Amos's face until they got him a good distance clear of the mill. The skin on his cheeks, forehead, and chin burned a livid red beneath blackened streaks of burned powder — at least, what Midge assumed to be burned powder. Flour. His eyes, closed, looked bare without their thick dusting of sandy lashes and unkempt bushy brows above.

Blackened holes tore through his shirt, displaying more burns beneath. His hands, where they rested at his sides, already showed signs of blistering. But he breathed steadily in and out, and his pulse, when she found it, beat strong and regular beneath her fingertips. "Oh, Amos." She smoothed a hand through his hair, wincing at the crisp of the locks up front.

It was only then she realized Marge and Gavin had left — most likely rushed back to extinguish the flames devouring the wooden structures inside the brick building. For a brief moment, she wrestled with the question of whether to go help them. But it was no choice — not with Amos lying helpless and unconscious before her.

"Midglet?" His eyes opened for a moment, dazed but determined. "Heart —" He sucked in a breath and shut his eyes. "Beautiful."

"You'll be all right." One of her tears trickled onto his forehead, but she knew better than to wipe it away. She gulped back a sob as he slipped back into unconsciousness. "You have to be."

"You aren't going back in!" His yell came out more like a croak, courtesy of the singed flour coating his throat, but that didn't diminish Gavin's determination as he halted Marge outside the mill door.

"If you're going, I'm going."

"No time to argue." He shoved — yes, shoved — her out of the path of the door, slid inside, and slammed it shut, barring it from within to keep her from danger. If the woman wouldn't listen to good sense, he'd see to it she had no choice but to abide by his decisions. *Effective — something I'll apply to other areas of our lives when this is over.*

For now, he rushed right, where the second water barrel stood waiting. Thick smoke clogged his vision and filled the room, relieved only by the sinister orange of the flames climbing up and across the beams to his ceiling, sliding their way to the grain stored above. He grabbed hold of a cotton blanket kept immersed in one of the fire barrels, the fabric made heavy with water as he flung it around the top of a wooden pillar, its weight and the force of his throw wrapping it around the top.

Gavin tugged it downward, smothering the flames on that brace, then rushed to repeat the maneuver. Smoke crept into his lungs, tickling his throat, teasing forth coughs he didn't have time for as he hauled soaked fabric back to slap at the wooden ceiling above him time and time again.

If he'd been able to leave the door open, he might've had more air. But Gavin breathed easier knowing he'd made sure of Marge's safety. The door to the sluiceway stood open, letting out some of the smoke, at least. Until the scant sunlight permitted by that opening became blocked by something. Someone.

A woman, moving slowly, as though encumbered by extraordinarily heavy skirts, headed for another water barrel. "Marge!" As Gavin watched, she lifted a bucket and splashed its contents on the rafters, ignoring him as she focused on the flames. He wasted precious seconds trying to determine how she'd gotten there, and deciding he wouldn't be able to force her out, he got back to fighting the fire with renewed desperation.

It wasn't just about saving the mill anymore. *If the building goes down, I lose Marge.*

They worked in silence, soaking and smothering every hint of flame and fire before Gavin took the time to reopen the main door. He would have done so far sooner had he not feared taking the time away from subduing the blaze. It was then, surveying the smoldering wreckage of every bit of wood in the room from the decimated gears and millrun to the now nonexistent hopper and the charred remains of the supports leading to the upper floor, that another heat unfurled within him.

She tried to muffle a cough, but it did no good. He heard. How could he not? How could she think he wouldn't know exactly how blistered, raw, and aching her throat felt? That knowing she experienced such a thing didn't make it worse by tenfold?

Gavin reached out, snagged her hand — a hand made rough with minor burns and scrapes coated with soot and burned flour, a hand he remembered as being soft and sweet mere days before — and led her outside. He dragged in a deep breath, ready to vent the rage of unrealized fears, only to pull up short when he realized he didn't have all the facts. "How did you get inside?"

Black streaked her cheeks, locks of hair wisped free from her habitually tidy bun to wave fiercely around her face, and her chin thrust forward in defiance. "I waded over and climbed the brace to the sluice gate walkway."

"You waded through the millpond and climbed up the walkway?" He wanted to shake her. He wanted to yell at her until she never put herself in danger again. Gavin looked at her, proud and disheveled and irresistible. *I want to marry her.*

But she wasn't looking at him. He turned to see Midge Collins kneeling at his friend's side, Dr. Reed next to her with his trusty black bag. Obviously the girl had run to fetch her adoptive father. Amos rested in the best of hands now.

That meant Gavin was free to confront Marge with the consequences of her actions.

As soon as Daisy released his fiancée from a hug that looked likely to strangle her, that was.

He coughed into his already-soiled handkerchief as Grandma approached, hoping to stave off the inevitable show of affection. It did no good. Before he could do a thing about it, Grandma had him and Marge in a clasp that would have done a jailer proud.

By then, he couldn't wait any longer to hear how Amos fared. Gavin walked over to confer with Saul Reed as the women held their own impromptu meeting, with Midge dispensing information.

"He'll live," Dr. Reed offered. "Good vital signs, and the burns aren't nearly as severe as they could have been, given what I suspect happened." Reed's words went a long way toward relieving Gavin's mind. "So long as we keep infection at bay and he doesn't succumb to lockjaw, Amos Geer should make a full recovery. Although I do wonder what we'll discover when he regains consciousness."

"What do you fear, Doctor?"

"Depends on what happened in there." Saul Reed jerked his head toward the still-smoking mill. "I've read that rye powder can be ten times as explosive as gunpowder but hadn't credited the rumors until Midge ran to fetch me and described what she knew, though she didn't witness the actual incident." There was no mistaking the look of relieved gratitude on the man's face.

"I've not had the opportunity to investigate, but this sort of thing happens when a small piece of metal finds its way into a sack of grain and feeds through the hopper. It sparks against the millstones, ignites the powder lying thick in the mill air, and flashes into an instant explosion." Gavin closed his eyes at the memory of the intense white light.

"So it is a flash burn. Then it's likely Mr.

Geer will suffer blindness." The doctor held up a hand. "In most cases, it's temporary rather than permanent. But forewarned is forearmed. I'll bandage his head and warn him as soon as he awakens so he isn't alarmed that he doesn't have his sight. That would be . . . disconcerting."

Gavin nodded. He could only imagine the sense of panic at losing his vision without warning.

"Although you seem not to have borne the impact of the explosion to the same extent as Mr. Geer, the fact that your vision remains unaffected beyond the effects of the smoke is highly encouraging."

"The circumstances of this accident are somewhat unusual. I expect to find that the piece of metal at fault is rather large — the scraping sound tells me the top millstone was knocked from the runner. I happened to be kneeling over a sack of flour at the time of the incident — judging by the location of the flames in the mill, at about the place where the stones collided once dislodged. It would have acted like a sort of barrier, guarding me from the brunt of the explosion."

"And directing it toward Mr. Geer?" The doctor caught on fast. "In that case, I won't make any expectations based on your condition, Mr. Miller." At that point, he turned his attention toward examining how Gavin fared after breathing in so much smoke, and repeated the inspection on Marge.

"Here." Dr. Reed gave him a rinse for his stinging eyes and a packet of herbs to make into tea. "This will help soothe the raw throat. You're both breathing fairly well. Don't try to stop the coughing. It's your body's way of getting out the soot." With that, he and Gavin loaded a still-unconscious Amos into the doctor's wagon, and he and Miss Collins took him back to town for further treatment.

"Marge, I don't know when the next stage comes, but I guarantee that we'll be on it," Daisy's voice rang out, shrill and demanding in the stillness left behind doctor and patient. "You don't belong in this forsaken place, full of dust and danger and . . . and . . ." She plucked a small notebook from the pocket of her full skirts and rifled through it before adding triumphantly, "Dilapidated machinery leading to explosions!"

"Gavin's mill isn't dilapidated!" Marge's outburst matched his thoughts exactly. Well, almost exactly.

"If you want to leave, be my guest, Daisy." Gavin slid an arm through one of Marge's and began walking, forcing her to keep pace alongside him. "But Marge stays with me."

CHAPTER 38

"Let her go, you . . . you . . ." Daisy rushed after them, searching for the right word. "Bully!" She reached over and tried to wrench his arm from Marge's but couldn't budge it.

"I'm no bully." He kept a firm grip on Marge's hand. "Tell her, Marge."

"You can't order someone to say you aren't a bully! Only bullies do that!" Daisy knew she was shrieking but didn't care. If her voice happened to be the only weapon at her disposal, she'd wield it until Gavin Miller let go of her cousin and clamped his hands over both ears to block her out.

"Marge?" He ignored her entirely, focusing on his captive.

"Do you know, Gavin, she makes a good point. You've issued a lot of orders lately." Marge attempted to tug her hand free but had no more success than Daisy had on her behalf. "That's a very poor record for someone who promised to meet his bride halfway. Particularly when he can't seem to decide which bride he wants."

"Not me!" Daisy vented her ire by whacking him on the head with her reticule, which startled him enough to allow Marge to pull free. "He doesn't want me, that much is certain."

"Agreed!" The brute reached for Marge again. "Now that we've settled that much, you can leave us in private while your cousin and I come to an understanding about what the future holds."

A private moment? "Never!" Daisy refused to remember the private moments Trouston insisted they share. "An unmarried woman should never be left unattended."

"I'm her fiancé!" Far from cowing her into obedience, his roar strengthened her resolve not to leave Marge alone.

"No, you aren't." Marge stepped beside her — away from him.

"You aren't anyone's fiancé, Mr. Miller." Daisy linked arms with Marge to point out the way they stood together — against him. *Me and Marge against overbearing men . . .*

"I will be, if you'd stop poking your nose where it isn't wanted." His scowl left no doubt in Daisy's mind that her cousin had managed a very narrow escape from a lifetime under the thumb of an overbearing ogre. "Marge and I have things to discuss."

"Marge needs a bath, some of the tea the doctor prescribed, and lots of rest." Daisy started toward the house, tugging her cousin along when she hesitated. "A certain miller lured her out into the middle of nowhere, toyed with her affections, and almost got her killed battling a dangerous fire today."

"She snuck back in!" His protest made no sense.

"I wouldn't have had to if you hadn't locked me out." Some of Marge's old spirit flickered to life again. "You can't control everything, Gavin Miller."

"Come back here, Marge."

"No." Now it was Marge sweeping Daisy back toward the house. "Because most of all, you don't control me!"

Burning. Heat claimed his face, his chest, his hands — a blazing pain sinking deep past the surface to set his very nerves aflame. Amos shifted, trying to escape, only to send a fresh wave of knifelike heat surging through his skin.

He held still, waiting for it to subside before opening his eyes. *Darkness.* He blinked, trying to dispel whatever blocked his vision, only to find no relief. Without conscious thought, he raised his hands to his eyes, sucking in his breath at the searing sensation caused by the movement.

"Don't move." Midge's voice came to him, cool and soothing. Close. "It'll make your burns hurt, though I'm sure you've discovered that."

"Burns . . . the mill." The memory of a blinding flash and intense heat knocking him against a stone wall came rushing back. He sat up and immediately wished he hadn't when discomfort churned to nausea. "Is Gavin all right?"

"Yes — lay down." He felt the pressure of her hand against his shoulder. Somehow, it seemed she'd found the one place that didn't hurt. Or maybe it didn't hurt because she touched him. Amos couldn't say for certain which was true, but he sank back slowly, trying not to trigger any more bursts of fiery punishment. "You've probably discovered that you can't see. Saul bandaged your face and eyes."

"Bandages." Relief coursed through him. "Thank God."

"God didn't put them there — Saul did. Dr. Reed, if you prefer." Her words sounded more clipped, controlled. "But if you're thanking the Almighty that it's bandages blocking your vision," she continued, her tone gentler, "you need to know that's not entirely the truth, Amos."

"Explain." He swallowed, unable to brace himself any other way as he felt her weight sink onto the corner of the bed beside him. "The bright flash of light — how bad is it?"

"We expect you to remain unable to see for a while, even without the bandages, but Saul says blindness caused by flash burns almost always corrects itself in a matter of weeks."

"Blindness." Amos blinked several times, as though to push away the darkness. Foolish, he knew — it gave him reason to be glad the bandages hid the desperate act from Midge.

"*Temporary* blindness." Her emphasis somehow made it more palatable. "You're young and healthy and may recover in as little as two weeks." The smooth rim of a glass pressed against his lips. "Drink this."

He swallowed. It took an effort to answer "yes" instead of nod when she asked if he was comfortable. It would serve no purpose but to set off the system of painful alerts warning against any movement. Not that he would be comfortable for a long while, but he knew that she meant it in a relative sort of way. "And the burns?"

"Not nearly as severe as they feel. Your

hands took the worst of it and will be slow-est to heal." She lightly touched his wrist as she spoke, the featherlight brush of her fingers affording a unique comfort. "You will heal, Amos."

A catch in her voice caught his attention. "There was doubt?" *And you care. Deeply.* He kept the observation to himself, but some of his restlessness eased away.

"You didn't answer when I called for you — lay so still when we carried you out of the fire . . ." Memories tinged her words with fear relived. "At first I didn't know if you'd survived." A ragged breath was drawn in quickly so he wouldn't notice — but it was too late. He'd heard it.

"Don't worry, little Midglet." He wanted to see her, reach out, hold her — but could offer nothing but the truth. "God watches over His own, and He kept me safe."

"Safe?" Her weight suddenly lifted from the bed as she jumped up. "*This* is how God watches over His own, Amos? *This* is the way He answers prayers for protection? *This* is what you offer me as proof of His love and grace?"

"No . . . what happened today makes one example out of many." He listened to the staccato clicks of her boots as she paced along the hardwood floor and surmised he must be at the Reed house.

"You're burned, blind, and could have died!"

"Exactly." He smiled and found the expression barely stung. "I'm here, not even badly burned, and only temporarily blinded according to all reasonable expectation. Things could be so much worse — how can I not be grateful?"

"Things could be worse." Exasperation underscored each word. "This is the basis for your faith? Things could be worse? Amos, what about the reverse side? Things could be so much better. Things *should* be so much better, if God really cared and protected His children as you claim."

Lord, guide my words to best reach this woman You've brought into my life. We've finally come to it — the real reason why she turns from You. Help me show her. . . .

"Why?" He waited one beat, then two, eventually counting out seven long breaths without any response from her. Even more telling, her skirts hadn't so much as rustled, telling Amos Midge hadn't moved a muscle since he asked the question.

"Why what?"

"Why should things be better, Midge?" *This would be so much simpler if I could see her face, Lord. If I could gauge her reactions and adjust my approach — temper my words to best reach her. Remember the tree? She thinks she harbors a heart of ugliness and corruption, not knowing the beauty within is only missing the fulfillment of accepting Your promise.*

"What sort of question is that?" Midge still didn't move. "It's what we always work toward — to make things better."

"Exactly." A rhythmic tapping let him know she'd begun to fidget. "We work to make things better. We earn the good things we attain — and that's as it should be."

"God could make everything so much easier. If He wanted to — if He loved as deeply and fully as He's supposed to."

Anger veiled the true motive behind her words, and if he'd been able to watch instead of rely solely on listening, Amos might have missed the deeper vein running beneath. The hollow note of betrayal burrowed beneath Midge's rage, eating away at the foundation of faith.

"We don't appreciate things that are given to us easily, Midge. It's the process of improving ourselves and the things around us for the people we love that makes us more worthy." He listened, realizing she'd gone still again.

"God judges the heart — sees deep inside

who and what a person is, and what he or she can become based on that." She started pacing again. "He doesn't need proof of whether or not we can be worthy — He knows it already. He knows what we think and what we need and when and how we hurt . . . and He lets it happen."

"We learn through our mistakes, Midge."

"What mistake did you make today, Amos?" Her steps moved farther away, until he heard the sound of a door opening. "What were you supposed to learn?"

"I don't know." His admission stopped her cold.

"Well, at least you know you don't have all the answers." She shut the door and walked back to his bedside. Looking down at him lying there, propped up against pillows, his face swathed in bandages, Midge felt rage rise up once more. "You didn't need to learn anything, Amos."

"There's a change I didn't expect." If she didn't know better, Midge would swear he smiled under those bandages. "A day or so ago you would've told me I have a lot to learn."

A grudging grin tugged at her until she realized he couldn't see it if she let it out. So she did — and it felt good. "That's not what I meant."

"You can't have it both ways, Midglet."
His voice went deeper, his speech starting
to slur from the medicine she'd given him
to help him sleep and ease the pain.

"Neither can God." She sank into the
chair at his bedside, suddenly weary beyond
memory. "He can't have a reputation for
being loving, forgiving, and all-knowing but
turn around and let the entire world stumble
and struggle and suffer. That's the worst
sort of hypocrisy I can imagine, Amos."

*Worse, even, than the men who abused my
sister then demeaned her for it.*

"But that's not God — that's Satan." It
looked as though he fought to remain
awake. "Midglet, don't ever forget we live in
a war. . . ." With that, sleep claimed him.

War? Midge left him to sleep. To heal as
best he could. *What does God have to do
with a war?*

CHAPTER 39

She'd won a battle against her own heart that afternoon, but Marge knew the victory to be hollow. Even now, she lay in bed beside Daisy, hearing her cousin's mutter in her sleep, as she always had; and her thoughts wandered to Gavin.

Lord, help me, please. I walked away this afternoon. Please help me give him up. Give me the strength to follow the path You put before me and be content with whatever I find it to be. Let me stop wondering what he would have said to me had Daisy not followed. Take away my worries about whether or not he's positioned his pillows just right so he breathes easiest after all that coughing.

"Not until we're married." Daisy threw out a full sentence before lapsing into incoherence once more. It sounded as though she were remembering fending off Trouston's overeager advances.

Marge wondered whether she should

awaken Daisy or if it was best to let her sleep. She still hadn't decided when Daisy spoke loudly enough again to be understood.

"You promised. . . ." Even in sleep, this sounded forlorn. Small. It made Marge frown and listen more closely.

If this counted as eavesdropping, she'd disregard it. Daisy hadn't explained the complete reason behind the abrupt end to her engagement, and obviously something deeply troubled her typically happy-go-lucky cousin.

More mutterings sank into silence. Then, "Can't leave me now!" The wail burst out so suddenly, Marge almost rolled out of the bed. "How could you?" This came so quietly, she could almost believe she'd imagined it. "Ruined . . ."

Ruined? Marge gasped. *Surely she can't mean what I think she means!* Yet no matter how intently she listened, Daisy would only repeat that one word every so often, as though unable to move past it.

"Ruined . . ."

If Marge had fallen asleep first, as she had the night before, she wouldn't know. *I shouldn't know now. Daisy didn't tell me.* Sadness shafted through her. *I didn't ask; I was too wrapped up in my own troubles to truly take note of how much she hurt.* She kneaded her pillow, trying to vent her guilt.

It didn't work. She lay there, turning the problem over in her mind, again and again, examining it from all sides. The facts didn't change. If her suspicions proved correct — and she held out little hope they wouldn't — Trouston had coerced or forced her cousin into giving him what should only be given to a husband.

"Ruined . . ."

Which means she'll have a difficult time finding a husband who accepts her past. Daisy wasn't the sort of woman to find her own way or push through on determination or grit. The simple truth of the matter came down to a bald fact: Daisy needed someone to watch over and provide for her. In short, Daisy needed a husband.

And Gavin needs a wife. Resolve flooded her, sweeping away most of the regret she should feel at the new plan working its way through her mind. *Lord, can it be You orchestrating this so my cousin wouldn't be left to fend for herself after her parents' deaths? If You mean Gavin for Daisy, I can accept that.*

She didn't like it. She didn't want it. But when faced with her cousin's need and God's will, Marge knew she could bear it. Even if the small box in her heart gaped wide open, the hope seeping away in small puffs of necessity, seeming to echo the one word on Daisy's mind . . .

"Ruined . . ."

The next day's sermon passed with agonizing slowness. With Amos laid up downstairs, Midge thought she'd found the perfect reason to avoid attending church . . . only to be outmaneuvered.

"I won't be the reason you don't go to church." Amos spoke up the moment she entered his room, somehow knowing it was her despite his inability to see. "Dr. Reed and I agree on that much, Midglet. I'll be fine for a few hours."

Maybe he's fine, she pondered, scowling as Parson Carter showed no signs of slowing down, *but what about me?* The longer she sat in that pew, the more Midge stewed. *Last night, Amos mentioned being in the middle of a war. He's about to learn how right he is . . . and that he picked the wrong opponent!*

Then something Parson Carter said caught her attention — something about fire. "Mr. Geer's accident brought to mind a verse that used to be one of my father's favorites. And while we keep Amos in prayer today, I'd like to read from Isaiah 48."

Midge sat up straighter, listening carefully

so she could pass along Parson Carter's message when she got home to Amos. But when the parson finished reading the verse, she felt so astonished she could scarcely credit it.

After entering her house following the service, she found herself stopping to pick up the Reeds' Bible and take it with her to Amos's room so she could read it and verify the message.

Amos still slept when she entered, but he must have sensed her presence, because no sooner did she begin turning pages than he stirred. "What are you reading, Midglet?"

"Searching for a verse Parson Carter read today." She could tell by his silence Amos wasn't sure how to respond. "In your honor. I think I must've heard it wrong, and I want to get it right before we talk about it."

"What's the verse?"

Midge consulted the scrap of paper where she'd scribbled the attribution. "Isaiah 48:10." She kept turning the thin, fragile leafs of the Bible as Amos lay there, waiting. When she finally found the right page, she traced one finger down the column to settle on the exact verse and read aloud.

" 'Behold, I have refined thee, but not with silver; I have chosen thee in the furnace of affliction.' "

To her surprise, she made it about halfway through before Amos began reciting the verse as she read it. "You know this verse? By memory?"

"Until you began reading it, I wasn't sure I had the right one in mind." He lay unmoving, a live corpse before her save the movement of his mouth. "But yes, I know it. And others that refer to the same idea."

"This is what you talked about yesterday — having to earn things and prove ourselves worthy. And today Parson Carter chose it because your ordeal reminded him of being put into the furnace of affliction." Midge stared at the verse until it became a jumble of letters. "As though it makes sense you needed to be tested like a precious metal to be found pure."

"No, Midge, put through trials to become refined into something more than the base metal I began with." His bandaged face turned toward her, and she clenched her hands to keep from ripping the coverings from his eyes. "The challenges we overcome shape us and prepare us to deal with those that await."

"I understand that." She shut the Bible and laid it on the bedside table. "I even respect it, Amos. But I don't see why God puts us through all of that if He's supposed

403

to be perfect in His mercy."

"Free will, Midglet. God gives us the choice and asks us to choose Him rather than succumb to the lures of Satan and live in selfishness. Many choose wrongly, and the world becomes a constant battle-ground."

"The war you spoke of?" She thought of it . . . examined what Amos was telling her, poked at it in an attempt to find a weak point — but it made sense.

"We fight for those we love, we fight to do what's right in the name of the Lord, and we fight against the parts of ourselves that want to stop fighting and indulge in all the things that look so easy or enjoyable." He lifted his hands then lowered them again as though anxious to enjoin battle once more. "That is our war — and one we wage so long as we value God's gift in letting us choose how we live out our days."

"No." She didn't bother to explain why that didn't work — hadn't figured out how to put it into words just yet — but knew enough to go ahead and refute what he said.

"No to what part? All of it? Some of it?" He raised his hands and spread them wide in a questioning gesture.

"The last part, mostly." If she thought about it, Midge could get behind the stuff about fighting for loved ones and battling against taking the easy way and doing wrong. "All that about the Lord giving us the gift of freedom. He's all rules and impossible standards and demanding you give yourself up."

I've worked too hard to keep myself together to do that.

"We need things to aspire to — you've already agreed to that. And God doesn't ask you to give yourself up. You're looking at it the wrong way."

Tears pricked her nose and eyes, clogged her throat, and made her breathing harsh. "What's the right way, Amos? He loves me in spite of the fact I lived in a back alleyway and Saul only just barely saved me from life as a prostitute? He loves me even though He let my parents and sister die?" She took in a great gulp of air and waited.

Now he knows the truth about my past. Now he won't want to talk to me or think I'm worth saving anymore.

Amos stayed quiet for a long time. "Jesus didn't condemn the fallen, and God sacrificed His only Son for our sakes." His words surprised her enough to dry up the tears. "You are precious in His sight, Midglet."

Midglet. He still calls me Midglet. But no more tears came. Instead, an odd calm descended upon her. "If He loves me so much and plans for me to keep my freedom, what does God want?"

"The same thing any of us want. Stands to reason, since we were made in His image." Amos shifted in the bed, turning his face just slightly so that it seemed as though the bandages stared straight through her. "He wants you to accept Him."

"As I am, He wants me?"

"To choose to accept Him. Yes." Every line of Amos's body seemed tense — with a hope Midge could understand.

"But it's my choice? I stay myself and gain an ally in fighting for what's good?" She waited for Amos's nod. "You're sure He already accepts me?"

"He already loves you, Midglet." She could see Amos swallow.

"In that case . . ." Midge got up and perched on the bed beside Amos, resting her head against the shoulder that hadn't been burned. "It's not hard at all for me to accept Him."

"And me?"

"Don't be silly, Amos." She smoothed his hair back. "I chose *you* ages ago."

"Good, because there's only one thing I want to see when my sight returns, Midge Collins."

"Oh?" Her hand stilled. "What's that?"

"You should've guessed." His smile made a mockery of the bandages swathing his face. "Freckles."

CHAPTER 40

Grandma cornered him a few days after the mill fire, while Daisy paid yet another visit to the mercantile and Marge ruled over the new schoolhouse. "Have you decided whether you take after my side of the family yet, or do you fancy the flibbertigibbet who pulled in here last week?"

"It would help if you let me know whether you leaned toward one or the other." Gavin kept a straight face as he answered. "Unless, of course, you bear no preference."

"Very well." The old woman chuckled and wandered over to her rocking chair. "If you've brains enough to be smart to your grandmother, I trust you've sufficient intelligence to choose the right Marguerite." She paused long enough to make Gavin wonder whether or not she'd leave it at that. "*This* time, at least." The final jab, when it came, earned her a smile.

"You can be sure of it, Grandma. I know

how fortunate I am that Marge misread the letter and came here. I don't plan on letting her leave." With that, he grabbed his hat and headed toward the schoolhouse.

Truth of the matter was, he couldn't blame Grandma for starting to wonder which cousin he'd decided to wed. Marge avoided him like the plague, whereas in direct contrast, Daisy seemed to pop up everywhere. Like a weed. It'd become ludicrous, the way he'd hunt out one cousin only to wind up stuck with the wrong girl.

The girl I thought I wanted to marry. Gavin shook his head. *Lord, I was blinded by a pretty face and cheerful laugh, when the true value stood right beside. Thank You for giving them the same name. I praise the day Marge stepped out of that stagecoach instead of Daisy.*

He wasn't sure he'd timed it right to arrive at the schoolhouse just as Marge let class out for the day, and as it turned out, he was early. Gavin glanced through the open door at the twenty or so students sitting inside — boys and girls ranging in age from five to about twelve — and decided to wait outside. Going inside would just disrupt things, and he didn't want a single thing to go wrong this afternoon.

Wandering around the side of the building, he heard Marge's voice through an open window and stopped to listen. It took him all of a moment to figure out she was reading a story to her students. Gavin rested one shoulder against the reddish brick of the schoolhouse and settled in to listen.

Marge spun the story of a boy named Henry Bond, whose father died and whose mother struggled with the cost of sending him to school. Her voice grew sad, her pace slow as she told of how Henry needed a grammar book but his mother couldn't afford one. A note of hope entered her reading, which picked up speed, as Henry woke to find freshly fallen snow and took the initiative to clear paths for his neighbors until he'd earned enough money for his schoolbook.

Satisfaction shimmered in the syllables as she read the end of the tale. " 'From that time, Henry was always the first in all his classes. He knew no such word as *fail,* but always succeeded in all he attempted. Having the will, he always found the way.' "

Just as I've the will to find my way into marriage with a certain schoolmarm.

Gavin straightened up as he heard Marge tell her students she would read a section of a poem to them and then they'd be dismissed for the rest of the day. Her voice took on a lilting cadence as she recited the first stanza to a familiar rhyme.

" ' 'Tis a lesson you should heed,
Try, try again;
If at first you don't succeed,
Try, try again;
Then your courage should appear,
For if you will persevere,
You will conquer, never fear;
Try, try again.' "

"Now remember, students, you can't expect to learn everything all at once. Sometimes you'll forget, sometimes you'll make mistakes, but that's all right so long as you do your best and don't give up. I'll see you all tomorrow!"

Gavin watched as the children filed out the door in clumps of two and three, some lingering far too long for his liking, before finally they'd all left. Only then did he venture inside the schoolroom, where he found Marge wiping down the blackboard at the front of the class. He walked up behind her and waited.

"Gavin!" The little shriek and hop made him smile. "You startled me!"

"I'd apologize, but the truth of the matter is I enjoyed it." He waggled his brows. "I've never seen you jump before."

"Sneaking up on someone tends to have that effect." With her surprise fading, she became all brisk and businesslike — as though brushing him away. "What brings you here, Mr. Miller?"

"I should think that would be obvious, Marge." For the moment, he ignored the way she'd reverted to using his proper name. Perhaps it had something to do with their standing in the schoolhouse. "I came for you."

"There's no need to walk me back to the house." Marge fiddled with the stack of readers on her desk, stalling for time. *Why is he here now? How do I talk to him about Daisy?*

"I want to." Somehow, his broad-shouldered frame swallowed all the space inside the one-room schoolhouse that managed to accommodate twenty children. "It's been difficult to spend time with you these past few days."

"With the start of school and Midge busy caring for Mr. Geer, there's been much to keep me busy." She skirted around the far edge of the desk — away from Gavin. "Besides, you've been repairing and replacing things as needed for the mill and haven't

412

had much time to waste standing around talking."

What little time you've had, I've done my best to make sure you spend with Daisy. Thus far, however, Marge saw no signs that her plotting bore any fruit. For a man who'd written and sent for Daisy to come out west and marry him, Gavin showed precious little inclination to woo her cousin. When it came right down to it, he showed no interest whatsoever. Marge fingered the chain to her glasses.

"You wear them when you teach?" His voice interrupted her thoughts, and it took her a moment to realize he referred to her spectacles.

"Only when reading." She snatched her hand away from the chain. *How many times has Daisy told me not to draw attention to my spectacles, not to wear them unless absolutely necessary? Men find them off-putting.* Except . . . Gavin didn't seem put off by her glasses in the least. Even now, he looked at where they hung near her waist as though wishing she'd don them.

Surely that can't be so. Marge blinked. *Even if it is, it shouldn't matter. Not anymore.*

"I've got a question for the teacher." A mischievous smile played at the corners of his mouth. "Will she explain something I've been wondering about for a while?"

"I'll do my best." It took a moment for her to identify the tingling feeling in her stomach as nervousness.

"Why is it," he began, tapping one knuckle on her desk with each word, making his way toward her while he asked his question, "that every time I turn around, you're foisting me off on your cousin?" By the time he finished, he loomed directly in front of her, brows raised in expectation of her answer.

"Foisting?" she squeaked. There really wasn't another word for it. "I don't know what you mean."

"Wrong answer." He took a step closer — a step she couldn't afford to give him without retreating a small measure herself. "Try, try again, Teacher."

She gasped. "You heard my reading to the children!" Heat swept up her cheeks at the idea he'd been watching her without her knowledge. It seemed so . . . intimate.

"I was waiting on you." Gavin ate up the step she'd retreated. "I still am."

"Daisy's the Marguerite you want." Marge couldn't believe she had to spell it out for him. "She doesn't think she wants to stay in Buttonwood, but you can change her mind."

"Who says I want to change her mind?" This time, he didn't move forward. He looked . . . puzzled. "Daisy's not the wife I want. You should know that, Marge."

The faint flutter of hope reborn made her giddy. And nauseated. *Not again. I can't keep going through the disappointment, Lord.* A dismaying notion chased away the other feeling. After all, he and Daisy had been spending more time together the past few days. Had her cousin confided in him?

"Is this because of what happened with Trouston?" She blurted out the horrible suspicion before considering the ramifications if he didn't know. "Because —"

He rested a work-roughened finger against her lips, effectively hushing her. "This is because of what happened with you, Marge. I don't want Daisy. I want the Marguerite who came to Buttonwood to meet me more than halfway."

"Daisy's in Buttonwood." It emerged slightly muffled, the words working around his finger before Marge tilted her head back. "Surely that counts for something."

"I'm not interested in counting. I'll leave the arithmetic to your students." One giant step on his part had her backed against her desk. "I care more about other things."

"Such as?" She found it difficult to breathe all of a sudden.

"Reading." He reached between them,

plucked her spectacles from the clasp at her waist, carefully unfolded the wire frames, and set them upon her nose with a tenderness Marge never would have expected. "I want you to read my face and see clearly which bride I want."

"No." She shook her head, spectacles sliding down her nose until he pushed them back into place with one finger. "You can't have changed your mind, Gavin. I'm —"

"Godly, kind, intelligent. Brave and foolish enough to wade into a millpond and scale sluiceway braces to stand at my side and fight a fire." His gaze didn't leave hers, staring with an intensity that gave the eerie impression he saw beyond her glasses and all the way through to the woman beneath. "You're many things, Marge. It shouldn't have taken me so long to see it."

She blinked. *Daisy is the beautiful, vivacious one every man wants.* "But I'm not —"

"Mine." He braced his hands on the desk, bracketing her. "Not yet." Then his lips found hers, warm and firm as they silenced her doubts. His hands slid from the desk to curve around her back, holding her close. When he finally let her go, he rested his forehead against hers. "Marge, I've only one more question to ask."

"Hmm?" She really ought to gather her wits, but they'd scrambled beyond repair anyway. "What is it?"

"How much longer will you make me wait before you become my wife?"

Her smile started slowly and spread until it felt as though every inch of her glowed with it. "Exactly as long as it takes for you to arrange the wedding."

"Done." Gavin angled his head for another kiss. "You'll be mine before the week is out."

CHAPTER 41

"I love weddings." Midge sat stock-still in the pew beside Amos, waiting for the ceremony to begin.

"Good." His smile could almost convince someone who didn't know him better that his eyes saw more than the varying shades of gray lightening the absolute black he'd walked in for a few days after the incident at the mill. Darkness still dodged his steps, but now Midge knew it wouldn't last.

God is faithful. She would've squeezed his hand but knew the burns there hadn't healed nearly so quickly as those on his face, so she settled for patting his shoulder.

"So do I." Daisy Chandler, the cousin who Midge could scarcely believe was related to Marge, much less shared her name, giggled from directly behind them, where she sat beside the Lindners. Midge didn't know precisely why the Lindners followed Daisy to Buttonwood, but if the admiring glances Mr. Shane Lindner cast in Daisy's direction were anything to go by, she'd assume he had marriage on his mind.

Parson Carter cleared his throat. "Before we begin the vows, Marge and Gavin have chosen to add something of their own. So bear with us as they do something they want to call "Meeting in the Middle."

The entire town started murmuring when they realized Gavin and Marge both stood at the front of the church — on opposite sides of Parson Carter's pulpit.

"She's wearing sky blue silk with simple lines — none of that overblown, fancy nonsense." Midge whispered the details so Amos wouldn't feel left out. "She's standing to the far right of the pulpit, he's to the far left, and they're looking at each other instead of walking down the aisle."

"I said I wanted a wife who'd be willing to meet me in the middle," Gavin spoke loudly enough to hush the crowd, "but the man is head of the household, so I take the first step." With that, he took a giant step toward the center of the church.

"For a man who's willing to give as much as he receives, I take another step." Marge's gown shimmered as she moved. "And add a second one in faith that he will match me."

"Two steps make a small price to pay

when the reward is a wife who will stand by my side for the rest of our days." Gavin moved forward again, reaching the pulpit as he spoke. "And I add a third in thanks she's come this far."

"One step to tell you no thanks are needed, only a promise to continue as we've begun." Marge's smaller stride meant she lagged slightly farther behind. "And three more to represent the three members of this marriage. Myself." She stepped forward with each name. "My husband." Another step, and she almost reached the pulpit — and a waiting Gavin. "And the Lord, who brought us together." The final step brought her to her fiancé's side, before the man of God.

"And so we meet in the middle." Gavin beamed as he spoke words that must have a special significance to the couple.

Midge thought about how lovely the whole thing was as they exchanged more traditional vows, waiting until Parson Carter pronounced them man and wife before whispering to Amos once more. "I'm sorry you couldn't see it."

"I liked what I heard." He shrugged. "Besides, I'm only concerned with seeing one wedding."

"Are you?" Midge couldn't tear her eyes

from him even as Marge and Gavin rushed down the aisle. "Which one?"

For the first time, he slid his arm around her shoulders, keeping her in the church for a moment after everyone else followed the newlyweds outside. He leaned forward, and even without the benefit of being able to see, unerringly found her lips with his in a brief, sweet kiss before answering her question. . . .

"Ours."

Without another word, keeping his arm looped around her shoulders, he guided her outside. "I want to hear this surprise you've been working on with the children."

"All right." Midge called them all around. "Is everyone ready?" She waited for them to nod, knowing that this would be their present to Marge every bit as it was her gift to the town — a way of sharing what filled her heart since the day Amos led her the last bit of the journey to Christ.

After all, she wouldn't have been on the path without Saul, Clara, Opal, Adam, and all the friends who'd prayed and showed her Christian love for four years. Their patience still astounded her, now that she knew the peace they'd wanted her to share. But if they'd pushed, she wouldn't have stayed.

Wouldn't have been here when Amos came calling.

Wouldn't be here now to listen to the students she shared with Marge recite the prayer she'd found in one of the McGuffey's Readers. Their voices blended in a celebration of the wedding, of the town, and most of all, of the Lord who watched over them all. When the townspeople insisted on an encore, Midge mouthed the words along with her pupils.

" 'When the stars at set of sun
Watch you from on high
When the morning has begun
Think the Lord is nigh.

All you do and all you say,
He can see and hear:
When you work and when you play,
Think the Lord is near.

All your joys and griefs He knows
Counts each falling tear.
When to Him you tell your woes,
Know the Lord is near.' "

"We know the Lord watches over you, Marge and Gavin" — Midge tucked one arm through Amos's — "so you'll have far more joy than tears." She couldn't hold back a tiny sniff as she leaned close to add something only Amos could hear. . . .

"And so will we."

Life doesn't wait, and neither does **Kelly Eileen Hake.** In her short twenty-six years of life, she's achieved much. Her secret? Embracing opportunities and multitasking. Kelly received her first writing contract at the tender age of seventeen and arranged to wait three months until she was able to legally sign it. Since that first contract five years ago, she's reached several life goals. Aside from fulfilling fourteen contracts ranging from short stories to novels, she's also attained her BA in English Literature and Composition and earned her credential to teach English in secondary schools. If that weren't enough, she's taken positions as a college preparation tutor, bookstore clerk, and in-classroom learning assistant to pay for the education she values so highly. Recently, she completed her MA in Writing Popular Fiction.

Writing for Barbour combines two of

Kelly's great loves — history and reading. A CBA best-selling author and dedicated member of American Christian Fiction Writers, she's been privileged to earn numerous Heartsong Presents Reader's Choice Awards. No matter what goal she pursues, Kelly knows what it means to *work* for it! Please visit her Web site at www.kelly eileenhake.com to learn more.